Diagnosing Sturgis: Examining the Annual Black Hills Motorcycle Rally

Good Medicine

The Secret Letters of William F. "Buffalo Bill" Cody and Dr. E.Y. Davidson

Chil Scoggin

Published in Boulder, Colorado by Charles Scoggin.

ISBN-13:978-1-951132-05-7

Cover Design by Mason Design

Cover Photo Credit: Buffalo Bill and Wild West Show photos courtesy of the Buffalo Bill Museum and Grave, Golden, Colorado

To Karen

Chil Scoggin

> *Buffalo Bill's*
> *defunct*
>> *who used to*
>> *ride a watersmooth-silver*
>>>>> *stallion*
> *and break onetwothreefourfive pigeonsjustlikethat*

>> *Jesus*

> *he was a handsome man*
>>>> *and what i want to know*

is

> *how do you like your blue-eyed boy*
> *Mister Death*
>> e.e. cummings

Contents

Editor's Note

I t started with a text message from Elliot Chaffee of the First National Bank and Trust of Denver, Colorado: *"I have something you might like to see."*
"?" I texted back.
"Letters. Buffalo Bill and Dr. E.Y. Davidson," Elliot replied.

I saw my reflection in the panes of glass to my right. Beyond, buds on trees. Looking back at the fingerprint-smeared screen of the phone I saw a different window open.

"When can we meet?"

∞∞∞

I first met Elliot two years ago at a December holiday party. I was standing alone in front of the host's fireplace, enjoying the warmth and sight of the natural gas flames. No real logs. I took sips of my red wine. It was smooth on my tongue, but still my mouth felt dry. My inability to make small talk frustrated me. Some think I'm on the coldish side, but it's more standoffish to avoid looking stupid. When I do get comfortable, I'm willing to risk planting my foot in my mouth or giving life to my personal aphorism, "There's no humiliation like public humiliation."

"I miss real wood fires." The voice came from a man my height. He had more hair and wore a camel-colored sweater over a blue shirt with the top button buttoned, grey flannel pants, black loafers with designer hardware, but no socks visible. He who goes out without socks in the Colorado winter has prepped somewhere east of Ohio. His hands were in pants pockets.

"Me too," I replied, holding back the temptation to talk about gas fireplaces and Denver's historic issues with air pollution, even going back to pre-European days when the Arapaho Indians called it, "The Valley of the Big Smokes." I can be seen as nerdish as a garnish to coldish.

Elliot introduced himself and asked what I did.

"I'm a doctor."

"Medical?"

"Yes, and you?"

"Banking."

"My name's Will Romine."

"Elliot Chaffee."

We shook hands. His was moist, but not slippery. Warm, not cold.

I saw Elliot suck in his lower lip, look to his left side, and then back at me. Whatever he was about to say had a windup before the pitch.

"Do you mind if I ask you a medical question?"

Here it came.

"Certainly—well, not really. I mean, I don't mind," I found myself stammering, and I hate that. I've learned to expect such questions once people find out I'm a doctor. Usually the best thing about free medical advice is the price.

In Elliot's case, I could help. He told me his wife was not able to attend the party because she was stuck at home with pain. "She has arthritis, mostly in her fingers and knees. It's kept her from skiing this year."

He also told me that she had developed a rash over her nose and cheeks.

A medical aphorism is, "When you hear hoof beats, think of horses, not zebras." But doctors who are good at making diagnoses recognize the uncommon presentation of common diseases—the pain in the back of the neck and a feeling of stomach discomfort and nausea can be the unusual symptoms of coronary artery heart disease cooking up in someone's chest.

Good doctors also spot the common presentation of uncommon diseases—the zebras. In Elliot's wife's case, the combination of painful joints and a butterfly rash on her face made me suspect lupus. I gave him the name of a specialist at National Jewish Hospital I trusted. I told him I would give her a call to alert her that Elliot might contact her.

I did, Elliot did, and she said she would.

Elliot followed up a few weeks after the party. Indeed, his wife did have lupus, and has so far responded to treatment. She's back skiing (but with a lot of sunblock—lupus doesn't like ultraviolet).

Since then, Elliot and I get together, usually about once a month. We like to share stories about our common interest, the American West. We discuss why the West held captive the imaginations of people throughout the world. Sometimes we talk about water as the life-blood of the West, other times about the clash of European and Native cultures. The Greeks had their heroes, and the West had heroic explorers, Indian chiefs, entrepreneurs of various flavors, and also outlaws, gun-fighters, and soldiers. Elliot and I had the good fortune of many good books about the West to read and discuss. I particularly appreciated having them at my bedside when I'm trying to decide whether or not to turn on the light or give one more shot at falling asleep. I resent those who don't know there's more than one two o'clock in the day.

Last year, over late afternoon beers in the Wynkoop Brewery, I told Elliot a story about a cousin who had married into the Latter-day Saints. She developed an obsession with genealogy. In her investigations, she'd uncovered a family connection to the Mayflower Plymouth Rock Colony, the reason a street through the University of Illinois at Urbana-Champaign bears our family name, and a newspaper article about a Romine child scalded to death when he fell into a caldron of boiling lye at a hog butchering facility. One of her discoveries that particularly got my attention was Dr. Edgar Y. Davidson, a prominent physician who practiced in Denver during the last century. Dr. Davidson proved to be a distant cousin on my mother's side.

Elliot and I ordered another round of beer.

I told him of my research in the basement of the Colorado State Medical Society, going through dusty, musty membership records until I found a large folder marked "Edgar Y. Davidson, M.D." I opened it. Some papers were stuck together, so I had to gently tease them apart. The glue holding some photographs on paper had deteriorated, so I was careful not to let them get separated from the text that described them. A corner table was piled up with old medical journals. I needed room, so off they went to the floor. Gravity did its thing, and they slid from stacks into a pile.

Dr. Davidson's history became a heap on the table top. I sorted and took notes.

Edgar Davidson's file contained a number of newspaper clippings, a rather detailed biography printed in the program for a testimonial dinner, and Davidson's handwritten, personal statement made when he applied for Colorado medical licensure in 1899. In the file I also found correspondence between the medical board and the University of Colorado pertaining to his appointment as a clinical professor of medicine. From all this I pieced together Dr. Davidson's story. I also found that the "Y" stood for "Yorick."

Charming and discrete, Dr. Davidson was doctor to the wealthy and benefactor to the poor. Through my research I discovered he liked to solve mysteries—medical and otherwise—such as one that involved a pregnant prostitute and a dead horse. He also invented a special device to help solve a common condition of women. And, he liked fast cars with color, curves, and chrome.

Dr. Edgar Davidson continued to practice medicine in Denver, Colorado, until his retirement in 1972. He served as the confidential physician and counselor to a number of noteworthy persons, including governors, senators, and a Miss America. In the course of this, Davidson was involved in some remarkable episodes of Western history, including a decisive confrontation with the Colorado Ku Klux Klan by Governor Billy Adams in 1925. Adams came across the Colorado prairies in a covered wagon with a brother who suffered from tuberculoses. The brother died, and Adams's family returned to Wisconsin, but Billy stayed and became a successful farmer, rancher, businessman, member of the Colorado Senate, and proponent of a balanced state budget and low taxes for economic growth.

Elliot said, "Billy Adams, my kind of Democrat."

High praise from a banker who did not let politics creep into conversations.

Adams was Colorado's only three-time governor. Adams never lost an election, and never learned how to drive a car.

I found a newspaper clipping with a photograph of Adams and Davison on horses. The caption read, "Colorado's Cowboy Governor; More Comfortable on a Horse than Behind a Desk." The article mentioned how Governor Adams and Dr. Davidson liked to go out on early morning horseback rides.

"Dr. Davidson has a longtime connection to my bank," said Elliot. "We manage a substantial trust he left. It's distributed anonymously to local causes, particularly those involving children and the poor. Dr. Davidson's son, Mason Davidson—adopted I believe—sat on the First National Board of Directors for almost twenty years."

∞∞∞

Six months ago, upon instructions left by Dr. Davidson that a particular trunk be opened in 2017, Elliot did so. When he saw the trunk's contents, he remembered my connection to Dr. Davidson and sent me the text.

I now sat in a small conference room in Elliot's Seventeenth Street downtown Denver bank. I might have detected the slight scent of money.

I noted a small, but significant difference between the conference rooms of lawyers and bankers. The credenzas of lawyers have a rack of the business cards of the firm's members. Next to them is often bottled water, soft drinks, crystal glasses, and an ice bucket with silver tongs. After 5 p.m., a bottle of wine or single malt scotch might appear. Bankers only have room-temperature water in a pitcher and offer plastic cups. No business cards, but rather, a listing of current interest rates for various forms of deposit. Bankers never offer alcohol.

The bank conference room provided to me had a westward view of the Colorado Rocky Mountains. Elliot's assistant said I could "dial 9" to get an outside phone line. She also gave me the number of her extension should I need her assistance. She also told me that Elliot had arranged for lunch to be brought in for me. She then left the room leaving no doubt that the door was closed behind her.

On the glass-topped conference table sat a brown trunk. Its wooden sides were banded with protective metal, and the edges and lid reinforced by large rivets. It reminded me in size and structure of the strongboxes demanded by stagecoach robbers in old western movies. The brass hasp was open, and a padlock with key inserted lay to one side of the trunk—alone and awaiting a return to duty.

Once I opened the trunk and read the introductory letter, I quickly lost interest in the view of the mountains and lunch. The trunk was full of letters, some addressed to Dr. Davidson by Buffalo Bill, others from Davidson to Buffalo Bill.

I started to read.

Like many Westerners, I knew the story of William F. "Buffalo Bill" Cody, but my knowledge was like a mountain stream in the late summer after the snow has melted and the runoff over—narrow and not very deep. I knew of the legends of Cody as a supposed Pony Express rider, buffalo hunter, frontier scout, and famed showman. In photographs I'd seen, he stood above most men around him and wore a Stetson cowboy hat, usually set at an angle, buckskin clothing, knee-high boots, and had a face of a man used to receiving adoration and giving orders.

I recalled reading about his marital difficulties, failed enterprises, fortunes lost, and elaborate funeral and burial outside of Denver. But the Cody in the letters to Dr. Davidson emerged as an individual struggling with life, moods, and sometimes his health. The letters covered the period 1899 to 1917. In contrast to today when patients and families often find it difficult to get the attention of busy physicians, Cody could not complain about access to his Dr. Davidson.

Dr. Davidson had his own issues as well, and as I scanned his letters, I saw a reciprocal—even therapeutic—relationship emerge between the two men.

The correspondence of both Cody and Davidson often involved a common element—the American West. Dr. Davidson brought the East to the West, first seeking health for his wife, but then seeking to improve healthcare and medical education. Cody brought the West to the East. I remembered I'd read a recent article in *Science* magazine in which a leading researcher warned about pushing the rules of human experimentation too far in the name of science. "This should not be a Wild West show," he said. Cody had introduced a term into the vernacular that persisted and bled over into modern science and medicine. Way to go Buffalo Bill.

I told Elliot that my instincts told me that what he provided for me to see was unexpected, unique, and most of all, important. We agreed; the newly found secret Cody–Davidson letters should not just become some archival website dying of loneliness on a server somewhere. They needed to be a book.

Elliot offered to help me defray the cost of publication. We both concluded it was a noble use of treasure.

My contribution has been to correct some spelling. Cody was definitely creative in his use of the alphabet—it reminded me of what my grandfather once told me, "I wouldn't give a nickel for a person who couldn't spell a word more than one way." I also reviewed the book drafts to assure faithfulness of transcription of each letter. I have also produced a table of contents of the letters. I found this helpful in following the thread of the Davidson–Cody correspondence.

I also solved a mystery. I noted that some of the back-and-forth letters were separated by only a few days. How could this be? Research answered my question. From after the Civil War until 1977, the United States Postal Service operated a complex, interconnected network named the "Railroad Post Office," or RPO. Skilled postal clerks would sort mail in specialized railcars as they sped along the route of what grew to 10,000 trains covering over 200,000 miles. RPO mail clerks were the elite of the postal service. They were expected to be able to sort 600 letters per hour and always carry a .38 caliber revolver. Thus, a remarkable rapid mail delivery system existed to support the Cody-Davidson correspondence.

Finally, some may cynically choose to challenge the validity of these letters. William F. "Buffalo Bill" Cody, on the stage and in the show-business arena, tilled the rich soil of human imagination. So much about Cody is already mythical; what is a little more fuel to this particular fire?

William Romine, M.D.
Boulder, Colorado

1972 Letter from Dr. Edgar Y. Davidson

June 23, 1972   Denver, Colorado

To Whom It May Concern:

I write this letter from my home of over seventy years. Through the open window I sometimes catch a choice word or two from the couple who bicker in their apartment across the alley behind my home. I am now in my tenth decade of life. Outside, the sounds of early Denver City—trolley cars, carriages, and the telling of the hours by the clock in nearby old city hall—have been replaced by the Denver rumble of buses, hiss and growl of automobiles, and the whine of airplanes overhead.

For the past two months my appetite has steadily decreased and so too has my weight. I have experienced shortness of breath, especially if I go fully recumbent. Curiously, my fingernails appear to have stopped growing. A cough has come to visit me with as much as a teaspoon of salty, metallic-tasting sputum raised after prolonged tussive paroxysms. On two occasions in the last week, I have noted blood in what my cough produces. A dull pain plagues me in my lower back.

Because of my discomfort, I have been carrying out an experiment with my old friend morphia. Two milligrams of sulfate of morphine given by subcutaneous injection brings me mild relief lasting three to four hours as noted by return to comfortable breathing, and also assuages the bit of anxiety I feel. My cognition remains clear.

Four milligrams, again subcutaneously, has the same duration of effect, but additionally eases pain and allows sleep. I have not yet had to go higher, but if circumstances necessitate, such as terminal distress, I plan on moving to at least 40 milligrams, delivered by my hand, intravenously—quickly.

I have now been watching this case with interest for two months, and I regret this is one autopsy I will not witness. My own chapter is near-written, but the story not yet finished.

I leave instructions that this envelope—and the associated archival trunk—be opened after 2017. That year that marks 100 years since I received, to my surprise, the enclosed letter cache from my good friend, and sometimes patient, William F. "Buffalo Bill" Cody.

I first met Colonel Cody when he sought my medical attention in 1899. I had only that year moved from Baltimore, Maryland, to Denver, Colorado.

Cody received my name from my father, who at the time was the medical examiner for the city of Chicago. Cody and my father had come to acquaintance during Cody's early career on the Chicago stage and later when Cody's Wild West performed outside the 1893 World's Columbian Exposition in Chicago.

Although Cody was twenty-seven years my senior, he and I fell into friendship. Much of it was practiced by way of the exchange of letters, the last of which I received in December 1916 shortly before Bill's death on January 10, 1917.

Cody seeking my care greatly flattered me.

Mr. Cody first called upon me for a consultation in my cramped clinic adjoined to my home. His handshake was firm, but not uncomfortably so, not one held a fraction too long and hard squeezed by a man trying to exert dominance. The skin of his hand was soft and warm, a sign I have found of men who, though they spend many the day in the sun—often doing rough work—conscientiously wear gloves. Cody's teeth were straight, and I detected a slight whiff of tobacco, not totally concealed by Sen-Sen breath perfume.

He and I shared a common height, at least half a foot taller than most adult men I attended to in my practice. While both of us had thinning hair, he wore his long in the back with rather large curls in which a few strands of silver sparkled. Our physiques differed in that I was slender, and his hinted at thickness around the middle. Placed side-by-side, I believe we would have looked like before-and-after images of the onset of middle age. While I was clean-shaven, he sported a well-groomed Van Dyke moustache and beard, thin but to the point.

To my surprise, he wore not boots, but rather well-shined, black toe-capped, lace-up oxford shoes that went nicely with his dark grey suit that looked to be of English tailoring. Cody's shirt was high-collared, double-cuffed, white, and starched with no wrinkle to be seen. His appearance was completed with a four-in-hand red tie and a Masonic lapel pin. I also observed one of his silk stockings had fallen down around his right ankle. He looked more like he planned to meet with a banker than a newly turned-out young doctor.

I asked that he undress so that I could carry out a proper physical examination. This he did, leaving on only his drawers, but removing a corset. "It's for my posture," he said.

My examination was only remarkable for the absence of any scars whatsoever, a finding I found surprising giving his rough-and-tumble upbringing and the many battles he fought, not to mention his long professional association with the dangers of the arena and presence of many types of firearms.

I made but a brief note of my examination. I have refused to let scribbling come between listening to, touching, looking closely for little clues, and even smelling my patients. The swollen neck might be from goiter, but a swollen neck with distended veins signaled obstruction of the superior vena cava, and shifts the search to cancer. Alcohol on the breath in a morning visit portended tragedy.

I took but a brief note of my findings. I wish to note my professional letters and other medical records were somewhat more detailed than one written by an early Colorado physician friend, who after examining a young chambermaid, wrote,

Diagnosis: Pregnancy

Recommendation: Matrimony

Examination charge: $5

At the conclusion of our meeting, after dressing, he donned his fur-collared overcoat and a broad-brimmed Stetson hat, which he set at a jaunty angle on his head.

I offered the famous man a ride to his hotel as he had arrived by taxi and the hour was now busy. He accepted.

Cody was quite taken by my new Columbia Electric Runabout and asked many questions about the vehicle once he was onboard. Throughout the ten-minute ride to the hotel, he returned the waves of the many people who recognized him. As we arrived at the Brown Palace Hotel, he nudged me in the ribs with his elbow, then grasped my right hand as you would in an arm-wrestling contest, but pumping it, first to the left then to the right then back again.

"That's Buffalo Bill's hearty handshake," he said, then cast one last, long look at my little car and entered the hotel, returning the doorman's salute.

A few days later, I received a letter from Cody, to which I replied. I was surprised from the beginning at the details Cody shared with me right from the first letter. I realized after reading the first one a few times, that Cody is the ultimate showman, that he couldn't let go of his persona at first, trying to "woo" me in a way to get what he wanted—my medical care and discretion. Moreover, at the time I did not realize that this entered us into correspondence that would last the reminder of his life.

On Christmas Eve in 1916, a messenger arrived at my doorstep carrying a thick packet. My housekeeper took it and left it in my study. When I returned from a trip, I opened the package. In it was all the letters I had written Cody. Ironically, I also kept his letters.

Over the seventeen years Cody and I corresponded, we

shared stories and secrets. Privacy and discretion are the duties of a physician toward patients. It was also the cornerstone of my particular medical practice.

So now on to the purpose of this letter.

I have practiced medicine all these years in Denver. I have made the acquaintance of a few, honest, reliable bankers—unfortunately, not so many lawyers with such virtues. For many years, I have been a satisfied customer of the First National Bank and Trust of Denver. For this reason, I have engaged the bank to take this letter and trunk into safekeeping. I made clear the 2017 opening. That year will mark 100 years after my receipt of the Cody letters and the centennial of Cody's death. I have confidence that the current president, David Morrison, will see that this charge is honored and passed on to his successors.

I believe that intervening century from Cody's death in 1917 will allow more than adequate time to transpire so as to assure no living person is in any way harmed by the contents of our correspondence.

I feel that these letters reflect the complexity of Cody, a man characterized on one hand as a philandering spendthrift fool by his business partner, Nate Salsbury, to the more sympathetic characterization by another business associate Gordon "Pawnee Bill," who simply said, "He was just an irresponsible boy."

No other individual is so symbolic of the American West than Buffalo Bill.

Within these letters you will enjoy and ponder words of a man revered by so many and still missed by me. To those that may choose to use these letters to denigrate the legacy of Cody, I close with the wisdom of Hippocrates who cautioned in Aphorisms 1, "Experience is fallacious and judgment difficult."

I should also disclose that my letters to Cody are self-revelatory. Reading through them again, I conclude that sometimes the patient is good medicine for the doctor.

A final request: I have always picked a current outside the mainstream on which to float. Rather than have these letters directly sent to the academy, I ask that they be first shared with the larger population of humankind. I believe it is the right way to present the relationship of two very different men, their wants, their struggles, and their times.

With humility and trust, farewell,

E.Y. Davidson, M.D.
Denver, Colorado

The Letters

1899

"I would kindly appreciate if you would conduct a medical examination."
October 14, 1899
Cody to Davidson

"I am most happy to be of service."
October 18, 1899
Davidson to Cody

"Buntline was quite taken with me."
October 22, 1899
Cody to Davidson

"I too look forward to our meeting and being of assistance to you."
October 28, 1899
Davidson to Cody

"I appreciate your taking the time."
November 15, 1899
Cody to Davidson

"I cannot accept explanations that revolve around moral weakness."
November 21, 1899
Davidson to Cody

"I have had many fine pards, but..."
December 1, 1899
Cody to Davidson

"I am intrigued by the opportunity for correspondence, and warm to experimentation."

December 15, 1899
Davidson to Cody

"My desire is to be as successful in business as I have been a showman."
December 21, 1899
Cody to Davidson

"Thank you for your kind remembrances of my father."
December 27, 1899
Davidson to Cody

1900

"What is life if we can't have fun?"
January 15, 1900
Cody to Davidson

"I used to fight Indians, now I fight speculators, government men, and lawyers."
March 30, 1900
Cody to Davidson

"I abhor gossip, and believe it dreadful and deceitful."
April 15, 1900
Davidson to Cody

"I hate to bother you, but...."
June 23, 1900
Cody to Davidson

"Your condition and need for remedy are shared by many."
June 28, 1900
Davidson to Cody

"I have taken your counsel."
August 3, 1900
Cody to Davidson

"Forgive me if I'm once again being too forward."
November 13, 1900
Cody to Davidson

"I greatly enjoy sharing advances in medicine."
December 4, 1900
Davidson to Cody

"My life goes better."
December 18, 1900
Cody to Davidson

1901

"*My wife is trying to poison me.*"
March 1, 1901
Cody to Davidson

"*I am in grief from the death of my wife.*"
April 5, 1901
Davidson to Cody

"*If Bill can help you, I'll ride slick to get you.*"
April 11, 1901
Cody to Davidson

"*Sometimes free advice is worth twice the price.*"
April 20, 1901
Cody to Davidson

"*A good horse is not very apt to jump over a bank.*"
June 10, 1901
Cody to Davidson

"*It is quite impossible for me to travel at this time.*"
June 19, 1901
Davidson to Cody

"*Good partners bring a lot, and common sense carries a premium.*"
June 25, 1901
Cody to Davidson

"*Nighttime though does bring a darkness that no lamp can chase away.*"
September 5, 1901
Davidson to Cody

"She showed me how a woman could do a man's work."
November 15, 1901
Cody to Davidson

"If you listen to the patient long enough..."
December 15, 1901
Davidson to Cody

1902

"*I promise it won't rain.*"
June 27, 1902
Cody to Davidson

"*I have made it a particular point to pay sincere attention to my young son's questions and observations.*"
July 7, 1902
Davidson to Cody

"*My old bones trust your care.*"
August 19, 1902
Cody to Davidson

"*Even a braying jackass eventually shuts up.*"
August 26, 1902
Davidson to Cody

1903

"My old partner, Nat Salsbury, had sacked his saddle."
January 20, 1903
Cody to Davidson

"I take pride in being a discrete physician."
February 1, 1903
Davidson to Cody

"I have been a good friend and father to my red brothers."
March 17, 1903
Cody to Davidson

"I have also taken the precaution of being armed and minding where I venture."
April 5, 1903
Davidson to Cody

"I have learned to enjoy the 'ups.'"
June 29, 1903
Cody to Davidson

"I am fortunate to have procured the services of women whom I trust."
October 15, 1903
Davidson to Cody

"Such picture shows will be nice little novelties."
October 29, 1903
Cody to Davidson

"Such extreme measures are constitutionally justified under the rationale of 'Greater good for all.'"
November 10, 1903

Davidson to Cody

"I feel like I have one big old sack of snakes."
December 15, 1903
Cody to Davidson

1904

"*I believe the natural tendency of the human body is to heal itself.*"
January 2, 1904
Davidson to Cody

"*I return from circumstances that try belief and hope for the future.*"
February 18, 1904
Cody to Davidson

"*There is no morphia for the soul.*"
February 24, 1904
Davidson to Cody

"*I was only trying to do what I thought best.*"
March 14, 1904
Cody to Davidson

Human relationships decay and unfortunate events and stories emerge—unfortunately, yours sells newspapers."
March 25, 1904
Davidson to Cody

"*I may be naughty, but I'm no hypocrite.*"
June 28, 1904
Cody to Davidson

1905

"I only wish God hears my side of the story."
January 10, 1905
Cody to Davidson

"I already have enough blood suckers in my life."
June 14, 1905
Cody to Davidson

"I have suffered through the direst of circumstances."
July 21, 1905
Davidson to Cody

"Perhaps our two sons play together."
August 10, 1905
Cody to Davidson

"Night times are the worst."
September 1, 1905
Davidson to Cody

"Time doesn't bring healing, just tolerance."
November 1, 1905
Cody to Davidson

"I continue somewhat at odds with my medical colleagues."
November 23, 1905
Davidson to Cody

Chil Scoggin

1906

"I value my privacy."
January 20, 1906
Davidson to Cody

"I must focus on the future and march forward."
February 20, 1906
Cody to Davidson

"Greetings from France."
March 5, 1906
Cody to Davidson

"What is money without health?"
March 24, 1906
Cody to Davidson

"Fresh air and exercise, combined with sufficient rest, are bet-
ter than any tonic."
April 22, 1906
Davidson to Cody

"Life continues to conspire against Buffalo Bill."
June 18, 1906
Cody to Davidson

"My practice flourishes."
July 5, 1906
Davidson to Cody

"Evidently money and printer's ink cannot buy every elected
office."
November 7, 1906
Davidson to Cody

1907

"It's been quite some time since I have heard from you."
February 19, 1907
Davidson to Cody

"Work I must."
February 28, 1907
Cody to Davidson

"But I am a bit low."
April 27, 1907
Cody to Davidson

"That you are so afflicted simply confirms that you have a conscience."
May 15, 1907
Davidson to Cody

"I still want to believe in a brotherhood of man."
May 26, 1907
Cody to Davidson

"Wherever I have gone, issues of race have confounded my own sense of justice and humanity."
June 13, 1907
Davidson to Cody

"In all my enterprises, the most difficult challenge is people."
August 29, 1907
Cody to Davidson

1908

"We've never been a family that has showed our emotions."
May 20, 1908
Davidson to Cody

"But in the end, there is only Buffalo Bill to solve problems."
September 7, 1908
Cody to Davidson

"I first thought it was you, knowing your taste for adventure and innovation."
November 19, 1908
Davidson to Cody

"I feel such relief."
December 27, 1908
Cody to Davidson

1909

"I have come to appreciate that the holiday season brings out behaviors in humans that at best, they regret, and at worse, require my medical attention."
March 10, 1909
Davidson to Cody

"I will pay back my debts, and be on easy avenue."
May 27, 1909
Cody to Davidson

"I have no problem than I cannot handle with the tonics of hard work, professional behavior, good books, and the occasional adventure."
June 30, 1909
Davidson to Cody

1910

"There are two jackasses in this picture."
February 20, 1910
Cody to Davidson

"I fear my Denver colleagues...will not be happy with me."
March 5, 1910
Davidson to Cody

"My cousin in Canada has been sending me some little powders."
June 23, 1910
Cody to Davidson

"I understand the bond between weakness and regret."
July 1, 1910
Davidson to Cody

"I wish my mood were as sunny as this place."
September 25, 1910
Cody to Davidson

It greatly saddens me to hear of your difficulties.
October 6, 1910
Davidson to Cody

"I am full of Arizona sunshine and enthusiasm."
November 1, 1910
Cody to Davidson

1911

"Every good actor should know when and how to get off the stage."
March 18, 1911
Cody to Davidson

"This is good for both of you since loneliness can be so deadly."
March 25, 1911
Davidson to Cody

"I don't trust happiness."
September 12, 1911
Cody to Davidson

"I realized my long-standing ambition to visit Summit Springs."
October 1, 1911
Davidson to Cody

1912

"Alas, I also think I have played Santa far too long for far less appreciative people."
March 15, 1912
Cody to Davidson

"I feel a part of my life has again been torn away."
April 30, 1912
Davidson to Cody

"What is now heartbreaking, I wager will prove providence."
May 6, 1912
Cody to Davidson

"I have lost a fortune and next year must return to the road."
December 15, 1912
Cody to Davidson

"I may be out of place, but felt moved to urge you caution in your dealings with these two."
December 29, 1912
Davidson to Cody

1913

"Oh, what treachery!"
July 27, 1913
Cody to Davidson

"Showman Cody Dead."
August 14, 1913
Davidson to Cody

"Now I have been caught."
September 17, 1913
Cody to Davidson

"Fatigue and lack of rest makes cowards of us all."
October 1, 1913
Davidson to Cody

"I feel like new money."
October 10, 1913
Cody to Davidson

"The hungry child needs attention, not the tut-tut of pity."
November 1, 1913
Davidson to Cody

"We both will know what it's like to be on display."
November 21, 1913
Cody to Davidson

"Medicine is a calling, not a business."
December 1, 1913
Davidson to Cody

1914

"*I feel like a dancing bear.*"
March 1, 1914
Cody to Davidson

"*It saddened me during our visit to learn of your father's death.*"
April 15, 1914
Cody to Davidson

"*The road to be walked between treatment and toxicity is narrow, and at some passages, treacherous.*"
April 25, 1914
Davidson to Cody

"*I am forming another company.*"
July 1, 1914
Cody to Davidson

"*I have continued on the outs with much of the Denver medical community.*"
July 8, 1914
Davidson to Cody

"*All is not as bleak as this tired old scout would complain.*"
August 6, 1914
Cody to Davidson

"*So often it appears that the public person may be a mirror reflecting the private one.*"
August 20, 1914
Davidson to Cody

1915

"I have high hopes for their success."
March 10, 1915
Cody to Davidson

"He was as fine a gentleman as I've had the privilege to know."
May 15, 1915
Cody to Davidson

"There is no doubt of the injustice being done to the Indian."
May 27, 1915
Davidson to Cody

"I dream like I never have before."
August 5, 1915
Cody to Davidson

"There is a physician in Vienna who is creating quite a stir."
August 20, 1915
Davidson to Cody

"Those were the days."
September 15, 1915
Cody to Davidson

"I find it laudable that the complexity of human behavior is being dissected and discussed outside of the usual revelations of scripture."
September 29, 1915
Davidson to Cody

"I found myself dreaming of my dear, sweet mother."
October 6, 1915
Cody to Davidson

"I trust you will keep this in confidence, just as I have your disclosures."
October 15, 1915
Davidson to Cody

"I have been told it is delicious."
November 6, 1915
Cody to Davidson

"To the road I must return."
December 23, 1915
Cody to Davidson

"I'm not sure I believe in God, but I certainly believe in the Devil."
December 29, 1915
Davidson to Cody

1916

"Now I have new excitement."
January 10, 1916
Cody to Davidson

"I remind myself that deeds, not words, define a man."
February 1, 1916
Davidson to Cody

"Spring has arrived, and with it hope for another new beginning."
April 1, 1916
Cody to Davidson

"I have continued to have problems passing my water."
September 16, 1916
Cody to Davidson

"I wish I could be more positive as it relates to your condition of most discomfort."
September 22, 1916
Davidson to Cody

"I am so tired."
October 2, 1916
Cody to Davidson

"Violence is everywhere; I hate it but I am so drawn to it."
October 16, 1916
Cody to Davidson

"Your 'taking inventory' and conflicted feelings place you within those members of our race who have conscience."
October 21, 1916

Davidson to Cody

"I can say that the expectancies of the world about the life of Buffalo Bill were only exceeded by my own."
November 11, 1916
Cody to Davidson

"Pain comes in many forms."
November 27, 1916
Davidson to Cody

1917

"I might honor us both by allowing the future to experience our past."
September 30, 1917
Davidson to Cody

1899

"I would kindly appreciate if you would conduct a medical examination."

October 14, 1899   Urbana, Illinois

Dear Dr. Davidson,

    I trust I am not being too bold in contacting you. My name is William F. Cody, also known throughout the world as "Buffalo Bill."

I am writing you at the suggestion of your father, with whom I have had a longstanding friendship due to our common interest in the theatre. He is a fine man who I first met while performing on the Chicago stage.

I have a possible issue with my health, and I would kindly appreciate it if you would conduct a medical evaluation.

I have occasion to travel to Denver this month during the week of the twenty-second, and I am certain that I can adjust my schedule to accommodate a day and time of your convenience.

I trust I am not presumptuous in my request.

Sincerely,

W.F. Cody

"I am most happy to be of service."

October 18, 1899   Denver, Colorado

Dear Mr. Cody,

    I am most happy to be of service.

    I practice out of my home located at 1320 Pennsylvania Street. Perhaps upon your arrival in Denver you could contact me via telephone. My number is Main 2906. I anticipate being particularly available between the hours of 9 a.m. and noon.

You may recall that I had the pleasure of meeting you at the Wild West at the 1893 Chicago World's Fair. You arranged for Father and me to visit to the grounds of the presentation, as well as wonderful seats for the performance. I particularly enjoyed meeting the Indians and cowboys as well as seeing the many animals under your charge. I had recently graduated from University of Illinois, and I had journeyed to Chicago to visit with my father. Meeting you was the highlight of my trip. I confess, as a youth I read the publications about your many exploits, beginning with Ned Buntlines' serial stories, "Buffalo Bill, King of the Border Men." Of course, Father has spoken glowingly about you, and I must admit I harbored a bit of jealously about his interactions with you.

I note that you write to me from the town of my birth.

With all best wishes,

Edgar Y. Davidson, M.D.

"Buntline was quite taken with me."

October 22, 1899   North Platte, Nebraska

Dear Dr. Davidson,

I regret that obligations at my ranch, as well as other business matters, have dictated that I delay my trip to Denver until November 1. Might I call you then?

Ah, Ned Buntline. We first met at Fort McPherson, just down the river from North Platte where my Scout's Rest Ranch is located. I was a scout for Colonel Carr and had just returned from the Battle of Summit Springs. I had a fine Indian pony that I had captured after the battle. I named him "Tall Bull," after the Indian leader killed at the battle. The horse was quite swift, and I won a great deal of money match-racing him at the fort. This was during my drinking days, and I am sad to admit I lost Tall Bull while gambling under the influence of Old Joe.

Buntline was quite taken with me. His real name was Judson. Later, he persuaded me to appear on the Chicago stage in his production of "The Scouts of the Plains or Red Deviltry As It Is." It was quite successful and launched my acting career. Our first production was December 11, 1872, and I remember it quite well. I stumbled and bumbled my way through, but the audience loved it. The critics carved me up, but the cash kept coming in.

As your father may have told you, it was during the performance of our "Scouts of the Prairie," where I first met Dr. Davidson. John Burwell Omohundro, also known as "Texas Jack," and I had a scene in the act where we simulated an Indian fight. We pledged to "wipe the redskins out," which thrilled the audience. Unfortunately, during the fight, W.J. Halpin, who played the role of "Big Wolf," was accidentally stabbed in the belly. Your father, who was in the audience, jumped on stage and immediately started to treat poor Halpin. He suffered throughout the week, and then died of the injury. Throughout this time, your father cared for him. The only good thing to come out of this tragedy was our friendship.

I look forward to our meeting.

With appreciation,

William F. Cody

"I too look forward to our meeting and
being of assistance to you."

October 28, 1899   Denver, Colorado

Dear Mr. Cody,

I quite understand your necessity to delay our meeting. I have also learned that a true admonition of my calling is, "The ill often burden the well." Not that you are burdensome. I too experience unexpected events in my personal life that dictated I adjust my calendar.

Kindly call me on the morning of November 2, and we will find a mutually satisfactory time at which to meet. In anticipation, I will tentatively reserve the time of 2 p.m. on November 3 at my home.

I too look forward to our meeting and being of assistance to you.

By the way, I have a keen interest in the history of the West. One of my goals is to visit the Summit Springs battle

site. I am impressed with how few people know the importance of this battle, particularly since it was the defeat of the
Cheyenne Indian Dog Soldiers and figured prominently in the
settlement of the West. One of the things that has distressed
me in moving from the East to Denver has been the Indians I
see on the banks of the Platte River as it flows out of this city.
Their camps are little more than lean-to shelters with frightfully poor horses and worse-appearing dogs. The children will
wave at me, but the women either turn away or hold out their
hands in search of coin. Smoke from their cooking fires burns
my eyes, and I know not what they cook. Of course, game is
gone, and those that come to the city rely on the charity of the
churches. I am told that the Catholic Church is particularly active, but priests trade poor beef for baptism.

Sincerely,

E.Y. Davidson, M.D.

"I appreciate your taking the time."

November 15, 1899   North Platte, Nebraska

Dear Dr. Davidson,

I enjoyed meeting you, and appreciate your
making the time to see me, particularly in your
comfortable home. It reminded me of my own North Platte
Welcome Wigwam that I purchased after the first one burned.
Good ol' North Platte. My business was crackin', so I also
bought the town band the best uniforms, filled the coffers of
churches, and donated the land for the fairgrounds and cemetery. Even the boy opening the door for me at the saloon
received a $5-tip from Buffalo Bill. I told my wife Louisa,
"Mamma, your Willie is generous to tribe and town."

Although we did not have a chance to chat, I enjoyed meeting your fair wife and infant son.

I was taken by your little horseless buggy, and I am con-
sidering finding one for myself. I have always been drawn to
the new, even as my career in show business has been about
recreation of the old. For instance, the electric dynamo has al-

lowed the Wild West to generate its own electricity.

I also found the view from your home of the new Colorado state capitol splendid. I believe there is talk of replacing the copper dome with gold, which would be most fitting for Colorado and its rich lodes of ore. Now if something could be done about the smell of horse manure in the Denver streets on a hot day!

My business partner, Nate Salsbury—ever the one to put numbers on things—calculated that when the Wild West played Madison Square Garden in New York City, each of our more than 800 horses in the show produced, on average, twenty-two and a half pounds of manure each day. At one point, our dung heap was the tallest mountain in Manhattan!

As I mentioned, I have recently closed the gates of the show season and have since been on the jump. I have of late suffered from fatigue, no doubt occasioned by my travel schedule and my many obligations. This year in the United States, the Wild West traveled more than 11,000 miles in 200 days. We gave over 300 performances in 132 towns and cities. Because so many people count upon me, and I need my health to meet this obligation, I thought it wise to seek your attention. Your affirmation that my health is tip-top provided me great comfort. I wrestled with a nasty bout of the typhoid fever a few months ago. It is my hope that having had typhoid, I am resistant to future affliction. As I move the Wild West from city to city and camp to camp, I always worry about contagion.

As to our conversation about temptation of drink, I will do my best to enter into the regimen you suggested. As I mentioned, I do not believe I have a great problem, but I thought it best to discuss it in confidence with someone before it, as we say on the Plains, "Starts to grow horns." With your permission, I will advise you as to my progress.

I enjoyed my time in Denver and rolling out my bedroll at the Brown Palace Hotel. Did you know that there is a little railroad from the Brown's basement to the Navarre building across Tremont Street? I went for a ride on it and found myself in a first-rate gentlemen's entertainment establishment! I did encounter one gent who was a bit too far into his cups. He recognized me and started to make a racket about how he was a better shot and how many Indians he'd killed. The Navarre proprietress was a woman formidable of bosom and standards. She did not take kindly to this, and her doorman, himself an awesome member of the African race, saw the man out the door, administering a whopping kick to his sit-down on the way out. The bigger the mouth, the better it looks shut!

It is my desire to remain vigorous so as to perform and support my various important ventures that carry me comfortably into my old age and bring me business recognition beyond just being known as a showman.

Sincerely,

Wm. F. Cody

"I cannot accept explanations that revolve around moral weakness."

November 21, 1899   Denver, Colorado

D ear Mr. Cody,
       Thank you for your recent correspondence. I enjoyed making the acquaintance of a man whose talents and travels I have for so long admired.

As to the imbibing issue we discussed, it is my strong personal opinion that so-called remedies being widely advertised and otherwise promoted are to be avoided. Some nostrums that are not just bunk are also dangerous. Unfortunately, I also am distressed to see attitudes changing in such a way as to move my profession away from understanding the nature of this affliction as we would any other human malady. I cannot accept explanations that revolve around moral weakness. When exposed to any external source of pleasure, the human body is often inclined to move from a state of pleasant response from occasional enjoyment to one in which ever-increasing sensation of thirst must be satisfied.

This produces profound effects on both body and behavior that cannot be simply brushed aside as symptoms of sin or moral turpitude. Therefore, I must once again reiterate that resolution of this issue will prove difficult, and it will only be through reaffirmation of sobriety and discipline, not just daily, but throughout the day—particularly during times of greatest vulnerability, eventide.

I found your mention of suffering last year from typhoid fever of interest. While a medical student at Johns Hopkins, I was involved in a number of cases from the typhoid outbreaks that have so long plagued Baltimore. My mentor, Dr. William Osler, had a special interest in infectious diseases, and regularly drilled into our head that humans are unique among creatures in that only we are susceptible to this disease.

Your concerns about contagion are justified. Typhoid invariably is from water or food, contaminated with the causal bacteria Salmonella typhi. The long-standing medical aphorism about transmission of typhoid fever is, "fingers, food, and flies," and the companion dictum to lessen the risk from food: "boil it, cook it, peel it, or forget it."

Other names for typhoid include "jail fever" and "ship fever." Both relate to the existence of confinement and non-hygienic conditions that promote the germ. One can imagine the hygienic challenges you face as you move the wonderful Wild West humans and animals from town to town and from campsite to campsite. There are good reasons typhoid has also been called "camp fever."

Lest one think typhoid is a risk only within primitive environments, outbreaks also occur in hospitals, and thus another ignoble name, "hospital fever."

As to the question of future bouts of typhoid fever, having recovered many months ago, you are beyond the risk of relapse; however, an attack of typhoid fever does not provide long-lasting protection from a future contracting of the same illness.

Again, it was my pleasure to meet you, and I close with

best wishes for continued good health and prosperity.

Sincerely,

E.Y. Davidson, M.D.

"I have had many fine pards, but..."

December 1, 1899   West-bound Union Pacific RR

Dear Dr. Davidson,

Once again, I was pleased to make your acquaintance on my recent trip to Denver. And, thank you for the lesson about typhoid. I will definitely keep the Cody guard up for a clean camp and hard-washed hands.

I must admit I have felt a bit foolish over my last letter to you. I know I prattled on, but I must tell you it felt good to be able to share thoughts without condition. I have had many "pards," a western term for "partner," But not enduring friends with whom I could share confidences. In my younger days, I did have those who I regarded as friends, but unfortunately this was fueled and fanned by drink, gambling, and a bit of sport. When I tempered, I needed to find a whole new group of friends. That has proven a challenge. I have worked with many on the stage, in the Wild West, as well as my various enterprises. Unfortunately, I've found business and friendship a bad mix.

In the past I've tried sharing private thoughts and circumstances with a minister or two and even a priest. While they do not trade in gossip, unfortunately it has been my experience there is a tariff on trust. I may share my secrets, but they want to share my purse.

I know doctors are oath-sworn to keep secrets, but I also sensed that you have an active mind that might enjoy this old scout's thoughts and experiences. Please jerk me up short if this is too bold.

Finally, in the spirit of forthrightness, I close with a small, but important observation. I have had the unfortunate occasion to deal with other members of your profession. All washed their hands *after* examining me. You, on the other hand, washed yours *before* you examined me, and this I greatly appreciate.

With best regards,

W.F. Cody

"I am intrigued by the opportunity for correspondence, and warm to experimentation."

December 15, 1899   Denver, Colorado

D ear Mr. Cody,

I am receipt of your letter of December 1.

I assure you that in no way did I find your letter in any way forward or offensive.

I am intrigued by the opportunity for correspondence, and warm to experimentation.

In fact, we share a bit of similar circumstance as it relates to absence of true friendship.

Because of my wife's health, we relocated from Baltimore to Denver. The salubrious climes of the Rocky Mountains are said to be particularly efficacious in the treatment of lung conditions.

I have had little correspondence with those I left in Baltimore, perhaps because of my choice of surreptitious marriage.

Beyond patients, the people I most commonly interact with on a daily basis are those that share my profession. In truth, I find many, if not most, poorly trained to the point that their bleedings, purging, and blistering are not just ineffective, but dangerous.

I too believe there is hazard in mixing friendship with profession. When disagreement arises, it doubles the consequences of a falling out. I most value people who respect me enough to disagree or correct, provided they are committed to truth. I know this sounds a bit the platitude, but nonetheless, it is true.

In contrast to the richness of your life, I fear you will find mine mundane. Beyond my wife's health and our new son, my biggest challenge of late has been starting my medical practice here in Denver. In the first few months, few people sought my attention. One day, the cook I employ said to me, "Doctor, I hate to be daring, but I would like to share something with you."

"Of course," I replied.

"Well," she said, "I know you are a fine young doctor, and have the best of training, but there is one thing."

"And what would that be?" I asked.

"When you travel to see a patient, you employ a horse cab, or you take the trolley."

"As transportation, they are quite practical madam. Plus, it avoids the bother of stabling a horse."

"Doctor, true that be, but when people see you using common transportation, they assume you cannot afford something better, because you are not a very good doctor."

I heeded her advice, bought the little electric run-about you so admired, and consequently, my practice has started to thrive.

I must also admit that I do find the little vehicle both convenient and entertaining. If more people drove them, they might do something about the dung and its smell that often clots on our streets. I might also note that talk of electricity abounds in Denver. Not far from here to the south in Colorado Springs, the noted electrical scientist Nicola Tesla has erected a huge apparatus to test his theory that electrical current can be transmitted over large distances, even from continent to continent, without the use of wires. He has chosen Colorado for his experiments in part because of our wonderfully pure air. I predict we will hear the name "Tesla" synonymous with electrical advances for years to come.

I look forward to our ongoing correspondence. While you and I are very different, not only of age, but of profession and experience, I find that appealing. I enjoy writing, and it is only made better by having someone to whom to write. To trust another is to risk betrayal, but trust we must.

With sincerity,

E.Y. Davidson, M.D.

"My desire is to be as successful in business as I have been a showman."

Decmber 21, 1899   Burlington Railroad

Dear Doctor,

I write to you as I travel to the new town in Wyoming that bears my name. It represents a grand step in the development of the Shoshone River basin and the West. Water brings farms, and farms bring families. When my plan is complete, I will have bought over 100,000 acres of old prairie under irrigation, and the water will stream to these families, and, as a consequence, money will also flow to my investors and me. It will assure accomplishing my desire to be as successful in business as I have been as a showman.

The road is rough, but the air sweet with the smell of sagebrush. I can almost taste the money I will make in this country and the happiness I will bring to prosperous new settlers and merchants.

Tonight, I will sleep at my T E Ranch outside of Cody. I'm sure I will dream of the fat cattle and fine horses my success will bring to its pastures. I will awake brimmed up with excitement and enthusiasm. Like most people, there are a few times when I feel a worn down by challenges and disappointment. But I've found the best treatment is putting my mind to work coming up with capital ideas and next getting on with the work of making them happen. Happy then is the heart of Buffalo Bill.

I've got a passel of projects going on in Cody. I'm starting a military school for young men. The mineral springs will provide health-giving waters. I'm even going in the oil business, and there's also plenty of good coal to be mined.

The name of the river near my town has been changed from "Stinking Water" to "Shoshone." There is a bit of the sulfurous taint to the water, but the new name certainly more respectable.

The railroad is on the way to Cody, and that will neatly knit everything together in my scheme.

I have designs for as fine a hotel as you will see in this part of the country—a hotel that will rival the Brown Palace. I also plan to provide other establishments of grand accommodation to those traveling to visit the wonders of Yellowstone Park, which is nearby, and only a short few days' wagon ride away from the town of Cody.

Doctor, one thing I will not tolerate in my new hotel is those Gideons who are now going around placing bibles in guest rooms. I often stay at the Hoffman House in New York, and entering my room recently, I saw a Gideon Bible sitting on the table next to the bed. I do not need or appreciate such reminders of morality and direction as to behavior. I called the bellman, and at my request, he removed it.

Of course, I would be most happy to have you as my guest in Cody, and should you find interest in in this most promising venture, I am sure I could find a way to provide a little room for your investment. I am prudent with my own money, as well as with that of my investors. I raise the money I need, and not a penny more. A bigger loop don't catch a better calf.

If you and your lovely wife are so inclined, I extend an invitation for her also to be a guest in Cody.

Finally, I am grateful for your interest in continued correspondence. In honesty, I am curious about your mention of the surreptitiousness of your marriage. My own has been anything but that!

I thank you for your time, and I ask that you send my best wishes to your father. He is a fine man, a patron to the stage.

Good cheer and hope for the future,

Merry Christmas!

Wm. F. Cody

"Thank you for your kind remembrances of my father."

December 27, 1899   Denver, Colorado

Dear Mr. Cody,

Thank you for your invitation to visit your town of Cody. I have only recently moved to Denver from Baltimore. My wife is quite ill with consumption, and in addition, we have an infant son. So, it is quite impractical for me to travel at present. Perhaps my family can make a visit when my wife's health improves, and my son is a little older.

I don't know how much Father has told you about me, but you might find some things of interest, particularly as it relates to my relocation to Denver.

In 1893, I entered the new medical school at Johns Hopkins University in Baltimore, Maryland. Earlier that year I graduated from the University of Illinois at Urbana-Champaign. When we first met at the Columbia Exposition, I was visiting father on my way to Baltimore to matriculate at Johns Hopkins medical school.

When I entered the school, it struggled financially and survived on the conditional benefaction of a local women's group —a decision more financial than philosophical. The condition for the advanced funds was Hopkins would admit women to the medical school. When Hopkins accepted the women's money, one revered and objecting faculty member, William T. Councilman, packed up and left for Harvard.

As a consequence of the admission policy, one of my medical acquaintances at Hopkins was Gertrude Stein. Although most found her loud, rather self-concerned, and foppish of dress, I was drawn to her through our common love of books. She was a rather short woman with the top of her head not even as high as below my shoulder. She wore her dark, somewhat wiry hair close-cropped. I recall a voice that sounded to emanate deep within her chest. She trailed a slight odor of clothing worn a day too long. Though a student of medicine, she always had many other books in hand and her rather large nose deep into them, even when she walked.

One of the surgical trainees I first encountered was a Dr. Harvey Cushing. Dr. Cushing arrived when I was a senior student on the surgical service. Although regarded as a brilliant student at Harvard who had interned in Massachusetts General Hospital, it was rumored that because of his particularly abrasive behavior, he was encouraged to look elsewhere for further training. Dr. William Halsted, head of surgery at Hopkins, and one of the most highly regarded surgeons in North America, agreed to take on the young doctor.

As a surgical resident at Hopkins, Cushing quickly proved to be both a hard, sarcastic taskmaster. But he also had a keen and innovative mind. The previous year, German physicist Wilhelm Conrad Röntgen demonstrated that rays produced by passing an electric current through a vacuum tube could produce an image of the inner bones of the human body. For his experimental studies, he enlisted his wife and displayed as evidence an image he produced of her hand with her wedding ring visible on the bone of her left finger.

Professor Röntgen named the rays produced by the tube "X-radiation" due to its unknown nature. Dr. Cushing had helped procure an x-ray tube for Massachusetts General, and he brought it to Hopkins.

One day, a woman appeared at Hopkins with a gunshot wound inflicted by her bartender husband during a family brawl. The shot to her neck partially paralyzed her. Dr. Cushing believed the site of the bullet could be determined using the Röntgen approach. To this end, photographic plates were positioned under the patient's neck, and while I turned the crank on a huge machine that generated the electrostatic current necessary to activate the Röntgen tube, Dr. Cushing directed the x-rays to the woman's neck. We made repeated tries, with Cushing developing the plates using a foul-smelling solution in a darkened room off the surgical theatre. Finally, an excellent image emerged, showing the bullet lodged in the vertebra next to the poor woman's spinal cord. It was a triumph for Dr. Cushing and the subject of his first medical paper and allowed him to help found the first radiological service at Hopkins. Alas, the woman's paralysis remained permanent. As I recall, her name was "Lizzie," and throughout our exploration she was very patient and brave.

At Hopkins, I became the protégé of Dr. William Osler. An icon of medical history, Osler changed medicine by bringing science into the study and practice of medicine.

In his famous medical textbook, *The Principles and Practice of Medicine,* Osler revolutionized the practice of medicine because he focused on describing diseases, not just promoting therapies of limited, if any, value.

As well as being an outstanding physician, Osler was a gifted teacher. The "Oslerian way" emphasized teaching at the bedside of patients and learning through their examination and care. I clearly recall him saying to me, *"Young doctor, in medicine, to not read is to set to sea without charts. To study medicine without patients is to not set to sea at all."*

This was revolutionary because in many medical schools, students can graduate with a medical degree having never seen a patient.

After graduating from medical school, I remained at Hopkins as Osler's intern. I aspired to a career in academic medicine, but fate had other plans for me, and herein rests an explanation why I characterized my early marriage as secret.

Medical students and interns were not allowed to marry. It was thought that marriage served as a distraction to learning. Even so, I had fallen in love with a young nurse, and we secretly married during my senior year in medical school. While some see "love at first sight" as a trope or figure of speech, it surely was the case when I first saw Jane. A long, starched dress and apron of her uniform covered her slight figure. Her blond hair was securely pinned up and covered on top by her nursing cap. I watched her at the bedside, kindly holding a woman's head with one hand while with the other spooning warm broth into the patient's mouth. The next day I found excuse for speaking to her. When she looked into my eyes, I felt our fates intertwine and thus, the marriage.

Unfortunately, not long after our wedding, Jane contracted pulmonary tuberculosis from one of her patients. By now I had taken a position as a new faculty member on Dr. Osler's Hopkins medical service. Sadly, at the same time we learned of this diagnosis, we also discovered that Jane was pregnant. Consumption is particularly dangerous during pregnancy. Osler counseled students and patients that becoming with child represented a condition to be avoided at all costs. We could have legally terminated the pregnancy as long as two physicians concurred that it was necessary to save Jane's life. Jane and I knew the risks, but we decided to carry on the pregnancy. I resigned my position at Hopkins, and with my ever-frailer wife, moved to Colorado in 1899.

Thank you for your kind remembrances of my father. He has spoken often about his friendship with you while you were on the Chicago stage. He was impressed about your raising funds to help those actors fallen on hard times.

You might find it of interest that my father is now the president of the Chicago "Whitechapel Club," an organization named after the area in London where Jack the Ripper preyed on his victims. The club meets for social reasons and to discuss notable Chicago murders. As the medical examiner, he always has some interesting medical fact or speculation to bring to a discussion. I remember that he said once you and he discussed the Jack the Ripper case and you were very upset.

Should I be of possible assistance to you in the future, please do not hesitate to contact me.

My best wishes for the New Year.

Sincerely,

Edgar Davidson, M.D.

1900

"What is life if we can't have fun?"

January 15, 1900   North Platte, Nebraska

Dear Dr. Davidson,

Best wishes and Happy New Year from W.F. Cody! We had quite the celebration here in North Platte. Perhaps a little too much cheer in that my wife is still a bit on the outs with me. But what is life if we can't have fun and shining times with good friends and family?

I wanted to thank you for your letter, particularly the words about your father and the Whitechapel affair. When Jack the Ripper started doing in those soiled doves in '88, as well as then carving up some of those poor dears, a rumor circulated that the killer might be one of my Indians who did not return to the States with me earlier that year. I was enraged then and even still when discussing that accusation, as your dear father so clearly remembers. To suggest that the maiming of the women was the mark of work by Indians is ignorant. To somehow equate the carnage on the women of Whitechapel with the work of Indians, still makes my blood boil.

Granted, Indians took scalps, but they learned it from the French. In 1876 after the Battle of the Little Bighorn, on the prairie of Nebraska, I procured the scalp of an Indian on Warbonnet Creek, held it in the air and proclaimed, "The first scalp for Custer." The troopers cheered, and my heart raced. My head felt a bit dizzy, perhaps because I had imbibed a bit of liquid courage as we rode out of Fort Robinson that morning. I recall that when I looked at the Indian's body, I realized this might have been the first man I had single-handedly killed, all my other gunshots having been sent in the smoke and chaos of battle. That morning I had dressed in the costume I often wore on stage, but this was not acting, and dead was my co-star on this particular stage. I kept the scalp, sometimes showed it on stage, and a friend displayed it in the window of his drug store.

Cutting up of bodies is nothing new. Following Custer's fall at the Little Bighorn, the Indians, primarily the women, had at the bodies of the troopers. What they did to the bodies of their enemies was directed by their religious beliefs about the afterlife. The reason they slashed the bodies and took off legs and the head was their trying to decrease the ability of an enemy to fight. It's been claimed that the Indian women pierced Custer's eardrums with needles so he would listen better.

It was not just the Indians who ravaged the bodies of dead foe. I am still sickened at the story of Chivington and his men returning to Denver in '64 after their attack on Indians at Sand Creek. His troops cut the Indians to pieces. They paraded through town displaying their rancid trophies of scalps, fingers, ears, and unmentionable parts from women they stretched over their saddle horns. To my thinking, them boys was the worst.

Enough of this. I will seal this letter and have it taken to the railroad yard to post in the RPO car. It's sparkling to think that the railroad postal service now connects this land, and this letter that I send today may well be in your hands tomorrow. Ain't progress grand!

Your Friend,

W.F. Cody

"Buffalo Bill"

"I used to fight Indians, now I fight speculators, government men, and lawyers."

March 30, 1900   North Platte, Nebraska

D ear Dr. Davidson,
I appreciate your taking the time to see me during my recent brief trip through Denver. I so enjoyed our meal at the Brown Palace. The beef was first rate, and just as I like it, rare enough that with a hot iron and caustic acid, I could have saved the critter. Doctor, I must say you looked so thin and drawn, but it was good to see you have an appetite. I hope your wife's health improves. I remember how my dear mother's illness brought stress to us all as we watched

her consumption march on.

I know my visit was unannounced and I hope not too intrusive. I apologize for my haste, but urgent business in Wyoming necessitated my attention and briefly leaving the preparation of my show for the upcoming season. I am in a damnable lawsuit over rights to my water. I used to fight Indians, now I fight speculators, government men, and lawyers.

When we talked over dinner, I told you how my journeys have shown me the rapid changes I see in the country and those in it. This was again evident from the window of the rail car as I traveled from Denver back home. From the Denver station I glimpsed good old Lookout Mountain that guarded the entrance to Clear Creek and the gold fields west of Denver.

My war bag is full of good old memories from those Colorado days as a footloose youngster on the tramp. Traveling north along the front range of Colorado to Cheyenne, the train stopped for water, and mixed with the soot and smoke of the engine, I smelled new-turned and sown earth from the many farms of Platte River Valley. How different from when I rode across these prairies as a lad.

When I changed trains in Cheyenne, in the terminal I saw immigrant families with bundles and babes. In the rail yards, trains with refrigerated cars for meat and fruit, and even special cars for the transport of oil scattered among the bawling masses of cattle cars. I remember when as a boy I traveled to Fort Bridger. The fort was located next to a large spring that produced oil used to lubricate the wheels and axels of wagons on the Oregon Trail and Mormon Road.

Cheyenne east to North Platte I witnessed how the farms now interrupted what was only a few years ago open bison range and the Nebraska Sand Hills.

I have been corresponding with my dear sister Julia. We agree that we are both getting old. Aches and pains have found new places to stakeout territory in our bodies. I now puff a bit on the top of stairs, and I do not like what I see in the brush when I neat up my hair. The book that sister Helen wrote about my life continues to sell well. It is so touching that Helen titled it, *The Last of the Great Scouts.* She is tender, dedicated to me, and kind.

I wish I could say the same about my valet, John Claire. A man easily looked down upon with crooked teeth and self-cut hair. I have to remind him to scrape under his nails. I have had a few words with him. He has become increasingly standoffish and seems to tut-tut about certain visitors to my private tent, even though I assure you they are of the most innocent nature. He needs to remember Buffalo Bill is the boss. If he does not improve, he will be kicked back to washing pans, mucking out stalls, and spreading manure.

Dr. Davidson, I do appreciate having someone with whom I can communicate. I am patient and you are doctor so I have greatest confidence in confidentiality.

Well, enough of this prattle from an old scout. I need to get down the trail. The Wild West opens in New York City in but three weeks. It's always good business in that city, and I greatly enjoy the restaurants. A particular favorite is Delmonico's. Their lobster Newburg is nectar. I have teased the chef for the recipe as I would like to feature it in my new Wyoming hotel. He has been evasive, but I'm sure it has lots of good butter, dollops of cream, yolk of eggs, cayenne pepper, and, a healthy splash of cognac. Just writing about it makes me relish and my innards rumble.

Yours in appreciation and sincerity,
WFC

"I abhor gossip, and believe it dreadful and deceitful."
April 15, 1900   Denver, Colorado

Dear Mr. Cody,
Allow me to reassure you that all my writings —from and to you—respects of the highest of privacy and privilege. I abhor gossip and believe it dreadful and deceitful. It is province of superficial souls try to convey to those who will listen their supposed superiority over those

about whom they chatter. I have found that the person who seeks me out to share gossip can only be trusted to do the same about me—and alcohol often sits at the same table.

I find you in good health, and given your age, you are remarkably vigorous. I am sure this will serve you well during your performances in New York. By the way, your description of the Delmonico lobster dish, "set my lips to smacking," as you might say. I hope to concoct some variation for my wife. The intake of good nutrition is so crucial for her health.

With appreciation,

E.Y. Davidson, M.D.

"I hate to bother you, but..."

June 23, 1900   Ambrose Park, New York City

Dear Dr. Davidson,

I know it has been some time since I corresponded with you, I have been mighty on the road making my business work. I hate to bother you, but I have been fiercely troubled by the piles. They particularly bother me at night. I wonder if you might have any suggestions, as everything I have tried has not worked.

Distressingly,

Wm. Cody

"Your condition and need for remedy are shared by many."

June 28, 1900   Denver, Colorado

Dear Mr. Cody,

Normally I avoid recommending treatment without first examining a patient; however, in the condition you describe, the symptoms are usually such that physical examination only confirms the obvious suspicion generated by a patient's complaints. I strongly feel that if you have not already been seen and examined by a competent physician familiar with piles (or as they are also called, "hemorrhoids") you should do so. On occasion other conditions can masquerade or present as the discomfort you are experiencing.

I wish that I might be able to afford you advice that will rapidly alleviate your distress, but I can assure that to my knowledge no speedy treatment exists. In general, I recommend taking a diet that helps soften the stool and prevents a decrease in bowel function and straining.

There are any number of nostrums and natural aperient waters that serve to stimulate the bowels. Prunes work well, and the cultivation of plums for prunes has become a major agricultural industry in California. This should assure you that your condition and need for remedy are shared by many.

If it is of consolation, you are in good company with your misery. Hemorrhoids reportedly prevented Neapolitan from mounting his horse at Waterloo. The Civil War General George Stoneman used hemorrhoids ("I cavalryman's complaint") as an excuse to retire from the field of battle and escape the wrath of his incompetent commander. King Alfred the Great, after a painful day's riding with swollen hemorrhoids, stopped in Cromwell at the shrine for a saint named Gueriir to pray for relief.

Did you know that sufferers from hemorrhoids even have their own patron saint, St. Fiacre, an Irish monk from the seventh century? That is why piles are sometimes referred to as "the figs of Saint Fiacre." A Catholic cardinal, suffering greatly from the affliction, made a pilgrimage to St. Fiacre's monastery, asked that the reliquary be opened, and the saint's bones applied to the area of his affliction. No claim of efficacy was recorded.

Karl Marx, whose works are now causing such international consternation, cursed his hemorrhoids while trying to finish *Das Kapital,* saying, "To finish I must sit down!" Dr. Livingston whom Stanley found in Africa, succumbed to the piles, bleeding to death, while kneeling in prayer.

But I digress.

As to treatment, sometimes sitz baths may give a degree

of relief. To accomplish this, you sit in a bath of warm water covering the affected area. At the same time, you place your feet in a tub of cold water. After three minutes, you reverse the process, with feet in warm water and distressed area in the cold.

If you are experiencing a particularly painful episode, application of ice may give some degree of relief and reduction of the inflammation. If possible, the pile should be gently reduced and returned within the sphincter of the rectum. Massaging in an astringent ointment of gallic acid and belladonna will facilitate this process as well as help cause the hemorrhoid to dwindle away. A competent pharmacist can provide you with the properly proportioned preparation. I have been told that dabbing on a cloth soaked in cider vinegar may provide some relief as well.

Of course, if none of these remedies work, then it may be necessary to move to surgery; although, I urge you to use all caution and allow patience in trial of other therapies before seeking such cure. I cannot over-emphasize the need to secure care from a competent surgeon who specializes in surgery of the bowel and rectum and provides suitable examples of a number of successful outcomes of his technique.

I apologize if I have gone into too much detail, and again urge you to seek care should your symptoms persist—particularly if bleeding is noted. Hopefully I have provided you with some information that will guide you in speaking with a fit practitioner. Finally, beware of the many charlatans promising cure. The quackery concerning cures of the affliction of the human body from fore to aft astounds me.

I close with words from the Book of Samuel, *"And the hand of Jehovah was heavy upon them of Ashdod, and he laid them waste, and smote them with hemorrhoids."*

Sincerely,
E.Y. Davidson, M.D.

"I have taken your counsel."

August 3, 1900   South Bend, Indiana

Dear Dr. Davidson,

I thank you for your letter to me providing wonderful advice. I have taken your counsel, found a helpful pharmacist, and can now report that the private pain has resolved, I can ride my horse into the arena without suffering, and I sleep like a baby lamb.

With appreciation,

Wm. F. Cody

"Forgive me if I'm once again being too forward."

November 13, 1900   Bridgeport, Connecticut

Dear Dr. Davidson,

I write to you from Wild West "Winter Quarters." My Indians have returned to reservation homes. I made sure that they had fine trunks in which to pack the goods they have bought, and they left with lots of jingle in their pockets. Most of the other men have returned to their homes, but some have stayed on in the East, and I have a bit of concern they will find mischief.

Again, I so appreciate your helpful suggestions for treatment of my piles. Your instructive and discrete response emboldens me to ask if you might have some suggestions for another sensitive issue involving affliction of the privy parts. Forgive me if I am once again being too forward, but this does involve an almost daily issue among the men of my troupe, and all too frequently impacts on their ability to perform. I hope to find a solution before the next travel season.

As you might imagine, I have a hardy group of men with robust appetites, used to rough and tumble. Even as a young man, I witnessed the comings and goings of men to sporting houses. I understand why my men have need to worship at the altar of Venus, but they all too frequently suffer the consequences.

No matter where I have taken my Wild West, we have had to deal with the gleet. The women where the Wild West sets up camp chase my men, particularly my Indians. The ladies of England were a bit reserved, those of France much more forward, but in Italy, I had to station guards around the camp. In spite of this, when daylight came, I witnessed an exodus of petticoats and stockingless legs.

The men complain to Dr. Powell of this itchy, runny, burny condition. Powell has great experience in this area due to his time as a contract surgeon to the army. He told me, "My main job in camp was treating the clap and confining the laundress."

Powell treats my men with a concoction of Indonesian peppers and balsam, and sometimes it seems to help. Others only respond to "tincture of time," with miserable weeks and even months of a prairie fire burning through their maypole when they pass water and have to wrap themselves with a kerchief to capture the foul discharge during the day.

Knowing you are a doctor knowledgeable of the latest advances in medicine, I thought you might have some suggestions I might share with Dr. Powell. He is not much of a scientist, but he is quick to jump to any new treatment that might bring him new patients, notoriety, and a bit of treasure. We are currently promoting a product called "White Beaver's Cough Cream" that Powell and I developed. It contains alcohol, chloroform, and opium. It is splendid for curing the cough of consumption and healing diseased lungs. Not only is it a fine product, but Powell and I will ring in the money, which is good because expenses are high, and I need to keep the creditors from making racket. At least I have my health and am "above snakes" and not residing in a coffin.

I look forward to hearing from you and assure you that you have my ever-abiding appreciation. I hope I am not producing an annoyance.

With gratitude,
William F. Cody
"Buffalo Bill"

"I greatly enjoy sharing advances in medicine."

December 4, 1900   Denver, Colorado

Dear Mr. Cody,

In truth, I greatly enjoy sharing advances in medicine, and find no imposition.

I understand the lustful ways of your men. As Dr. Osler told me, "The natural man has only two primal passions, to get and to beget."

Too often the importance of common diseases of sexual passion, such as those caused by the gonococcus, are underappreciated by the public, and, I fear, the medical profession. If gonorrhea could be eliminated from the wedded life, gynecology as a specialty would shrivel so as to be but a trifling portion of all medical practitioners.

Gonococcus infection is of great interest to me, first because so many people have sought me out for treatment. Second, the discovery by Neisser of the characteristic organisms was an important landmark in understanding the disease—particularly the rather remarkable experiment that proved the germs he found caused the ailment. When he inoculated them into the urethra of healthy men, he reproduced the disease. A victory for science, but a troublesome consequence for the experimental subject. I note that the famous Scottish surgeon, John Hunter, performed similar experiments regarding the transmission of syphilis in the eighteenth century. There persists a rumor that Hunter used himself as a subject. It is possible that in inoculating himself with pus from a patient with gonorrhea, became himself infected with syphilis.

Gonorrhea raged in the population served by the Johns Hopkins Hospital. It was as common as respiratory catarrh. As students assigned to the urology clinic, one of our responsibilities was to conduct massage of the prostate gland and seminal vesicles of gonorrhea patients. I can assure you, this was not a pleasant experience for either student or patient. Inserting a finger into the patient was invariably accompanied by a scream when the swollen, tender gland was touched. This was followed by the poor patient sobbing and sweating. I add that some suffering was on the student's part as well as he kneaded away in attempt to express and clear the infection. Some took an evangelical moment to discuss with their suffering patient the sinful consequences of their carnal carelessness. Fortunately, our female compatriots were spared from this experience, but they had substantial challenges in their own clinic providing comfort and counsel to the women afflicted by this malady. As the saying goes, "Under microscope we search for germs shaped like cocoa bean and find them in harlot and in queen."

Mr. Cody, this condition provides fertile territory for quack remedies. Treatments for gonorrhea—or "gleet" as you called it—include injections of silver, application of electric current to the genital region, or just walking on a cold floor in bare feet. The use of hemp extracts on the swollen, weeping member or the smoking of hashish has been promoted as providing relief; although, in my opinion, the aphrodisiac properties of the latter promotes propagation of the infection, not cure.

Some physicians irrigate the urethra and bladder with various solutions including nitrates—used to cure bacon as well as gonorrhea. None have proven definitive in relief. In the absence of an effective armament from the apothecary, my mentor, Dr. William Osler, simply relied upon "good food, good air, and open bowels."

You asked as to anything new, and to that I can bring good news. Dr. Albert Barnes of Philadelphia is a physician but trained as a chemist. He has developed a mild solution of silver nitrate for use in irrigating the festering urethra. He markets it under the name "Argyrol," and the reports have been encouraging.

Of additional particular importance, when the Barnes solution is placed into the eyes of infant children, it appears to be effective in preventing sore eyes and blindness caused by the gonorrhea infection entering newborn eyes as they pass through the infected birth canal.

Given the success of smallpox vaccination, efforts are now underway to produce a vaccine against the gonococcus germ. This effort is certainly a worthy scientific undertaking. If successful, and made mandatory in the male population, then I would predict that gonorrhea will eventually be relegated to the annals of medical curiosity.

Mr. Cody, there is another important point for you to consider. To quote Dr. Benjamin Franklin, "An ounce of prevention is worth a pound of cure." As it relates to gonorrhea, abstinence is a fool's recommended remedy. Men driven by the mission of passion are unlikely to take the time or have the inclination to determine if infection lurks in the object of the coupling. But a solution exists, even if imperfect. Condoms will protect men from both receiving and giving the infection. Those produced from internal animal tissues have limitations of cost, and for useful fit, they should be obtained from a physician who can assure proper size. The discovery by Charles Goodyear of the process called vulcanization has had many marvelous applications, one of which is to produce an elastic, well-fitting condom in an inexpensive process. The availability of these male shields—"rubbers" as they are now called—is an important advancement in the control of both gonorrhea and syphilis. While sensation is decreased, if properly used, it represents a wonderful way to avoid the near and far consequences of fornication. From a practical standpoint, because they are constructed of rubber, not the parts of animal bladder or bowel, they may be easily washed and reused again. You might well consider making these appurtenances discreetly available to your men. I recommend a Cody endorsement as to wisdom of use. You might provide further incentive if there exist consequences as to employment if infection follows from failure to practice practical prudence. Incidentally, I note that in my Sears Roebuck catalogue you endorse the rubber horse halter manufactured here in Denver by the Gates Rubber Company.

I wish you luck in your promotion of the White Beaver's Cough Cream. I strongly suspect the key ingredient is opium since both alcohol and chloroform are volatile, and when taken by mouth, as they are breathed out, they will irritate, not calm the inflamed airway. In contrast, opium—and its derivatives morphine and codeine—is a long-known suppressant of cough but suffers from the curse of physical addiction.

But this leads me to a final piece of good news.

The German company Bayer has developed a new form of morphine that is many times more potent than codeine in suppressing cough, particularly in those with the lungs of those who suffer from consumption, as well as patients with asthma, pneumonia, and bronchitis. As a cough syrup, it allows those with debilitating coughs to find relief, relax, and get much needed sleep. Furthermore, according to the experience of Bayer and physicians using this new drug, it has no toxic effects and is completely free of the risks of addiction. For this reason, this drug is now considered to be a medical breakthrough. Not only does it remarkably treat cough but restores great feelings of vitality to those so treated. It takes its name from the German word "heroisch," meaning "heroic." It is marketed under the name, "Heroin." While this new drug is just now being marketed in America, it might provide some competition to the White Beaver's concoction.

I trust you mind this information useful. I enjoyed sharing it with you.

With respect,
E.Y. Davidson, M.D.

"My life goes better."

December 18, 1900 North Platte, Nebraska "Scout's Rest"

Dear Dr. Davidson,

Thank you for your letter.

My health continues good, and I continually

appreciate your counsel regarding diet and treatment of my back-of-the-lap affliction. Natural cures are the best. In my trips to California, I have seen the plum orchards and walked among the fragrance of the blossoms. I can also note the odor of the fruit being dried into prunes.

Dr. Powell and I have conspired to develop many products. In addition to our cough cream, we also developed a coffee substitute for marketing to the Mormons. The German product causes me no concern. I have fattened on competition. My business partner, Nate Salsbury, and I have fought many "circus wars." It was critical that we lure customers and their money away from competing shows. Each customer counted. Our weapons were ink, paint, and paper. We sent out advance men ahead of the show to pass out handbills, buy advertising in the local newspapers, and put up posters. Our most effective poster was simple. It showed my image over a running buffalo and the words, "I am coming." It made people sit on their money and the circus eat empty seats. Our 1895 battle with the Ringling Brothers Circus cost Nate and me $16,000 but cost them $60,000. Hah! We won!

I also appreciate the information about the clap. Many years ago, in New Orleans, I had the opportunity to make the acquaintance of some young Englishmen touring America who definitely savored the sporting life. One of them contracted a carnal infection in his eyes and was forced to wear a set of goggles that allowed the bathing of his inflamed eyes in a treatment solution. I assure you that it gave a great laugh to all of us, but it did not seem to dampen his quest for the flesh.

I so thank you for the letter and assure you that I will take your recommendations most seriously when it comes to the care of my men. I am aware of the personal items you recommend and will consider ways by which they might discretely be made available to the troupe.

I have endorsed many products, but the rubber halters you mentioned are among the best. I became aware of them while in winter quarters in Denver when I was approached by a man named Gates who made them. He is the owner of the Gates Rubber Company that you mentioned in your previous letter. We tried a few, and then a few more. They were pretty much unbreakable, which was a great value. When our mustangs have to be kept confined in a train car for a couple of days, they are often reluctant to leave the car down the ramp. With the rubber halters, we just snap a pole to the mustang's halter, attach it to an elephant, and drag the beast out of the car.

My life goes better, and I am spending more time in Nebraska. I truly would rather wake up in the middle of nowhere than any city on earth. I take to this country like a horse takes to oats.

My wishes for the Merriest of Christmases and Happiness of New Years.

All the very best,
William F. Cody
"Buffalo Bill"

1901

"My wife is trying to poison me."

March 1, 1901   North Platte, Nebraska

D ear Dr. Davidson,
I am writing to you with great urgency as I must communicate with someone who is an expert in science and duty-bound to confidence.

I fear my wife is trying to poison me. Three days ago, she insisted that I drink a "special cup of tea." To stop her constant badgering, I agreed. It was bitter, and burned like bad whiskey, but I choked it down. A few minutes later, my poor head felt like it was about to explode, I broke out in a fearsome sweat, cascaded my breakfast, and then lost consciousness. My head still aches, and my breath has a frightful odor that would turn back a badger.

Once I recovered, I found in the kitchen a bottle of a liquid in Louisa's basket of potions bearing the label, "Dragon's Blood." When I removed the bottle's stopper, I noted that it smelled like the tea Lulu asked that I drink. Pouring a small amount into a tumbler, I saw it had a bright red color and coated the sides of the glass—I can only imagine what it did to my insides. When I confronted the woman, she screamed, "I bought it from a gypsy woman camped near the rail yard. I was only trying to recapture your love," and fell into a swoon.

As I think about this, I believe she must also be putting it in my whiskey—which I only take sparingly to help rest my nerves at the end of the day. I have experienced sweating and a turning stomach, which I attributed to my general weakened condition, and perhaps a bit of advancing age. I intend to challenge her. For now, I am bunking in my fine barn, and controlling my temper.

Louisa and I have been on the outs. My travel, particularly to Europe, has separated us by time and distance. I have, however, made sure that our home is as fine as can be. Now at Scout's Rest, there is a beautiful and comfortable mansion sitting on 4,000 acres of the best pastureland in Nebraska. I have populated it with top thoroughbred horses and purebred

Shorthorn, Angus, and Hereford cattle. One bull, Earl Horace, is widely considered the finest of his breed. Imagine my distress when I learned that much of the money I sent to my wife was used by her—without my knowledge or permission—to purchase land and livestock in her name only.

I also have had to deal with her powerful appetite for food, and other vices, resulting in her ever-expanding girth.

She also has a thunderous temper. At times she has also sent my guests fleeing from the ranch with her cursing and threats. When I brought this up, she rained tears and woo-woos, saying, *"Oh Willie, I was only trying to be the best wife for you and protect you from people taking advantage of your kind and generous heart."* Two days later, she exploded at two old boys I'd invited out to the ranch. We were enjoying a snort on the porch, discussing some dollar opportunities. Louisa nixed our little talk, and the next thing I know, she was coming across the yard at them with an axe, yelling, *"Get you rascals, get!"*

Doctor, it's hard to build a business when the wife is on the warpath.

By my truth, I have some regret that I abandoned my petition for divorce a few years ago. I put a halt to it when little daughter Orra Maude died of fever, and we buried her next to her little brother, and my son, Kit. Is there a greater pain than when the child dies before the parent?

I feel sadness and regret for once what our marriage was. I first saw Louisa astride a fine horse. It suddenly ran away with her, her long, black ringlets of hair flowing and flying. I rode like the wind to save her. (I have wondered if the "runaway" was her way of gaining my attention. Later I made a proposal to her, and even though my service to the Union intervened, I honored the commitment and we married. This was somewhat to the regret of her parents, given her community standing and me as just a veteran of the War of Separation, and a Union one at that.

I tried to provide for her, as my father had done when he moved from Iowa to Kansas. William Rose, a contractor for the Kansas Pacific Railroad, and I staked out a town at a location the westward moving railroad was sure to pass. We decided we needed a grand name for our new town and called it, "Rome." Louisa and I started a hotel at a location I was drinking a bit, and I fear it made me both too confident and a bit stubborn. When I refused to share my town with the railroad, they sent the route around me, started a new town, "Hays City," and my business failed.

Yep, Doctor, "The rise and fall of Rome."

What's the old saying—"pigs get fat, hogs get slaughtered"? A great disappointment, but from that came opportunity for Will Cody. I started meat hunting for the railroad. Someone even came up with a little chant,

> Buffalo Bill, Buffalo Bill
> Never missed and never will
> Always aims and shoots to kill
> And, the Company pays his buffalo bill.

While I was hunting, Louisa with child returned east.

Separation strains the best of marriages, and the time it took to return home from my hunting and guiding obligations made visits rare.

When my career on the stage emerged, my travels took me throughout the country, and this continued as the Wild West became the world's premiere educational presentation. This brought many nights on the road and attendant separation. I have used the substantial funds I have generated to improve Louisa's circumstances. I provided a wonderful home in Rochester, New York, and returned to her when I could, and felt sorrow when support of the family required my leave-taking.

The delightful children we still produced during such visits speaks to our then affection.

I must close.

What might you tell me about this poison? Will the effects linger? I note that the red still stains my teeth, but that appears to be resolving. I worry about my innards.

What can one do under such circumstances in my home? I

am getting my show together for the road, but this taxes my brain and greatly strains my nerves.

I leave for New York, but my mail will be forwarded.

With appreciation and distress,

William F. Cody

"Buffalo Bill"

"I am in grief from the death of my wife."

April 5, 1901   Denver, Colorado

Dear Mr. Cody,
 I apologize for lateness in responding to your letter, but I am deep in grief from the death of my wife.

Dear Jane, in spite of her phthisis, she successfully brought forth a fine son; however, her consumption marched on. In addition to broken lungs, she suffered from a broken heart because the disease meant she could not suckle our infant or ever dare cuddle him in her arms.

Mr. Cody, this was a woman of remarkable self-assurance and will. Dr. Harvey Cushing, whom I helped produce the first Hopkins x-ray image, was known to drive nurses to tears. He would have fits of temper and belittle their competence. He tried this once with Jane. Jane calmly replied, "Dr. Cushing, I do not appreciate your words or their tone. However, I do know you have been long hours in the surgical suite, and the outcome not to your liking. I will forgive you, provided you retire to your quarters, get some rest, and pledge never to address me in this manner again." Cushing did not reply, but cut his rounds short, and left the ward.

Word of Jane's confrontation and courage spread like wildfire through the hospital, with resultant nods of "hear, hear," as she passed nurses, students, and aids in the hospital halls.

Despite his moods, Dr. Cushing and I worked well together; I believe because of a common dedication to patients and search for better methods of treatment. When he learned of my marriage and necessity to leave Baltimore, I feared his denunciation. Rather, he gave her a soft travel blanket and a me a copy of Vesalius' *On the Fabric of the Human Body*, originally written in the sixteenth century. I read it on the train west and cherish it to this day.

In dealing with Jane's illness, I utilized all rational methods for treatment and avoided the siren call of quack remedies. Great the temptation of humbug. Even I came close with a trial of the zomotherapy of raw minced meat given in generous portions three times daily. It only seemed to increase my wife's struggles with finding appetite. Better she tolerated the fresh buttermilk and kefir I obtained from the Montclair molkery dairy. Throughout this, a staple was bed rest in the fresh air and cool nights of our sleeping porch and the daytime warmth of the sunroom.

Unfortunately, my wife's disease did not relent. Fever smoldered, and her weight declined. Syrup of codeine did help quiet her tussive spells, particularly at bedtime, and allowed her some night's sleep without cough.

I enlisted the help of a colleague, Dr. Leonard Saltzman, of our Denver's National Jewish Hospital. National Jewish opened the same year Jane and I came to Denver as a national charitable hospital for consumptives. Its motto is, "None may enter who can pay—none can pay who enter." Dr. Saltzman's keen interest in tuberculosis is matched by a strong distrust of bunk and great respect for reason and science. Watching him care for patients and discuss difficult cases with me, I came to a conclusion that may be the highest praise one doctor has for another: "This is a person I can trust."

Dr. Saltzman agreed to attempt the air treatment developed by Dr. Carlo Forlanini of Italy. In 1882, the same year that Robert Koch discovered the tubercular bacillus as the causative agent, Forlanini described how partial collapse of an infected lung with injected air could improve the disease. Together Dr. Saltzman and I, using a large hypodermic needle, gently introduced air, and later nitrogen gas, into the space between my wife's left inner chest wall and lung. She so bravely tolerated the agony of our ministration. This technique, "pneumothorax," appeared to decrease both the amount and product of her cough. Her temperature taken by mouth returned to normal. I judged her asthenia to be improved. I must also mention, that even with such results, both Dr. Saltzman and I were subject of objection and near-censure by the Denver Medical Society for our performing what they felt to be a dubious experimental treatment.

Although she experienced a few months of clinical improvement, with the coming of spring, my wife's fever returned as did general weakness. With her gradual failure of strength, ever increasing amounts of blood appeared in her sputum. Late in an afternoon of the Monday in the third week February, a day when the snow melted on lawns as it fell, she began to hemorrhage freely from her lungs. I called Dr. Saltzman to our home. Sadly, before he could arrive, the dark bloody tide from my wife's lungs increased, her pulse weakened, and her gaze waned. She died in my arms, holding my hands for comfort as she passed over the horizon to I know not where. Dr. Saltzman and I both concurred that the disease had ulcerated and progressed to an aneurismal erosion into the pulmonary artery, a somewhat rare, but known cause of tubercular death.

The only thing that keeps me moving forward now is my work, so to address your question:

I believe it would be outside my purview to comment on your domestic circumstances; however, I can tell you the Dragon's Blood might be of two types. The first is a bright red plant resin used to treat "morbid impressions in the blood" since the time of the ancient Greeks. *Morbid impressions of the blood* is somewhat of a grandiose, and non-selective, phrase for any affliction ranging from fever, weight loss, and weakness to loss of human libido. It is also possible that the Dragon's Blood you report to have found is not from a plant, but rather cinnabar, red sulfide of mercury, which was called by the same name as the plant resin.

I favor the cinnabar mercury explanation because of your complaints of acute toxicity manifest by vomiting, collapse, and loss of consciousness. In contrast, the Dragon's Blood resin can be used for such things as violin varnish, and when taken by mouth, it is apparently quite benign. According to my copy of Thompson's *Handbook of Poisons, Preparations, and Treatment Thereof,* cinnabar in Dragon's Blood is quite toxic, inducing sweating and, in high enough dosages, brain, liver, and kidney damage, and even death. There is good news of sorts, assuming one survives the acute toxicity. Dragon's Blood's effects do not linger.

As to your teeth, you might try applying large amounts of soda powder, followed by vigorous brushing.

Perhaps we can discuss all this in more detail should you feel it appropriate when we meet again.

In addition, I have an infant son, Willis, for whom I have been arranging care.

With Sincerity,

E.Y. Davidson, M.D.

"If Bill can help you, I'll ride slick to get to you."

April 11, 1901   New York City

Dear Dr. Davidson,

It saddened this old scout's heart to learn of your wife's death. I lost my dear mother to consumption. I watched her wane and weaken as she struggled to care for her fatherless children. May God take a special likening to you and your son. I falter as I reflect on my own situation and how I burdened you in my last letter. I must say that having someone in whom I might confide does help suck out poison. If Bill can help you, I'll ride slick to get to you. You have my word on it.

Sincerely,

William F. Cody

"Buffalo Bill"

"Sometimes free advice is worth twice the price."

April 20, 1901   New York City

Dear Dr. Davidson,

My hope is this letter finds you somewhat better in the tragedy of your loss. I find from my own experiences that if grief does not become all-consuming, time does indeed provide healing. I felt this after my brother was killed in a horse accident, the loss of my father, Mother's passing, and little Kitty's death.

I write to you from the city of New York. The heat and humidity are already oppressive as summer has already replaced spring. We have to constantly soak the coats of our poor suffering animals with water to give them a few cool minutes. In the city, horse cars are unable to run because it is impossible to haul adequate food to the beasts. It is said that 250 horses died in one day, and many still lie in the streets and stables where they collapsed, their bodies progressively swollen and blistered. The air reeks of carrion.

In spite of all this, we have enjoyed great success in presenting my educational extravaganza of the Wild West at Madison Square Garden. I had a capital idea of adding a special new presentation to the International Congress of Rough Riders. Following the war with the Spanish, the concluding act for the Wild West portrayed the Battle of San Juan Hill. I came up with the new idea of depicting another important historical event. I replaced the Cuban battle with a re-enactment of the rescue of Europeans from the Chinese. Like good fodder for cattle, business feeds best off fresh ideas.

I thought the audience would enjoy my recounting of the success of civilization in quelling the Boxer Rebellion in China (and my Indians were more than willing to play the role of Chinamen.) Well, old Mark Twain came to see the show, and to my astonishment, walked out during this new presentation, telling all that would listen that he intended to skin my hide. I have no idea what got into Sam. I meant no harm, but rather wanted to honor those brave souls who suffered and died bringing civilization to that part of the world.

I found out he has a big burr under his saddle about the whole China situation, with foreign troops invading, and what Christian missionaries may have done in response to the Boxers. Sam has come back from his year in Europe with hay in his horns. He sees the U.S. just becoming another colonizer, like the English. Last year, he sailed back and told the *New York Times* that he was an anti-imperialist, and "I am opposed to having the eagle put its talons on any other land."

While critics may scoff, and Sam censure, the audience of the Wild West loves my portrayal of historic events. I bring news to them in a way no newspaper ever can do. I saw this whole Boxer thing as an event my audience could only barely imagine before I dressed it up and added bang and smoke. And, like I said, my Indians got a kick out of playing Chinamen. Sam has been a great fan of the Wild West, loved seeing the Indians, the Custer Battle, the Deadwood Stage, and, of course, the climax with the burning and saving of the settler's cabin. Maybe old Sam would have been happy if I'd somehow worked in the alleged looting and extortion of the Chinese by Christian missionaries. I do believe in God, but I don't necessarily buy into what those of the missionary stripe lay on people who have lived forever on the land, like my Indians. Sam don't need look at what is happening in China to get all wrapped up feeling all preachy and pious; he could stay here at home and look at the Indian situation. It's a hard fall off a high horse. And that's all I'm going to say about that. Buffalo Bill doesn't need a fight with Mark Twain. It distresses me if I offered offense. It was he who, when I first started the Wild West, suggested that I take it to Europe. Sometimes free advice is worth twice the price.

Well, enough of this letter. It did feel good to write it and get my mind in a better bunkhouse for the night. My personal situation is exhausting my tolerance, but I'll ride that haired-up broncho tomorrow.

When I am next in Denver, I would greatly relish the opportunity to again partake of your counsel.

Oh, how I miss the smell of sagebrush and campfire smoke.

With hope,

Wm. F. Cody

"A good horse is not very apt to jump over a bank."

June 10, 1901   Binghamton, New York

Dear Dr. Davidson,

I write to you from a quiet camp, although I hear some distant drumming from my Indians as they are want to do around a fire in the evenings. We are camped on the outskirts of town. We have been on the road almost a month, find ourselves in a quite comfortable location with dry sandy soil and large trees providing shade, although the cotton from them falls like snow and gets into everything, including our cooking pots and skillets.

I've been thinking much about you and your loss. Again, I am grieved for you and your son. Have you found a caretaker yet for him? Since you say that focusing on work helps ease your grief or at least distracts from it, I am taking the liberty during this difficult time to ask your advice. Should it be too much at present to reply, I will understand.

Good Doctor, my business partner, Nate Salsbury, is quite stricken by stomach troubles. As a consequence, he had to leave the Wild West and return to home in the East.

I greatly miss his contributions, particularly his genius for moving and sustaining my show. It is no small task. We have two trains of at least 50 cars each to transport our own electrical power plant; over 1,000 horses; 100 Indian men, women, and children; 30 buffalo; 25 cowboys; a dozen cowgirls; the Deadwood stagecoach and mules, tents, and tepees; and seating for 20,000 people. On our 15-acre show lot, Nate arranged for our kitchens to serve three hot meals a day. We even had a barbershop! I'd learned a good horse is not very apt to jump over a bank if left to guide himself. I let mine pick his own way. I treated old Nate the same way. Perhaps I was remiss in not overseeing Nate more. I could have seen that he was suffering and offered help before he was so sick that he had to leave the show.

I would deeply appreciate it if you would arrange to examine and provide consultation to Nate. He currently resides in New Jersey. Of course, I will personally cover all your travel costs and professional fee. Please advise me as to your availability, and I will contact Nate.

The heat that has gripped the East since spring continues. Man and beast suffer, but the crowds for the Wild West continue good, as people come out at night.

With thanks,

Wm. F. Cody

"It is quite impossible for me to travel at this time."

June 19, 1901   Denver, Colorado

Dear Mr. Cody,

I would be happy to see Mr. Salsbury; however, it is quite impossible for me to travel at this time. While I have competent women assisting me with his care, when I am not working, I spend time with my lad. He has learned how to walk, and every day says more and clearer words, often with questions. The one I cannot answer is, "Where's mommy?" He asked the nursemaid the question, and she replied, "Your mother is in heaven." That resulted in the boy asking me, "Daddy, where's heaven? Can we go visit mommy?" I had a stern talk with the nanny I have employed, and I told her that the nursemaid should refrain from any religious references, general as they may be. I simply can't have my son indoctrinated in beliefs I have come to question. Unfortunately, following my instructions to her, the nanny discharged the nursemaid, and now I struggle with my actions having put the poor soul on the streets.

The care of my son is only one issue precluding my ability to travel. I have obligations to my patients, and I do not have a reliable way to provide care for them in my absence. I do hope to employ a nurse to assist me, and I anticipate being able to identify another physician whom I trust and can share coverage when necessity dictates his or my absence. I should also tell you in honesty, that my heart remains heavy from my loss, and it saps both interest and energy for travel. I feel better confining my grief to the home even though in every room I still find memories of my wife followed by thrust of the reality that I shall never see her again. I must work through this process, and it is my hope that time does indeed bring healing. Until then I will focus on my son and profession, and trust this will soothe sorrow lest it degenerate into darkness, and worse yet, bitterness and shirking of my responsibilities.

I regret that I am not able to provide service to Mr. Salsbury, but since he now resides on the East Coast, should he be willing to travel, I would be happy to arrange for a consultation with physicians at Johns Hopkins. I have the greatest confidence in their skills.

Of course, should Mr. Salsbury find himself in Denver, I can perform my consultation in my home.

Please stay in touch as time and circumstance allows.

With best wishes and regards,

E.Y. Davidson, M.D.

"Good partners bring a lot, and common sense carries a premium."

June 25, 1901   Akron, Ohio

Dear Dr. Davidson,

The heat is somewhat better now that we have escaped the East and traveled to the Midwest. Things promise to be very busy. We have shows lined up in towns and states, and I may not timely receive correspondence, and will no doubt be hard-pressed to respond quickly.

I understand your difficulties of travel, but I will pass along your suggestion of the Johns Hopkins to Nate Salsbury. I hope he will follow the advice, but we have been a bit on the outs. He disagrees with some of my decisions about the Wild

West, and our venture in Wyoming land has been a bit rocky. Business may build fortunes, but not necessarily friendships.

I first met Nate in New York City when that damnable scoundrel dentist Carver and I first put the Wild West on the road in 1883. Carver proved entertaining in the arena with a gun but knew nothing about putting on a show. We came upon one another at Fort McPherson in Nebraska. I was scouting for the army, and Carver was practicing dentistry. I should say, "playing" rather than practicing, in that he seemed to enjoy imbibing the laugh gas himself when he wasn't snatching teeth. The army doesn't pay much attention to teeth, other than a historical requirement that a soldier has enough front teeth to tear the top off a paper cartridge. When I scouted for the army, I saw many a poor trooper with a toothache treated by a shot of whiskey and a twisting yank by a medical orderly.

Carver did become a rather good shot, and when I organized the first Wild West, I invited him as a partner, as well as investor. Little did I realize his involvement and investment in the Wild West would turn into a ransom when he started his own show and tried to steal the name "Wild West." He hooked up with Adam Forepaugh, a circus man and swindler. When P.T. Barnum claimed to have a white elephant, Forepaugh whitewashed a regular gray elephant and called it "The Light of Asia."

Carver and I fought over the Wild West name, and we both lined the pockets of some lawyers before we reached settlement, but long I had to chase him to make him actually give back the name.

Unlike me, Carver never stood on the stage and acted out a story to an audience's satisfaction. We did suffer through that first season of the Wild West. We had a segment in which cowboys rode buffalo. The crowed loved that one. There was one bull I called "Monarch." The cowboys wanted nothing to do with trying to ride the old boy. I took the challenge and ended up two weeks in hospital. Many a nose has been broken by a big mouth. I returned to the Wild West sober of mind and alcohol.

I had no further interest in buffalo than to re-enact shooting them. Likewise, after that first year I wanted nothing more to do with dentist Carver. We quarreled, and his first reaction to every suggestion I made was argue, and then when I proved right, claim the idea as his. Too bad you can hang for stealing a horse, but not an idea. You can get the horse back.

Nate was a seasoned showman, having taken his group of troubadours throughout the country after he was mustered out of the Army of the Republic. Much like me, he fell into show business. He ran out of money while going to business school. He started doing a little acting and got hooked. He had a good voice and gift for comedy on the stage (but not necessarily off it—he was, as the saying goes, "all business.")

Nate was not kind to my first efforts to bring the story of the frontier to the American people and wanted nothing to do with the Wild West when he first saw it. Later, after seeing how the crowds flocked in, Nate got that I was on to something. He loaned me $5,000 and brought in some of his own ideas. In my mind it was clear that Nate, in his wisdom and keen eye for what captured imagination and purses, saw something special in my Wild West.

I must tell you that upon first meeting Nate, I was a bit taken back by his teeth. They were filed down almost to the gums, a thing done by some people to correct crooked teeth. In Nate's case, it made his smile startling.

In truth, Nate was right about the first show. I got rid of Carver. In 1884, with Nate's guidance, I put together a first-rate spectacle. I brought him in as my partner because it seemed like the right thing to do and because I needed the brain and experience of someone steeped in show business like me. He helped me secure the rights to the Wild West name in spite of Carver's efforts to swindle me and drag my good name through the mud from St. Louis to Providence. We were a great team. I could bring people into the show to see "Buffalo Bill." Nate knew how to build the scenes and stories that both entertained and educated. Nate was as good at organizing as I was riding a horse. I remember that when we toured Germany, the system that Nate devised for unloading railroad cars was of particular interest to the German Army. He linked flatcars together with planks so that they could be quickly loaded back to front.

Doctor, Nate was of great value to the Wild West and to me. We needed a manager to make the idea of educating people on the American West degenerate into work. Nate used his considerable experience to handle logistics, acts, and people. He also provided me great counsel. Although I saw promise in adding additional attractions, such as sideshows and a place for affable gambling, Nate advised against because he felt sideshows and games-of-chance would make the Wild West a less friendly place for families. Running a clean show would as well make us different from the vulgar circuses that so crowded the country. Good partners bring a lot, and common sense carries a premium.

The new show went gloriously good with money in the till. It went so well, in fact, that in 1886, rather than retire to winter quarters, I had decided to keep the Wild West on the road. That was a mistake as I lost a great deal of money, partly from weather, and also because we lost equipment and animals in a steamboat accident on the Mississippi. Nevertheless, I pulled things together in New Orleans, as "the show must go on." There I met Evelyn Booth. I believe I have already mentioned him to you—Booth, quite the young Englishman on "grand tour" with several of his friends. They favored hunting, drinking, and sporting houses. At times I was astonished by both their sexual appetites and different varieties of practice. Those boys from England would put to shame a troop of cavalry on payday.

Even though we came from very different societies, Evelyn and I fell into enjoyable company, and even put on several contests of shooting. Wild West business was not all that great; Nate and I feared we would not be able to start back up in the coming show season. After we closed in New Orleans—

in exchange for a part of future proceeds—I secured $30,000 from Booth. The Wild West was relaunched, and away we went. And, I proudly say, Evelyn got every dime of his money back.

In closing, I must say I have had many partners, but dear Nate was the best. When people inquire of me as to my secrets in business, close to the top I put "Find your Nate Salsbury."

My very best,

W.F. Cody

Buffalo Bill

"Nighttime though does bring a darkness that no lamp can chase away."

September 5, 1901   Denver, Colorado

D ear Buffalo Bill,
        I have been remiss in writing to you. I've found grief to have a paralyzing effect, but I am doing better. I progressively get out of bed each day with a little more energy. I look forward to coffee and biscuit. I am coming to believe that appetite is a barometer of enthusiasm.

I want you to know I greatly enjoyed learning about your partnership with Mr. Salsbury. The success of the Wild West is evidence enough of what you have accomplished. I am among the many people the American West serves as power-ful attractant. I salute you not only bringing excitement, but also appreciation of the different cultures, including those of other nations. I am taken with how the horse plays such a prominent role, and in my mind, I am trying to understand the power of this particular creature in the souls of men, beyond just being a necessary form of transport.

As an aside, while walking down Broadway, I saw a man beating on a horse, trying to make it arise. The poor beast could lift its head, but not body. I quickly crossed the street, and I seized the man by the arm, twisted away his whip, and commenced to give him a trashing. Thankfully the police ar-rived, and they stopped me, for I'm not sure I could have contained myself in my anger. Thanks to efforts of a man of great prominence in Denver, our city has some of the strongest laws against the abuse of animals and children. The vile man was led away in handcuffs to face judgment for his cruelty. Sadly, the police were forced to dispatch the pitiful horse where he lay.

Enough of my aside. Please understand that it greatly affected me, and I have now found it a help to just relate the story to you. Authoring seems to both settle my mind and mood.

I liked your closing advice in the letter about "finding your Nate Salsbury." The business of medicine is quite different. When I left Hopkins, William Osler counseled me, "Young doctor, remember, the practice of medicine is an art, not a trade; a calling, not a business." Now that I am out of the academy, into the world, I find many of my fellow practitioners regard our profession as less a calling and more a trade. I retain hope that some wise minds should be able to show a path forward that satisfies Dr. Osler's aphorism.

Dear Dr. Osler, trim of stature, neatly balding, a walrus mustache, and black eyes. I swear those eyes could penetrate into a patient and take inventory of every organ in the body. Occasionally I would hear his Canadian roots through the increased cadence of his speech and raised vowels when he said "aboot this patient," rather than "about." Sometimes he would self-correct back into American pronunciation, but the brisk pace of his professorial expounding always persisted.

Having had to leave Johns Hopkins and the academy, I do find myself lonely for the camaraderie and commitment I shared each night at 10 p.m. when we'd gather in the dining room to discuss the patients admitted each day, as well as interesting cases seen in clinic. The kitchen was kind in providing their leftovers from the day to us bachelor students and young doctors. It was a comfort to have access to the power of the gathered mind of my peers and the occasional senior physicians that might join us. If I had a vexing problem,

I could present it to the group for consultation—I remember one fellow saying, "The unappreciated power of having a consultant, is someone to share the blame."

Unfortunately, here in Denver, I'm much on my own. The medical society meetings I first attended seemed to be dominated by self-congratulation and exercises in moral superiority.

Most of the scientific sessions were discussions of the prevailing obsession with electromagnetism as a primary factor in human health and disease. Never mind that there is not a shred of evidence beyond some observational studies better suited for the gypsy séance than a medical scientific report.

I was drawn to one presentation entitled "Sanitary Horseback Riding." Not knowing what to expect, I sat in my seat wondering if this had something to do with hygiene and the horse. As it turned out, it concerned the beneficial effects on consumptives of riding in the crisp Colorado air and exercise associated therewith. The primary thrust of the speaker's presentation proved to be a strong argument against the use of sidesaddles by women, going so far as to say they should be outlawed. I did question in my mind whether or not this was of sufficient importance to require legislative action, but I could imagine debate by elected officials obsessed with appearance of action and not substance of subject. I gave the speaker credit for having raised the issue of women and saddles, and an argument that their structure and physiology required a posture similar to that of male riders. He then presented a detailed discussion as to what he felt would be a better design suitable for women.

I did leave the session scratching my head as to why, with all the challenges of controlling and treating the female consumptive patient, this particular session garnered a standing room–only crowd. I left the meeting dispirited that doctors discussing sanitary issues in phthisis would concern themselves with ladies' saddles and not simple, but important, general benefits to the public. If physicians really wanted to affect the health of women, they would promote paper cups and paper towels to replace the dreadful shared communal counterparts now common in railway stations. I would add the necessity to post vigorous and various reminders to people not to spit on sidewalks. It would protect man and woman alike.

This professional isolation is made all the worse by the void in my life with the loss of Jane. The care for my son, as well as what satisfaction I gain from service to my patients, give me energy to start and work through each day. Nighttime, though, does bring a darkness that no lamp can chase away.

With sincerity,
Edgar Davidson, M.D.

"She showed me how a woman could do a man's work."
November 15, 1901   En route to Chicago

Dear Dr. Davidson,
Oh, the troubles for Buffalo Bill!
We have had to cancel some shows this fall out of respect for the assassination and funeral of President McKinley, and those shows that did go on suffered from low attendance due to our national mourning.

Because of the size of the Wild West, this season we have been traveling divided into two trains. On October 28, in North Carolina, the second section of our Wild West train collided head-on with a freight train.

I was retired to my private car and was deep in thought, as well as pleasure, envisioning how the success of this year's season will allow me to get on with my many business projects, those in progress and those of the future. Suddenly, I was thrown from my berth. I hit the floor hard. The train was stopped. It was inescapable that a calamity struck. In the darkness, I pulled on boots and trousers, opened the vestibule door, and jumped down, and felt my knee wrench as I landed. There was a bit of a moon, and I could see that many of the cars were off the rails and down on their sides into a creek. I yelled, but what I heard was the screaming of horses, some suddenly silenced by gunshots.

What a disaster. One hundred and ten horses were killed, including my wonderful horse, "Old Pap." Also slain in the accident were the mules used to pull the Deadwood Stage and "Old Eagle," another star horse. I wept like a child over their many bodies. It will cost me a fortune to replace my losses— over $60,000—and I am suing the railroad. My greatest loss is "Little Miss Sure Shot," as Sitting Bull called her. Annie Oakley's injuries have already required two surgeries, and the doctors tell me she will require several more. A few years ago, she left the Wild West to travel with Pawnee Bill's Near East Show but returned to the Wild West for the next twelve years as my little star. On the stage, her name was "Annie Oakley," but outside of that she insisted on being called "Mrs. Frank Butler," who was her husband, great love, and also a remarkable marksman in his own right. She tolerated my calling her "Annie."

Like me, Annie came from an impoverished childhood due to her father's premature death, and again, like me, supported her family by killing and selling wild game. I will always remember her skipping into the arena with skirt and rifle and breaking glass balls. Next to me, she was the highest paid performer in the Wild West. Unlike me, she was frugal beyond belief. She used her talent with needle and thread to make her own costumes. It was rumored within the troop that she'd siphon off lemonade from my tent carafe, then buy her own!

She is off to Hot Springs, Arkansas to partake of the healing waters. I hope she is soon able to return to the Wild West. She showed me how a woman could do a man's work. I strongly believe women should receive the same pay as men for doing the same work. My dear sisters are forceful in their marriages and lives. I felt the same for Louisa when we first wed. I know life was not easy for her as we tried to make a go of it in the hotel and land speculation business. Perhaps my absence from the home, first as a hunter and scout, and later on the stage, led to

the change in her affection for me. Even with our current difficulties in the marriage, it does not diminish my appreciation
for strong women, although their stubbornness can become
a bit contentious. When Annie left the Wild West, it was because of her fractious relationship with Lillian Smith. Rather
than help me find solution, she joined Pawnee Bill. Oh, how
happy I was to later welcome her back, and I hope to do so
again soon when she has recovered.

I am suing the Southern Railway for all my losses, including animals, equipment, costumes, and, of course, the rev-
enues (as much as $10,000 per show) from cancelled engage-
ments. Whatever the railroad pays, it will not repair every
broken part of the Wild West or mend the hurt to my heart. I
still wonder if the rough justice I sought might provide some
salve when I first grabbed a shotgun and went looking for the
freight train engineer. I recall the punishment I inflicted on
that poor Indian after Custer's death did not provide lasting
satisfaction. I am glad that cooler heads prevented me from
seeking violent revenge after the railroad wreck. That said,
when I think of my losses and the suffering of my animals, I
relate more to the retribution of the Old Testament than the
forgiveness of the New.

Wish I had Nate Salsbury to help rebuild. I quite understand why it was impractical for you to attend to him. His
health, particularly problems related to digestion, necessitated his leaving my Wild West. In Nate's absence, I engaged
Mr. James Bailey, an experienced showman himself. This necessary move aggravated Nate and led to a bit of falling out.
Nate finally agreed that the Wild West needed expertise in the
complexities of moving our troupe, animals, and equipment,
and Mr. Bailey certainly brought such experience from his circus.

Nate may still grumble over my selling Bailey an interest
in the Wild West without his direct approval, but the need
was urgent, the terms attractive, and Nate difficult to contact.
My decisions preserved both the Wild West and Nate's invest-

ment.

I know you still suffer the pain of your great personal loss. It is my hope you don't find my sharing of my own troubles as insensitive to your circumstances. I am powerfully mindful of your sorrow, and hope that with each day, a little more sunshine seeps in.

I plan to return to North Platte, and then on to Cody while the Wild West is repaired and returned to glory. I plan visit you soon and will telegraph ahead when I expect to arrive in Denver.

Before I see you again, I wonder would it be possible for you to send or tell me what you believe to be a proper potion to treat my rheumatism. Of all my years in the company of horses, I have only been injured by one once, and that was in England when one stepped on my foot as it went into the arena.

Lo though, the hours, days, weeks, and months in the saddle appear to have settled in my bones. Over the years, especially when I was young, I slept a lot on the ground, and I don't think that has helped. The romance of the outdoors life fades when you're shivering, soaked, and trying to use a saddle for a pillow. Life has shine when you're dry, warm, and headquartered in a soft sack.

With sincerity and soreness,
William Cody
"Buffalo Bill"

"If you listen to the patient long enough..."

December 15, 1901   Denver, Colorado

Dear Buffalo Bill,

Indeed, I read with distress the newspaper accounts of your train wreck. It is remarkable that no human was killed. The reports stated that Miss Oakley was severely injured and in a comatose state for several days. I trust there is no residual paralysis.

I would indeed be happy to see you when you are next

in Denver. Rheumatism is a common affliction. Indeed, many of the hot springs in the Rocky Mountains make wondrous claims of the treatment of rheumatism based on both soaking in and partaking their water. I regard most of the claims dubious and can assure you that ingestion of the mineral water, particularly those sulfur-laden, have more effect on bowel than bladder.

When we meet, I will learn more about your symptoms, and also perform a physical examination. With that information, I hope to make recommendations that are of benefit to you. Absent that I cannot recommend or provide remedy. Good practice of medicine must be in the presence of the patient with keen attention to not just the body, but speech. I have found that if you listen to the patient long enough, they will eventually tell you what is wrong.

Finally, I appreciate your continued correspondences and condolences, and I look forward to seeing you.

Sincerely,

Edgar Davidson, M.D.

1902

"I promise it won't rain."

June 27, 1902   Troy, New York

Dear Dr. Davidson,

I send you greetings from a damnable and wet New York. I regret my language, but as you have no doubt seen in the national newspaper accounts after a fine opening in New York City in Madison Square Gardens, so far this summer has been nothing but rain, rain, and more rain. It keeps the customers away, and the canvas is so sodden, men and beast struggle whenever we set up or break camp. All the time we are in so much mud that I even long for the Sand Hills of Scout's Rest Ranch. Those old prairies soak up water like a dollar sponge in a Turkish bath.

I also miss Annie Oakley, but Missy has not yet recovered from last year's train wreck. I trust that the injuries and surgeries have been successful, particularly those involving her head. As you mentioned in a previous letter, she was unconscious for several days after the accident. That smiling face, when she entered the arena, brought the audience to their feet as they clapped and whooped. She was pretty as a milkmaid, but no milkmaid ever shot like Annie Oakley.

On my way to New York to start the season I did visit briefly with your father in Chicago. He and I both spoke glowingly about you. I don't think I am breaking any confidences, but a letter, or even better, a visit from you, would cheer his old heart. He's shrunk a bit, and I noticed a tremor of his hand when he took the cigar I offered him. Nevertheless, I did see a twinkle in his eye when the senior Dr. Davidson and I reminisced about the old Chicago theaters.

I recalled my meeting Edward Judson ("Ned Buntline") while I was a scout for General Nelson Miles. I believe I mentioned this to you in an early letter to you. I told him of my adventures, and he was moved to write a wonderful recounting, *Buffalo Bill, Frontier Scout,* which sold so well that "Ned" put on a show at the Bowery called "Buffalo Bill, King of the Border Men." I traveled to New York to see it, and there was this actor playing me. When the audience found out that the real Buffalo Bill was in the audience, the whole place stood up and cheered. Later that evening, the owner of the theater invited me to stay and star in the play. Well, at that time, having never appeared on the stage, the thought of acting was about as uncomfortable a sharing a two-hole privy. I got out of there as fast as I could and went back to scouting for the Third Cavalry.

Judson kept coming after me, telling me how much money was in the theatre. He pestered me so mercilessly to travel to Chicago to act in his play, "Scouts of the Plains," that I finally agreed. Plus, the money sounded good. Just as you can't have too many friends, I've also discovered you can't have too much money. The critics found fault, but the audience hooted, hollered, and shook the house with their stomping feet. It launched my stage career that allowed me to make enough money that I could purchase and develop dear old Scout's Rest Ranch. These were high times, Doctor. Buffalo Bill had a fine ranch and jingle in his pocket.

Speaking of Scout's Rest, you know that you are always welcome there. My sister Julia and her husband are managing things quite nicely, and I'm sure they would be more than happy to provide you hospitality if you look to layover on a visit east. No need to worry about my wife's temper. We are still on the outs, but Louisa now lives in North Platte town. If you stay at the ranch, my dear sister will see that you enjoy sunny hospitality. Of course, you are always welcome at the T E Ranch in Wyoming or at a first-rate hunting lodge that I plan constructing outside of Yellowstone National Park.

This November we will dedicate the Irma Hotel in Cody. It will be as fine a hotel as there is in the land. The beautiful cherrywood bar is a gift of Queen Victoria. I have had all the stone quarried locally and combined with river rock to construct the walls. In addition, I had fossils put into a magnificent fireplace. I will make sure you get an invitation. I promise it won't rain. You have Buffalo Bill's word.

Your sodden friend,

Wm Cody

"I have made it a particular point to pay sincere attention
to
my young son's questions and observations."

July 7, 1902   Denver, Colorado

Dear Mr. Cody,
I hope that this letter finds you experiencing better weather and the benefits to your business that goes with it. We are enjoying a splendid summer in Colorado. The temperature rarely gets above 90 degrees, and there is never the oppressive humidity I experienced during the summer months of Illinois, and particularly in Baltimore. Each afternoon, there is a pleasant rumble of thunder followed by a brief rain shower that cools the day as we move into evening. When lightening sparks, it leaves the air scented similarly to the delicious smell of my housemaids fresh pressed laundry.

Thank you for your kind invitation of hospitality. Should my travels take me through North Platte, I hope to avail myself of the generosity of your family. Unfortunately, I will not be able to attend the new hotel opening, but I wish you all the very best. The hotel sounds splendid.

I appreciate your mention of my father. When I last saw him, I too detected some signs of advancing age. Of course, he brushed aside my questions as to his health, saying he was "just fine." I am quite accustomed to his discounting of my thoughts and opinions. My mother related to me that his father behaved similarly toward him.

I do know that father was greatly troubled from his service during the Civil War. Not only was there the horror of amputations without benefit of anesthesia, but the triage of determining who would live and who would die presented a great burden for a young doctor, only having recently graduated from school and conscripted into the army. He related how those patients who developed "the sweet smell of death," due to what we now know as pseudomonas infection, were placed outside the hospital tent because death was inevitable. Also, I know that he has never been able to put aside his suspension from the army due to charges that he abandoned the wounded on the battlefield. I believe that his interest in the theatre allowed him to experience a few hours of escape from those dark memories.

With the absence of Willis' mother, I have made it a particular point to pay sincere attention to my young son's questions and observations. Although he is only three years old, his mind is active and curious. In this I find satisfaction. Occasionally, he delights me with something unexpected and with it its own form of charm. To quote the Bard, "When a father gives to his son, both laugh; when a son gives to his father, both cry."

In the meanwhile, I look forward to seeing you again in Denver.

> With every best wish,
> Edgar Davidson, M.D.

"My old bones trust your care."

August 19, 1902   Baker City, Oregon

D ear Dr. Davidson,
      I thank you for the brief visit in Denver. As the Wild West moved on to shows in Oregon, I could not help but break way in Cheyenne to come down to see you, as well as visit my sister May.

I've done one show after another since we started April in New York. Even though the weather started to favor the Wild West, this economy is the pits. It is playing hell with my finances. All the creditors are as nervous as a pig in a bacon factory.

Like a hard-worked horse, it helped to have a day to "just take off the saddle and take a relaxing roll in the dirt."

I was distressed to learn from you that Henry Brown may have to sell his fine hotel, the Brown Palace, to satisfy the holders of the mortgage. G.D. these bankers! I know Henry and others were mightily hurt in the Denver Depression back in '93 when the bottom of the bucket fell out of the silver market, and people have been holding on by the skin of their teeth. If I didn't have obligations in Cody and my new Arizona mine, I'd help Henry out. I know a thing or two about hotels, having stayed in the grandest all over this country and Europe. I now own my own, and I'm sure I could give him some useful tips. The Brown Palace has been the site of a many fine meal and libations for me and my guests. It truly is the supreme hotel between Kansas City and San Francisco, though my Irma Hotel in Cody will eventually share this honor. I greatly admire Henry Brown as a man of generosity, particularly his gift of valuable Denver acreage for the construction of the state capitol. I too have delighted in generously giving land for civic purposes in North Platte and Cody. Brown and I have never asked for anything in return, but I wouldn't mind if a statue might someday show up somewhere.

The Colorado capitol is almost as nice as Wyoming's, although I grant you the sandstone for its construction came from Colorado, as did the gold for its dome. Oh well, it's a sort of fair trade. I have told people, "If you want to experience the freedom and wholesomeness of Colorado, come to Wyoming."

As to my health, I follow your recommendation for warm tub baths and, when possible, Turkish baths and massage. My old bones trust your care.

Nature does conspire against me. If it's not rain, it's blight. Try as I might, we have yet to be able to bring the Wild West to the banks of the Charles River because of the continued smallpox outbreak in that city. Oh, how the pox has plagued me. In addition to Boston, it has kept me out of San Francisco since 1900. In 1889, in the midst of a successful tour of Europe, we sailed to Barcelona and got trapped by a smallpox quarantine. What a nasty city. I recall one of my Indians looked at the Barcelona statue of Christopher Columbus, and said, "Damned bad day for us Indians when he discovered America."

In Barcelona, the smallpox raged. No one dared come to the show, even the King and Queen of Spain were scared away, which was poor for our business. Royalty acts as a Wild West magnet. Poor little starving waifs raided our dustbins looking for food. Frank Richman, the finest orator and ringmaster ever, caught the grippe and died. Finally, after a month of suffering in Spain, we bribed the captain of a wretched ship, and the Wild West escaped to Italy.

Other than my rheumatism, I feel exceptionally fit, full of energy, and dipsomania does not darken my door. I have always agreed with the old saw, *"Drink makes you see double and feel single,"* and that I do not need in my life. My wits are my best weapons against the daily challenges of being Buffalo Bill.

Your friend,

Bill

Wm. F. "Buffalo Bill" Cody

"Even a braying jackass eventually shuts up."
August 26, 1902   Denver, Colorado

Dear Mr. Cody,

Thank you for your recent letter. I was sorry to read of your troubles, particularly having to contend with the effect of disease on your business. As wise Seneca, tutor and advisor to Emperor Nero, observed, *"Disease is not of the body, but the place."*

I found your mention of the smallpox epidemic in Boston of interest. The medical world, particularly the *Boston Medical and Surgical Journal,* has been fairly buzzing on the issue.

The Boston Public Health officials have decreed that vaccination should be offered to the entire city, and those reluctant for vaccination would be "encouraged" to receive vaccination. "Vaccination squads" have fanned out throughout the city. In one *Boston Globe* recounting, a man was only successfully vaccinated when one Boston policeman sat on his legs, another on his chest, and a third pinned his arms as a doctor applied the vaccination. The vaccination campaign appears to have had the necessary effect. Few people now bear the scars of smallpox.

But this particular epidemic has stirred up controversy. Some ignorant foes of vaccination argue that forced vaccination violates personal freedom. Others evoked religious arguments stating that to prevent disease through vaccination breached the will of God. Dr. Emmanuel Pfeiffer, a Danish immigrant ardently objected to vaccination, even to the point of questioning the infectious nature of smallpox. Dr. Pfeiffer felt the cure of disease lay in fasting and hypnosis. It is insane to question both the science of smallpox and the overwhelming evidence for the life-saving benefit of vaccination. A free society dictates that the voices of the ignorant not be silenced, but that doesn't not mean they should be listened to. Even a braying jackass eventually shuts up.

As regards to smallpox, I think you will like the following story about Dr. Pfeiffer. It appeared in the Boston newspaper, *The Evening Traveler,* and was sent to me by a medical colleague.

Many of the persons stricken with smallpox are quarantined in a hospital on Gallops Island in Boston Harbor. Dr. Samuel Holmes Durgin, chairman of the Boston Board of Public Health, frustrated with Dr. Pfeiffer's public and vociferous objections to vaccination, happily arranged a visit by Dr. Pfeiffer to the smallpox patients on Gallops Island. He reasoned, if Dr. Pfeiffer's doubts about the infectious nature of smallpox were true, then the unvaccinated Dr. Pfeiffer would not be at risk of contracting smallpox. Along with the physician in charge of the Gallops Island hospital, Dr. Paul Carlson, Dr. Pfeiffer toured the smallpox ward. At one point, Dr. Carlson even suggested that Dr. Pfeiffer take a particularly close whiff of the breath of one smallpox victim. Ten days later, Dr. Pfeiffer became deathly ill with smallpox. A newspaper headline read, "Pfeiffer Has Smallpox. Anti-vaccinationist May Not Live." Assumedly, upon his possible recovery, Dr. Pfeiffer will recant on his doubts about the infectious nature of smallpox.

My best wishes,
E.Y. Davidson, M.D.

P.S. I noted your characterization of Miss Oakley in your letter of June 27. Prior to vaccination, women who survived smallpox almost invariably had facial scars. European women with uncommon beauty were said to be "pretty as a milkmaid." A saying derived from cowpox infection protecting milkmaids from smallpox and its facial scarring.

1903

"My old partner, Nat Salsbury, had sacked his saddle."

January 20, 1903   Cody, Wyoming

Dear Dr. Davidson,

I write to you from the T E Ranch. Thick frost covers the windows, and fresh snow blankets the ground. The cloudless blue sky makes a perfect Wyoming day. The ponies stand in the corral letting the sun warm them, and steam glints off their backs.

This morning I sat at my desk and began to sort my mail. As part of my necessity to keep up on events of the world, I have the *New York Times* mailed to me when I am in Cody. I opened the copy of the December 25 issue, and there to my distress was an article bringing the word my old partner, Nat Salsbury, had sacked his saddle. As to cause of death, it only mentioned "stomach trouble," a condition I previously mentioned to you that had plagued him for years and caused his leaving the Wild West.

If I in were your company, Doctor, I would raise a toast or three to Nate and tell you more about him than I have already shared. So, allow me the indulgence reminiscing as if you and were in the Brown Palace lounge with our glasses on high.

Nate did have his moments of becoming impatient with me. He usually traveled with his wife and family. His daughter Rebecca was born while the Wild West was in England. This was in contrast with my family situation. Louisa did not like the road; therefore, I first set the children and her up in a fine home first in Rochester, New York, and later in North Platte. The road is a lonely place, particularly when an ocean and many months separates one from his loved ones. Because I was Buffalo Bill, people greatly enjoyed my company, and I also enjoyed theirs. I also admit, that I did become particularly social when I was "into my cups," so to speak. This seemed to grate on Nate, and he sometimes made comments that one might consider "ungentlemanly." For instance, when in Rome, we visited the Pope and the Sistine Chapel. I had with me a lady who I sought to share the experience. As we got out of the carriage, Nate came up to me and he whispered, "I see you brought your concubine." Well, it was loud enough for the young woman to hear, and believe me, I had quite the time of soothing those particular ruffled feathers.

Even though we sometimes squabbled, we did a lot of business together. In 1895, we decided to put on a show called "Black America." It featured all sorts of opportunities for people to see of the better sides of the Negro race. Nate and I thought that just as people were drawn to the Wild West, they would be interested in learning about the southern Negro and his life in the South. For some reason, white people seem to have a particular fascination with the black. We only hired authentic southern blacks. On the show grounds, a plantation was recreated, including a cotton field. The cast lived in authentic cabins that the public could visit and interact with the inhabitants. Negro cavalrymen, including Buffalo Soldiers, encamped and drilled daily for the audiences. The show also presented minstrel shows and blacks playing such games as baseball and concluded with a chorus of over 300 voices. Unfortunately, the show proved very expensive given the cast of over 500, as well as construction and other costs. There were also those who felt the slave market and whipping-post re-enactments a bit too unsettling a reminder of this part of American history.

Nate was also very much involved in my Wyoming irrigation venture. His business experience and tight rein on expenditures were valuable as we brought water to the land and its settlers. As the project stretched out, he did turn his attention to his eastern land investments and their development, perhaps due to his failing health and inability to travel.

On the positive side, Nate also understood my need to provide support for those that joined our unique group of committed performers. My desire to do this went all the way back to 1889 when I launched the organization in Chicago to provide financial relief for actors and other associates of the theatre in need.

My desire to help went beyond just the performers. I lost my father when I was just a lad, and I needed to support my poor mother, brothers, and sisters. My childhood slipped away. I vowed to help children, and, at my insistence, the Wild West distributed free tickets to orphanages and other organizations supporting children. At the World's Columbian Exposition, at the suggestion of the Wild West publicist, Major Burke, the urging of the Chicago mayor, and with Nate's concurrence, I declared a "Waif's Day." The Wild West provided free train tickets out to the Exposition, admission to my show, and free ice cream to 16,000 children. Nate needled me about my generosity. I told him, "When you die it will be said of you, 'Here lies Nate Salsbury, who made a million dollars in the show business and kept it.' But when I die, people will say, 'Here lies Bill Cody, who made a million dollars in the show business and distributed it among friends.'"

Well, Nate held up his end and died a wealthy man, but dead he is.

With sorrow, I remain sincerely yours,
     Col. William F. Cody
     "Buffalo Bill"

"I take pride in being a discrete physician."
February 1, 1903   Denver, Colorado

D ear Mr. Cody,
          I send you condolences for the death of your partner, Mr. Salsbury. Given how long he was ill, and the oft torture of aliments of the stomach, he is now free of suffering.

I appreciate your candor in further sharing of your business dealings and relationship with Mr. Salsbury. I struggle to fully appreciate the intricacy and costs of your business undertakings.

In contrast to the complexity with which you deal, mine is a simple cash business. This also allowed me to exercise my own justice in determining how much I charged for my services. I have tried to live the dictum of my mentor, William Osler, *"No one should approach the temple of science and medicine with the soul of a moneychanger."*

Following the death of my dear wife, I have decided to dedicate my medical career to the treatment of Denver's many indigent patients, supporting myself through a lucrative side-practice caring for wealthy patients. In a small way, it is a model of what the Mayo brothers are doing in Rochester, Minnesota. The Mayo's' cost of removal of the thyroid gland goiter of a member of Chicago's Armour family might be $10,000, but a poor Minnesota farmer pays nothing.

I take pride in being a discreet physician, but I also factor this into my charges to the well-to-do. I found that patients seeking my care, particularly for nervous disorders or the consequences of sexual indiscretion, were more likely to pay substantially for confidentiality as well as quality. My sin of pride begins and ends with having never betrayed a patient. This might serve as an eventual epitaph on my gravestone.

I wish you to know how I appreciate your forthright correspondence with me, and pledge to provide similarly to you.

Most sincerely,

Edgar

E.Y. Davidson, M.D.

"I have been a good friend and father to my red brothers."

March 17, 1903   Bridgeport, Massachusetts

Dear Edgar,

I write to you as the Wild West prepares to embark on another tour of England.

First, I feel a bit awkward in my use of your first name in this greeting; however, since that is how you closed your last letter, I will use it with caution, but at the same time urge you to use my first name. In that regards, people seem to have a hard time settling on whether it should be "William," "Will," or "Bill." I have been of little help in this regard since I have no particular preference. Just so you know, only my wife calls me "Willie." Also, there may be times when I feel the formality of "Dr. Davidson," is more comfortable. I have always regarded that professional attainment should be respected. In this regard, sometimes I like to be addressed as "Colonel Cody," a rank bestowed upon me by the Nebraska National Guard. Major Burke particularly likes to refer to me as such in his promotion of the Wild West.

Second, allow me to express my thanks for your continual willingness to listen to my frustrations as they relate to my blasted home situation. Though I know you are a man of ideological temperance, particularly when it comes to matters of medical speculation on patients you know only through the tales of others, I'd much appreciate any light you could shed as to the nature of Louisa's volatility.

Louisa is impossible. I feel against the wall. I walk the floor at night. We continue estranged, and I contemplate divorce. When I told her such, she flew into a red rage. Among other things she screamed she would use my treatment of my Indians against me. She said I made them live in mud and eat what was left over from the white man's mess.

It so set me off. I take pride in how I have respected and provided for them. Everyone was equal in the Wild West chuck line. The agents from the Federal Office of Indian Affairs who have visited the show to check on the Indians admitted that conditions for the Indians in the Wild West were superior to those on their reservations, and touring with me made them civilized. There are those, however, who would rather keep them prisoner on the reservations, and not allow them to make an honest dollar. I paid Indians fairly and promptly. I even paid the Indian children who participated in the Wild West. People particularly liked to visit the children in the Indian village part of our camp.

I have been a good friend and father to my red brothers. I say "brothers" because we have often helped one another. The wonderful beaded clothing I wear was made for me by Indians. Once when I had guzzled a bit too much, Indians found me asleep on the prairie and brought me home. When Frank North and I ranched together in the Dismal River country, the local Indians protected our herd from raids by other tribes. When Iron Face developed blood poisoning from a broken wrist and was also found to have consumption, I sent him home at my expense. I well recall the situation of poor Kills Plenty when we performed in Sheffield, England. One day, as this splendid young man rode his pony out of the arena during a performance, the beast stumbled. Kills Plenty's ankle was trapped beneath and severely dislocated such that the bones were visible. We immediately transported him to the Sheffield infirmary where he received the very best of care. Unfortunately, he developed fever, sweating, and the most severe of spasms. The attending doctors diagnosed lockjaw, and poor Kills Plenty died, with his last words, "Jesus, Jesus." I procured a fine coffin for him and transported his body to London. When the train arrived, I had the Cowboy Band play the funeral dirge as he was taken the London Indian burying grounds.

Kills Plenty, like all Indians, was a fine performer and equestrian. In addition to demonstrating their skill in hunting and displaying their dances, the Indians of the Wild West re-enacted attacks on the Deadwood Stage, the Pony Express, and their defeat of Custer at the Little Big Horn. I suffered great criticism for such exhibitions, and people accused me of perpetrating the bloodthirsty nature of Indians and preventing their absorption into society. To my mind, what some are doing in perpetuating the deplorable conditions on the reservations, especially taking Indian children from their families and placing them in schools, is a form of great cruelty. I may be accused of exploitation, but I say its preservation in the face of those who say in the name of Christian assimilation, "Kill the Indian, save the man."

When the Indians traveled with the Wild West, they were allowed to speak their own language and wear their traditional clothing—things the government either discouraged or forbade when the Indians were on the reservation. When not performing, the Indians were free to leave the grounds to visit local attractions and sightsee. I paid members of the Indian troupe to act as police, even giving them badges and an additional monthly wage, to assure the safety of the Indians and prevent drinking, gambling, and fighting. I loved my Indians, and know they loved me. One of my proudest accomplishments was being honored with the Indian name "Pahaska" ("Long Hair") and some called me "Great Father."

Many called them "Show Indians," and that they were —they even referred to themselves in such way. But they "showed" the nobility of their race.

I still feel sadness to this day.

> With sorrow,
> Bill
> Wm. F. Cody
> "Buffalo Bill"

"I have also taken the precaution of being armed and minding where I venture."

April 5, 1903   Denver, Colorado

Dear William,

Thank you for your letter. I trust your show goes splendidly in England. Sometime in the future I hope to travel there, as well as throughout Europe, with my son. He's doing well in his studies, and when I take him places, he is keen to inquire about things, such as how the trolley cars work and why we need policemen. Yesterday, when I took him to the Denver City Park, he was particularly curious about all the men loitering there—their clothing soiled and tattered. I explained they were people who worked in mines, but now there was a great argument about how they should work and what they should be paid, and they had no homes.

William, my son's question and my answer are because of a dark time in Colorado. Miners and smelter workers have gone on strike for better pay and shorter hours. The working hours prove to be quite contentious. Despite a referendum of voters supporting an eight-hour day, under lobbying by owners, the state legislature and governor refuse to implement it. The mine and smelter owners have brought in strike-breakers, as well as Pinkertons to spy on the unions. Immigrant workers have been targets of both the unions and mine owners. They have been attacked both physically and in articles and editorials in newspapers. There are those who argue for wholesale deportation as a solution.

The Western Federation of Miners union has advocated socialism and taking the mining industry out of private hands. It is possible that the dynamitings that have occurred in places such as Idaho Springs and Cripple Creek might have been organized by the WFM. On the other hand, the Pinkertons brought in by the owners have no doubt been behind the beatings, and worse, of strikers. Yesterday, a photograph appeared in the *Rocky Mountain News* of a union man chained to a telegraph pole in Telluride. Violence in the mining towns has become such that the Governor has brought in the Colorado National Guard, but it is not clear how much of their mission is really controlling violence versus breaking the strike.

I have cared for some of the sick and injured as they have made their way to Denver, but yesterday a note appeared on my door—unsigned I might add—advising that I best mind my own business. I do not plan to do so, but I have also taken the precaution of being armed and minding where I venture, particularly when it becomes dark.

Faithfully,
Edgar
E.Y. Davidson, M.D.

"I have learned to enjoy the 'ups.'"

June 29, 1903   Banbury, England

Dear Pard Edgar,
Greetings from jolly old England where the crowds are spectacular as they cheer and stomp

throughout our show. Many come "backstage" to see my Indians, smell the roasting of beef, and inspect all my fine animals.

I am sorry to learn of the troubles in Denver that even threatens you. I wish Buffalo Bill was there to be your bodyguard. The scoundrel who threatened you would prove to be the coward I'm sure he is. I know you are a sensitive man, and I can well imagine that this situation must weigh on your mind. I'd also knock some heads together to make the workers and owners sit down and get their issues solved and come to treaty.

I enjoy England and the people that I meet and the recognition I receive, but I do miss my ranches and enterprises. When my mood gets a bit dark (particularly after writing to reassure those holding my credit), I work to shoo it away with positive memories. Yesterday I thought back on how splendidly went last November's opening of the Irma Hotel in Cody. I sent out more than 1,000 invitations embossed with a golden buffalo. Punch flowed, and I had two kinds of soup—consomme and my favorite, chicken giblet. This was followed by fish, beef, and all forms of vegetables. Most vegetables were canned, but even up here in Wyoming, the cook's garden yielded a few hardy Wyoming newcomers. I personally liked the cabbage and Brussels sprouts. Both made better by bacon drippins'. We finished with desert, and, of course, coffee and cigars. A smashing night in just the sweetest hotel ever.

The railroad has arrived in Cody, and will bring more and more people to area for homesteading, enterprise, and to visit nearby Yellowstone National Park. I am constructing a marvelous hunting lodge to be called "Pahaska Tepee." The name comes from one given to me by my Indians, meaning, "He of long hair." The lodge will also serve as a waypoint for those on their way to the park. I will also have the finest in transportation to make their journey both educational and comfortable. I am excited to see it in finish when I return this fall.

We will complete our stay in London, and then I will take

the show throughout England and Wales. We plan to fold the tents in October before winter sets in.

I will be back in Cody for some hunting, business matters, and see my daughter and her husband who run the hotel. While the hotel dining room is famous for its roast prime rib, I plan to insist that we have lobster Newburg for Christmas dinner!

I have learned to enjoy the "ups" since they help make the "downs" tolerable. As the cowboys say, "Give the calf a pat 'cause the cow's a comin'."

Well dear doctor friend, Cheers!

Wm. F. Cody

"I am fortunate to have procured the services of women whom I trust."

October 15, 1903   Denver, Colorado

Dear Mr. Cody,

It is a glorious fall day in Colorado. From my window I see the thick coating of snow now covering Mount Evans. This is a beautiful place to live, and in spite of the loss of my dear Jane, it is the proper place to raise my son and practice my profession.

Yesterday I drove my little automobile by the medical college in downtown. I hesitate to bestow the honorific of "college" on this piece of excrescence. It runs for the financial betterment of its so-called faculty of local physicians, certainly not the betterment of its students or the profession. I have refused to lend either my time or expertise to this charade. The college was formed this year by the merger of the Gross Medical College with the Denver Medical College.

The former is such a contrivance. It was named after Samuel Gross, a prominent Philadelphia surgeon. He had no connection with Colorado, and the closest he probably came to the state was somewhere on horseback in Iowa. I might also mention that Dr. Osler married Grace Revere Gross after Dr. Gross's death. She is a force herself and the great granddaughter of Paul Revere.

The Denver Medical College was founded by Dr. John Evans when he was appointed Colorado Territorial Governor by President Lincoln. Seeing the college caused me to think of Governor Evans and reflect on what I have read and heard about him. I conclude he was a man of convolution. He brought railroads, hospitals, and the first college, as well as medical school, to Colorado. But then I recalled your letter to me about the Indians in your show. Evans did good things, but he also allowed the atrocity against Black Kettle and his people at Sand Creek. History will prove the Sand Creek massacre was the blackest of day on the state of Colorado. I still shudder when I think of those poor people escaping across the crusted snow of our plains on a bitter December night. A cruel consequence that only the affected suffered, while the perpetrators warmed themselves by the fire and bragged of their foul trophies. I am reminded of the words of Dr. Charles Eastman, a Santee Sioux. After caring for the victims of the massacre at Wounded Knee on the Pine Ridge reservation, Dr. Eastman characterized it as "a severe ordeal for one who had so lately put all his faith in the Christian love and lofty ideals of the white man."

So, like you, I have remembrances and thoughts that trouble me and cause my mood to become a bit dark. This is a particular problem at night, but also during the day. Sometimes what helps me release from such thoughts, especially when they seem overwhelming, is to focus on sensory things in the present. For instance, now I smell the tangy smoke from the burning of leaves in my yard. I also hear the happy shrieks of my young son being swung in a swing by his new nanny. She is quite the trim young Irish woman. She has proven reliable, and also willing to stand up to my housekeeper and cook. There are challenges to being a father alone, and I have considered whether or not I should remarry, but right now, I am not ready, and there is the practical reality of no attractive candidates. I am fortunate to have procured the services of women whom I trust and derive their own satisfaction as they dote on Willis. Sometimes I worry that he will become spoiled from all the attention, but then I think about all the poor urchin children I see on the streets of Denver. My small concern about Willis is a blessing, not the hell that is theirs.

With sincerity,

Edgar

E.Y. Davidson, M.D.

"Such picture shows will be nice little novelties."

October 29, 1903   New York City

My Dear Doctor,

How thoughtful of you to remember me. I am back in New York City recovering from our pitching and rolling as we thrashed our way across the ocean from Europe. Nothing has quite the smell of seasick men and sour animals.

The smallpox still keeps us out of Boston, but thankfully, our educational triumph was welcome in England and Wales, and I shall return next season. Business there was good, and I continue with high hopes for my many investments. I am in dire need of relief from worry, and the success of my show still provides cash to satisfy my creditors.

I understand and related to your mention of dark thoughts, particularly in the night. Sometimes I come awake and battle to get back to sleep. My mind returns to my wonderful West, but oh, the changes. Yesterday morning, the Hoffman House bellman brought me the morning paper, and I read the news that Tom Horn is going to get his neck stretched in Cheyenne next month. I guess he will receive justice for the dirty deed he did in killing that poor settler boy. The forces of the Wyoming cattlemen who hired him as a "stock detective" appear to have no faith or patience for taking their perceived injustices to the courts, and must resort to execution. I guess it's cheaper to hire killers than judges. I might mention that when I first started to assemble the Wild West, I had occasion to approach Horn. He was a champion roper in Arizona. He could really throw the hondo. I thought his skills might be top rate in my production. Unfortunately, he was a braggart and inclined to seek the bottom of the bottle.

You might find of interest that two nights ago I attended one of those moving picture shows, "The Great Train Robbery." It was made by a gent named Edwin Porter who started off working for Edison as a handyman. That boy knew how to move up. I found his result entertaining and it got me thinking. First, it was all set in my West (although I'm told it was filmed in New Jersey). Second, there was no sound, and following the story, short as it was, in any depth, required literacy, because you had to read cards to follow the story. The audience enjoyed the novelty of the show, but for education and pageantry, it cannot hold a candle to my Wild West. I predict that such picture shows will be nice little novelties. (Perhaps I can find a way to integrate them into my presentation of the International Congress of Rough Riders.) Back in 1894, Thomas Edison made a moving picture of me, along with Annie Oakley and my Indians. The Indians performed the Ghost and Buffalo dances. Annie did a find display of shooting. Major Burke thought it would help to sell tickets, but Edison never did anything with it.

When I scouted for the army looking for hostiles, I didn't know what would turn up around bend or over hill. I feel about the same way as I leave for Wyoming tomorrow.

I remain, your faithful friend,
Bill
William F. "Buffalo Bill" Cody

"Such extreme measures are constitutionally justified under the
rationale of "greater good for all."'
November 10, 1903   Denver, Colorado

Chil Scoggin

Dear Bill,

Thank you for your letter. I have had the occasion to see these moving pictures and must admit that I was quite taken. The images are striking, but I noted the weakness you mentioned. The person sitting in front of me read the written narrative as it appeared on the screen. She did this for the benefit of those with her who were apparently illiterate. This was quite distracting in that she had to speak loudly to be heard over the cacophony of piano music being played as well.

There is news about the Boston smallpox outbreak. I believe you will find it of interest. Since the epidemic began in 1901, there have been 1,596 confirmed cases resulting in 207 deaths. Yet more has come of the Pfeiffer affair. Some citizens of Boston have threatened lawsuit against Dr. Durgin and the Board of Health because they allowed a presumably infected Dr. Pfeiffer to leave the island and live among them before Pfeiffer became obviously ill.

As I write this, it is my understanding that the mandatory vaccination of citizens will be argued in front of the United States Supreme Court maintaining such extreme measures are constitutionally justified under the rationale of "greater good for all."

One hopes the wisdom of the Court will enthusiastically support this reasoning.

It occurs to me that I can close a circle. In a previous letter to you I mentioned Dr. John Hunter's use of inoculation to study venereal disease. Dr. Edward Jenner was a protégé of Hunter and from Dr. Hunter he learned the technique of inoculation. Jenner's discovery of protection against smallpox by inoculation with cowpox traces to Hunter's experiments with inoculation and the transmission of venereal disease. Perhaps when vaccines against venereal disease are soon found, the circle of Hunter and Jenner will open to admit these new scientists.

With all best wishes for your health and happiness,

Edgar
E.Y. Davidson, M.D.

"I feel like I have one big old sack of snakes."
December 15, 1903   Cody, Wyoming

Dear Edgar,
As I mentioned to you in my previous dispatch from New York City, I have been spending some lay-up time. I now write to you from my T E Ranch, where it is now "time to chop winter wood." Fall has fled, and the winds and snows of winter have set in as my horses hair-up. I did manage to get in a fine hunt two weeks ago and procured a massive buck deer and cow elk. Both animals, as well as those taken by other members of my party, are processed and salted, with some in the smokehouse. This will provide fine fare as we move further into the winter.

I did take a quick detour to Denver while traveling back to Cody last month but found that you were on a trip to San Francisco. I trust you received my calling card. Unfortunately, my trip to Denver was for a very difficult family business. My daughter Arta Lucille became widowed last year. She had married Horton Boal, a splendid member of a prominent Chicago family who was most approved by me, her father. Unfortunately, Horton suffered from severe melancholy, possibly precipitated by being thrown from a horse. Horton subsequently took his life, leaving Arta with two infant children. As you probably imagine, this has been a heavy burden for our dear daughter, and I regret that my absence had prevented me from comforting her.

I learned that in her grief she had started seeing a Dr. Charles Thorp, an army surgeon returned from the war in the Philippines. In truth, from my years in the army and on the frontier, I have come to not hold army surgeons in much regard. If confronted with a wound or fracture, and even the occasional snakebite, the surgeon's first reaction was to reach for the saw. Many seemed to spend more time with the laudanum bottle than with patients.

When told that Arta and the surgeon planned to marry, I was dead against it.

I understand that this surgeon has now left the army and plans to join his brothers in the practice of medicine in Denver. I thought you might be able to tell me more about his clan.

I feel like I have one big old sack of snakes, and it's all I can do to keep the top tied.

The worst thing is my marriage to Louisa. She continues on the warpath. I wish that she would listen to reason. We both should be trying to help Arta, but all Louisa can do is to blame me for everything wrong in her life. She won't fight fair. To hear her talk, Satan has taken up residence in the skin of Will Cody.

After much consideration, I have decided to file, in the State of Wyoming, a petition for divorce.

I have tried to preserve the relationship—Major Burke has been quite adamant as to the importance of my domesticity and my North Platte home. People appreciate that I am grounded in being a stable and generous member of that community. At his urging, I have sponsored the town fire brigade and helped in the construction of a fine opera house. I even hope to construct a new Masonic Lodge in North Platte, having attained the esteemed rank of thirty-second degree. Throughout this time, I have wanted Louisa to be proud of me. I provided support for her, but with little in return. She refused to live at the ranch, offended my guests, and, as you know, even tried to poison me. I am certain she purposely poisoned the fine staghounds I received from the Czar of Russia. It broke my heart to learn of the dogs' deaths and their suffering with burning guts and non-stop fits.

The only way I could stand her was to drink. It has only been through strong constitution and warnings from doctors that I have freed myself of its grip.

I have been patient and generous, but she has been, "Hell with the hide off." After she had made life miserable for my ranch managers, particularly sister Julia's husband Al Gooding, I turned over the ranch to her to take and run to suit herself.

I last visited North Platte and the Scout's Rest Ranch in 1901. We had a fine Christmas dinner, and spirits were high. Louisa said, "Oh, Willie, it is so good to have you home," and gave me a big old hug. However, when I later made a simple request that she sign a few papers allowing me to sell some of our land in Wisconsin and provide me some needed financial relief, she refused. When I climbed on the train on Christmas night, I knew I would never return.

This has simply come to a point where knitting back together the blanket is out of the question, and we both must divide up the herd and move to different pastures.

Of course, Louisa intends to fight, and I'm sure she is gathering an army of attorneys, as am I. I fear she will take her battle to the newspapers, who will lap it up. They know that any mention of Buffalo Bill will sell papers.

When I first saw that little girl with black curls riding a big horse in Missouri, she stole my boy's heart. Now, I scarce can believe what has happened to us, to my Lulu. But life is short and the grave cold, so I must do what I can to find a little happiness for us both, even if it means some pain right now. Cuttin' the bull calf makes for a fatter steer.

Well, enough of this. I wish you a Merry Christmas and the Happiest of New Years.

Your friend,

William

"Buffalo Bill"

1904

*"I believe the natural tendency of the human
body is to heal itself."*

January 2, 1904   Denver, Colorado

Dear William,

It so distresses me to learn of your difficulties. What a difficult way to start the New Year.

I cannot tell much about the Thorp brothers. They are part of the many doctors of Denver who practice for their purses. I believe they are allied with the homeopathic movement. As you may know, homeopathic practitioners espouse a patient's aliment can be treated by administration of something that causes similar symptoms. For instance, they will give dilute solutions of arsenic to treat complaints of indigestion. They will also use vapor of red onions to induce the watering of eyes that occurs in some patients during the spring season. Most of their remedies are as benign as they are ineffectual; however, some zealots have gone too far in their claims. For example, proposing with the use of homeopathic drugs, appendectomies and most other surgeries are unnecessary. While I do share their tenant of "The Wisdom of the Human Body," and I believe the natural tendency of the human body is to heal itself, scientific evidence is the physician's lodestone to draw together the best treatments for patients. That said, I do not doubt that homeopathic practice will remain on the fringes of medicine, due to its simple, if scientifically unfounded, doctrine of "like cures like." Simple solutions for complex problems are best first examined with distrust.

In addition to your daughter's situation, the news about Annie Oakley no doubt adds to your distress. When I saw the headline in *The Denver Post,* "Famous Woman Crack Shot…Steals to Secure Cocaine," I wondered if she had become addicted due to the injuries she received in the North Carolina train accident. It now appears that the article had been picked from the Chicago Hearst newspapers. The whole story is steeped in sensationalism, based on mistaken identity. A Chicago burlesque performer, who goes under the name of "Amy Oakley," was arrested and jailed for stealing to support her cocaine habit. In order to protect her good reputation, Annie Oakley is suing the Hearst papers, as well as those newspapers that picked up and printed the erroneous story. The first cases are scheduled to start to go to court this year. All the papers, other than Hearst's, have printed retractions. I have heard from one of *The Denver Post* reporters for whom I provide medical services that Hearst sent detectives to Annie Oakley's home state of Ohio to dig up dirt on her, but they came back empty-handed.

All of this makes me to be steadfastly suspicious of what I read in newspapers. I assure you that anything nefarious I may read about you in the papers will be treated with appropriate suspicion.

Your friend,

Edgar

E.Y. Davidson, M.D.

"I return from circumstances that try belief and hope for the future."

February 18, 1904   Chicago, Illinois

Dear Friend Davidson,

I so appreciate having someone to whom I can communicate during times when my head and heart ache, and this is such a case.

I write to you from Chicago as I return from circumstances that try belief and hope for the future.

As I mentioned in my letter of two months ago, I have sought relief from my marriage. This greatly upset my daughter Arta Lucille, and against my wishes she went forward with her marriage in Denver to that Dr. Thorp on New Year's Day. After a brief honeymoon, they moved to Spokane, Washington, where he intended to become a physician for the Great Northern Railroad. I then received a telegraph from Arta that she was very ill and did not expect to live. Word followed that she had undergone surgery for appendicitis and succumbed to complications.

I made arrangements for her poor body to be shipped back to Rochester for burial in the family plot. I met Louisa in Omaha, Nebraska. In spite of our shared grief, she refused to speak with me, but rather shrieked to anyone who would listen that I was a murderer, having broken my daughter's heart.

We traveled in separate sleeping compartments. It occurred to me that this tragic circumstance might allow reconciliation, and to this end I approached her and swallowed and choked down my pride. When I suggested that we find a way to be together and put aside the pains of the past, I received a full charge of Louisa's venom. She roared at me in a screaming fit, and she pledged to denounce me at the gravesites of our children, Arta, Orra Maude, and dear Kitty. The *graveside* Dr. Davidson! What sort of person would do such a thing over the bodies of her dead children? Nevertheless, I asked Major Burke to also approach her about a civil solution, but this only set her off again. She told me I am so low that even the dogs would not bark at me, and pledged to ruin my career.

And then there are the newspapers. The *Chicago Daily Tribune* headlined, "Buffalo Bill at Last Stand," and, "Buffalo Bill Reads of Love." One report in the red rag, *The Denver Post,* described me as being a "good kisser," insisting that the girls in my theatrical shows kiss me good-bye at the end of season, and call me "Papa." This report only serves to inflame Louisa.

Louisa is ripe with her own faults. Some for me in the legal proceedings have testified to Louisa's drinking habits, as well as abusive language to household help. Although Louisa in testimony was said to be a very religious person, she consults astrologers and gypsies—one of whom gave her the poison she used on me.

Doctor, that poor woman could be so strange. I have told you of her behavior toward people who visited me in North Platte. I still cringe at the memory of a time she tried to break up a party by appearing in old and soiled wearing apparel, cursing, and screaming, our dogs hiding under tables and the piano. My guests fled before her threats and breath.

I know I am but a man, and I certainly have my shortcomings. I am willing to ask for forgiveness, but it seems Louisa would rather cut my throat (or other parts) than cut me some slack.

What am I to do?

With dejection,

Bill

William F. Cody

"There is no morphia for the soul."

February 24, 1904   Denver, Colorado

Dear William,

Thank you for your letter of last week.

I wish I could provide comfort and solution for the challenges with which you cope. The loss of yet another child, with its painful grief, now compounded by the severing of matrimonial bonds surely must torture you. I wish that I could provide you relieve of such pain, but there is no morphia for the soul.

I know that the Gnostic literature speaks of marriage between man and woman as "two into one." While that mystical imagery also hints at the carnal, it does not speak to the challenges of maintaining unity in the daily trials of life, and the reality that time and circumstance may create a situation in which one becomes two again after travails. Unfortunately, our society does not look kindly upon attempts to break the marriage contract. I sense that you have tried to find rationalization for the necessity for divorce and feel that time will prove your decision both practical and wise, but the words of Voltaire come to mind, "Optimism is the madness of insisting all is well when you are miserable."

When you are next in Denver we can dine together. Even if I cannot provide helpful counsel, I'm sure we will enjoy each other's company. I am anxious to learn of your plans for the future.

Most sincerely,
Edgar
E.Y. Davidson, M.D.

"I was only trying to do what I thought best."
March 14, 1904   Cody, Wyoming

Dear Doctor,
     I appreciate your taking the time to see this worried scout while I was in Denver on my way to Wyoming. As I mentioned, the Caldwell remedy, recommend by a close associate, has helped my constitution as she said it would.

As always, your first advice was also well taken, and I assure you that I am a new man, although the events of the next few weeks will no doubt provide more than enough excuse to seek refuge in the damned bottle, though I teetotal.

I am sorry to have spent so much of our time lamenting this ongoing home situation. Try as I will, watching my private life pass through the meat grinder of the press has left more scars than from a wet and muddy saddle cinch on a tolerant horse. Every time something more gets thrown on my back, these hurts fester up again. I should have taken a lesson from the trials of Oscar Wilde. I met him during my first tour in England. In fact, we enjoyed tea together, and laughed at one another in our velvet pants and silver belt buckles. I smiled and nodded when he said, "I can resist everything but temptation."

I guess his novel, *The Picture of Dorian Gray,* really got people stirred up; although, Wilde told me the editor of *Lippincott's Magazine* "took out the good parts." Like me, he was tortured by the press and courts, and we both made the mistake of believing tolerance has evolved in a so-called civilized society.

I've read in the Bible that sodomy is a sin. Well, there was all sorts of sin in the West, but no one made much out of it.

Chil Scoggin

It was a reckoning with reality. I personally say it's a glandular thing. There were hog farms around the military posts where I served, as well as along the Cheyenne to Deadwood Stage route (something we did not re-enact in the Wild West!). I remember when the McPherson army post chaplain tried to get commanding General Bankhead to erect a wall around the pleasure palaces outside the fort. The General said, "Reverend, a stiff cock can break down a brick wall."

Out on the prairies, I saw that cowboys sorely suffered from lack of women. If they wanted to have a dance, they'd divide up, and those who played the "she" had a triangular patch over the front of their trousers. Truthfully, not much was made of the whole thing, even the bachelor marriages some cowboys entered into. Given my own marital circumstances, I know what it's like to be sat in judgment. Minding my own business is like telling the truth—you don't have to remember what you said.

My marriage remains a source of anguish and dissatisfaction. With Louisa, I was only trying to do what I thought best. I trusted that justice would see that that poor, ordinary woman would be better off. Alas, it was not the only time I have found disappointment rather than gold at the end of a rainbow on a stormy day.

This month, I have been giving depositions in support of my request for divorce. While it makes my head hurt and my heart break not a little. I leave for England and France, and there is the possibility I will not return.

Your hopeful friend,
Bill
Wm. Cody

"Human relationships decay and unfortunate events and stories emerge—
unfortunately, yours sells newspapers."
March 25, 1904   Denver, Colorado

My Dear William,

As always, it was my pleasure to see you as well, although it distresses me regarding your ongoing personal situation. I wish I had a salve that could assuage the situation.

I well know the Caldwell concoction. It is alcohol, sugar, and the German compound "salicylate" distilled from coal tar. Its most profound ingredient is senna, which serves as a laxative. I shake my head when I read the label and its purported benefits range from the treatment of heartburn to bad breath. I must place it in the category of the cough cream you mentioned when we first met. As Dr. Osler taught, "The desire to take medicine is one feature which distinguishes man, the animal, from his fellow creatures."

I have found that even with the trivial illness that would respond to diet or simple tincture of time, the expectation of patients and their family are such that the visit to my office or mine to their home, is not thought to be complete without the provision of a prescription.

As I mentioned, I am sorry to learn from you that your domestic difficulties persist, and I can only wish a speedy resolution. Their impact is on your well-being more than your public image.

As to the accusations by the court of the press, one can only suffer through as a matter of our pride, but know that we suffer more if we know them to be true. Human relationships decay and unfortunate events and stories emerge—unfortunately, yours sells newspapers.

I did smile when I read of your meeting with Oscar Wilde, as well as your comments about certain acts around the needs of the human species. I am reminded of a scene in Melville's *Moby Dick*. Prior to sailing out on the Pequod whaling ship, the narrator, Ishmael, describes his night in a rooming house. It was the custom for men to share beds. Ishmael crawled into bed. He watched as his bedmate, South Pacific Islander Queequeg, undressed, showing tattoos across his massive muscles. "Oh well," Ishmael mused, "better to sleep with a cannibal than a drunken Christian."

I wish you a pleasant voyage. I hope that time brings news of improvement in the pain from which you suffer. Even if you remain in Europe, we should continue our correspondence.

Sincerely,

Edgar

Edgar Davidson, M.D.

"I may be naughty, but I'm no hypocrite."
June 28, 1904   Gainsborough, England

Dear Doctor,

I feel I was a bit too emotional in my last letter to you, and for this I apologize and ask your tolerance. When I wrote it, I felt like a whipped horse; I couldn't get my head down low enough to make the beating stop. I do appreciate your words of support. They help salve my tender hide.

Please be assured that I have worked hard at preserving my marriage over the years, but it has been a trial, particularly as Louisa has become so demanding as well as hateful in her speech toward me. She fails to appreciate the many obligations I have had and sees my attempts to help others, particularly women as somehow an affront to her.

For example, at one point she was angry at my attempts to help Katherine Clemmons, a talented young actress I met during the Wild West's first tour in London. Like me, Miss Clemmons was a child of the American Frontier, skilled on a horse, and able to drink like a man. I provided her financial assistance during her tour of England. I also helped her to come to the United States and debut in the play, "A Lady in Venice." It cost me a great deal, but when the play was attacked by critics and had to fold, I did not ask for financial reimbursement at that time. Later, as my circumstances—and hers—changed, I did partition her for a $10,000 return of my investment. Unfortunately, she refused, and I dropped the whole thing.

Lulu's lawyers have made a big deal out of my relationship with another woman, poor Bessie Isbell. Like Miss Clemmons, she was a superb actress, but without resources or sponsorship. My association with Bessie was one thespian helping another. She also traveled with me as my press agent, and I believe was a great asset to Major Burke in this regard. In New York, Louisa made a huge fuss because when she made a surprise visit to me, Miss Isbell answered when Louisa knocked on my hotel door. Louisa would not listen to my insistence that Miss Isbell was only assisting me in dealing with some correspondence. Louisa's rampage resulted in damage to her hotel room and caused me a pretty penny to make right. When Lulu's fuse gets lit, she's short to go off, and when she does, she can do more destruction than three drunk Irishmen or one sober German.

Louisa was also angry that I provided accommodation to Bess at the T E Ranch. She would not listen to my explanation that I both needed Miss Isbell's expert assistance in dealing with the press, and I believed that the Western climes would prove beneficial to Bessie's health. I admit that I had a few cattle branded for Bessie as she had no financial resources, and I thought the cattle would give her a bit of personal wherewithal. To make sure there was no mixing of Cody cattle with hers, I even registered the Wyoming brand "Bar BQ" in her name. I also gave her a small parcel of land, again, as a way of compensating her for her services to Buffalo Bill. To make sure that all was on the up and up, I asked that she pay me one dollar and other valuable considerations in exchange. That damned lawyer of Louisa's asked me about the "valuable considerations," but for the life of me, I could not recall. Poor Bess's health has continued to decline, and I fear she suffers from consumption. She is now in Denver, and I have taken the liberty of giving her your name.

One thing in all this mess that confounds me is knowing how I have always promoted women. I shared the spotlight with Annie Oakley. She helped fill my stands and treasure in my poke. And I made a pretty penny for her, too. As for the female gender as a whole, I have gone on record saying women should have the right to vote. Believe me, I have endured a lot of hell for that. You also have Buffalo Bill's word that he has never forced a woman into a compromised position with either promises or threats. Too often I have seen men of power in show business use their position to satisfy their lechery.

If all this wasn't enough, I have now received word that my Masonic brothers in North Platte are threatening to expel me from the organization over "issues of moral character." What two-facedness! Many are the nights that I have witnessed them drunk and debauched. If I were a spiteful man, I'd let it be known that I have seen Freemasons, regardless of officership or degree (including I might add, the Worshipful Master), in the repose of wickedness.

I may be naughty, but I'm no hypocrite.

With frustration and disgust,

Bill

William F. Cody

1905

"I only wish God hears my side of the story."

January 10, 1905   T E Ranch, Wyoming

Dear Dr. Davidson,

I am back in my wonderful Wyoming after a solid successful season in England, Scotland, and Wales. I avoided repeating my 1903 unscheduled dismount in Manchester where my horse stumbled, I tumbled, and my ankle sprained. For several weeks, I could not mount a horse, and the audience had to welcome Buffalo Bill in a buggy.

I plan to return to Europe. There I will prepare to start up the show in France and then tour the continent. Before I leave in March, I am to give more depositions in Omaha in my petition for divorce. I will also rebut the acquisitions that will no doubt arise from Louisa and others as we prepare to go to trial. Louisa maintains she never tried to poison me, and it was me poisoning myself with liquor. She also alleges that it was me that caused her cruelty, and in spite of all she said I did, she still goes to sleep each night with a portrait of me above her bed.

When my show was pummeled by rain, winds, and mud, I once told Salsbury, "God, Christ and the devil are against me." I did not find myself on knee asking for salvation from the situation. I questioned the role of God in my life. Up until recently I've been pretty much an Ingersoll man figuring his atheism meant he believed in something—that there is no God.

Given how long this has gone on with Louisa, and newspapers throwing out stories like red meat in front of slobbering hounds, I find myself tempted to ask for help from a higher power. I have no doubt that my soon-to-be former wife has already tried to bend the ear of providence. I only wish whoever is up there hears my side of the story.

A belated Happy New Year to you, Doctor.

God bless you,

William

"I already have enough blood suckers in my life."
June 14, 1905   Elbeuf, France

My Dear Dr. Davidson,

No doubt you have read that the district judge in Sheridan denied my request. He noted that in Wyoming, incompatibility is not grounds for divorce. Louisa's and my counterclaims of cruelty did not wash it with him, so I'm stuck. I am in correspondence with my lawyers regarding filing an appeal, but that may be once again me throwing good money after bad.

I write to you from France. What a splendid morning, listening to the Wild West come alive, and smelling the brewing coffee and frying bacon in the cook area. It is the best part of the day.

We are on tour after a superbly successful stand in Paris. We averaged overflowing crowds of 17,000 or more each show.

I so love Paris. When we did the 1889 Exposition, we packed in the French and banked lots of French dollars.

I remember the strict laws about importing gunpowder. Annie Oakley smuggled in her favorite English powder hidden in hot water bottles under her bustle!

I have no doubt you would approve of our Paris show site. We were camped on the same grounds where Napoleon marshaled his troops before going off to war. The Eiffel Tower was in our front yard.

The French really like my addition to the Wild West, "Carter, the Cowboy Cyclist." Cycling is quite the rage in France, and we sometimes stage races between a Frenchman on a bicycle and a cowboy on a horse. The cowboy always wins.

Soon we will have more fresh cut summer hay for our poor animals. Oh, how they have suffered. It appears that glanders has broken out, and the French authorities have placed the horses of the Wild West under quarantine. They now threaten that all will have to be destroyed, although we have only seen one possible case within our herd, and that beast recovered without apparent spread to others. I fear the cure for glanders, and the saving of my ponies, is the greasing of palms. Bailey fears the damn Germans will threaten to make me kill the horses and burn all the harnesses, saddles, tents, and other things associated with my horses before they'll let me into the country. If I have to do this, I'll have to raise a lot of cash to replace it all, and that will be both difficult and painful. I will keep you informed, as I know of your interest in infections and their course.

In spite of the glanders, I have had time on my hands, and have finally gotten around to reading the book, *Dracula,* you suggested. I have had it for years, carried it with me, and planned to see what all the fuss was about. It does have significance to me. During my London stay during the Wild West's first tour of England, I met that fellow, Bram Stoker, who wrote it. He was involved in the London stage, and managed a famous actor I paled around with, Henry Irvine. Old Bram was a bit jealous. I found him a nervous fellow, and his book is a queer sort of thing. One of the characters in Stoker's book, a Texan by the name of Quincey Morris, was a hunting guide who favored Winchester rifles. By gad, he reminded me of me! I plan to tour in the eastern portions of Europe, and I hope to not encounter any kind of the creature Stoker describes. I already have enough bloodsuckers in my life! Hah.

Dr. Davidson, I must tell you that it troubles me that I have not heard from you for so long. Have I done something to offend you? Has my griping about my marital circumstances gone so far as to have you, too, shun me? Have I been too familiar? If such is the case, I apologize in the sincerest way, and beg your forgiveness.

Yours in trust,

Bill

William F. Cody

Good Medicine

"I have suffered through the direst of circumstances."
July 21, 1905   Denver, Colorado

Dear William,
Thank you for your letter, and you are due an explanation for my lack of communication.
I have suffered through the direst of circumstances.

My son has died, and I was the vile vector who brought him the diphtheria.

It has been a dreadful time in Colorado. The demand for an eight-hour workday led to continued deadly confrontations between miners, militia, and those damnable Pinkertons brought in by mine and mill owners to break the Cripple Creek strikes. The close, cold conditions of the strikers' high mountain tent camps with limited hygiene, and the even poorer diets of inhabitants, led to an outbreak of diphtheria in the children. By autumn, it spread to Denver.

When I answered the call to the hospital fever wards, I knew it prudent to minimize my chances of carrying the diphtherial bacteria beyond the bedsides of the stricken children. To this end, I practiced what I felt to be the most stringent of precautions. When in the presence of the sick, I wore linen overalls that were afterwards boiled in lye soap water and then hung to dry in the sun before reuse. Upon leaving the ward, I thoroughly washed my hands and face in Lister's solution. I even washed my mouth and gargled my throat with antiseptic chlorine water.

In spite of these measures, I brought the germ to my son.

Within a week of the first Denver occurrence, my son fell ill. I sat by my son's bed throughout the night, listening to the course whistle of his breathing and dabbing at the tears from his eyes. I admit my tears mixed with his, and I recalled a similar vigil four years ago at the bedside of his mother and my wife.

Watching him struggle as the dawn began to seep through the east windows, I was joined by guilt, and I wondered how

149

I might have better protected the boy. I deduced, blameful or not, that I could not have done differently lest I shirk my duties and oath to the sick. As dawn fully broke, I knew that now I could only care for my son. I changed his sleeping gown, placed new clean covers on the bed, and opened a window to allow the entry of fresh air. I placed a cold compress on his forehead and once again wiped away tears.

Throughout the day, the child's breathing became more labored with retraction of the intercostal muscles of the chest.

I asked him to open his mouth, and bravely he obeyed. Gently using forceps to tease up the edge of the membrane in his throat, I saw a pulsating ulcer portending risk of erosion into the carotid artery. The horror. The devil himself hid under a putrid blanket in the throat of a child. The ceilings and walls closed in as I stared at the loathsome thing. I heard no ticking from the clock in the room. I willed my hand not to shake as I withdrew the forceps. In my mind came the vision of how his mother coughed forth the blood of fatal consumption. I found myself praying to the god whose existence I so questioned when she died.

As light from west windows in the room faded, my son's face became increasingly blue with cyanosis and lack of oxygen. I noted the pulse irregular. In spite of increasing the anti-toxin dosage to 50,000 units, my poor boy no longer responded to me, went into vascular collapse, and died.

I brought my hand away from my son's cooling brow, bit into the index finger of my fist, and tasted blood as I swallowed the sob in my throat.

As is proper with such cases, I wrapped his body in a sheet soaked in corrosive-sublimate solution and placed him in a tightly sealed coffin. I held the most private of funerals and laid him to rest beside his mother in Riverside cemetery where someday I will join them.

I have joined the families who, as a physician, I had heretofore but watched suffer the agony of the death of a child—doubly dead because they had died so young.

The door to my son's room is across the hallway from mine. His toys are still scattered on his room's floor—a cup-and-ball, marbles, a small popgun with tethered cork, the acrobatic wooden monkey he so loved, the skittles set with its balls and pins we both liked to play together, and neat piles of the books I had given him. In the corner of the room sat the blackboard on which his governess had written a list of words to be learned. I cannot bear to change a thing.

With apology for my lack of communication,

I remain faithful,

Edgar

E.Y. Davidson, M.D.

"Perhaps our two sons play together."

August 10, 1905   Lyon, France

Dear Dr. Davidson,

Oh, how it pains me to learn of the death of your son, and the memories it brought back to me. In April of 1876, I was appearing on the stage in Massachusetts when I received a telegram from Louisa telling me that my children were stricken with scarlet fever. My son, Kit Carson Cody, was near death. I rushed home to Rochester and was able to embrace my angel boy, Kitty, before he died. God took from me my only son, and I can only conclude that he was too good for this world. God sent the angle of death to take him to a better place.

Please accept my most heart-felt condolences and assurance that your son, too, is now in heaven, and perhaps our two boys play together.

With sorrow,

Bill

William F. Cody

"Night times are the worst."

September 1, 1905   Denver, Colorado

D ear William,
 Thank you for your thoughtful note.
 I remain in sorrow. Night times are the worst. I find myself questioning over and over, especially what would have happened if I had obeyed the rules at Hopkins, not married, and not had the son. I could have remained in an environment in which I had experienced success, and from that had a predictable and stable career. I don't deny my love for Jane compelled me to marry, but what if my head would have ruled over my heart? As my life has unfolded, I appear to have traded a bright future for daily darkness. I know not the reward for such decisions, but moreover, the "why."
 Sincerely,
 Edgar

"Time doesn't bring healing, just tolerance."
November 1, 1905   Marseilles, France

D ear Edgar,
 I trust that you are feeling better. Having lost loved ones, including my brother Sam, my father and mother, and more recently children, I have learned the wisdom of the old saying, "Time heals all wounds." But I also know that the wounds may scab over a bit, but they are still there. Time doesn't bring healing, just tolerance. I have had to fight slipping into perpetual darkness and anger.

In a few days I will return from a wonderfully successful season in Europe as judged by the crowds and the money that has flowed in. Unfortunately, it has also flowed out.

As I wrote to you earlier this year, the Wild West has been plagued by glanders. Shortly after we left Paris, horses in the bronchos developed fever, became listless, and refused to eat. This rapidly turned into a nasty discharge from the poor beasts' nostrils. Ulcers in their throat, mouth, and skin appeared. Their eyes became swollen, giving them an even more pitiful appearance. French government veterinarians called to care for the animals diagnosed glanders, a very contagious and often lethal disease. The only solution was to shoot those horses that were sick, and make sure none of other stock came in contact with the bronchos herd. Over the course of the season, an additional 200 bronchos were killed, leaving us only 100 as we completed the tour in here in Marseilles. Yesterday, Mr. Bailey and I decided to destroy the remaining bronchos and burn all the tack and trapping that came in contact with them. As a result of all this, I am deeply in debt due to the necessity of importing new animals for the coming season.

Like you, Doctor, through this trial, I have asked why this was all happening. As I said, the show has been the greatest success, but ever since we left Paris, the early optimism and success has turned into continued worry that the Wild West would be shut down by the French government. We have had to kill fine animals. One was "Dolly, The Laughing Horse." She was a crowd favorite, and I shook my head and swallowed a sob when I saw her fall to the ground with the gunshot to her head. She twitched, tried to rise up, and went still. I fight to get the image out of my mind.

I plan to spend the next few months in Winter Quarters at the T E Ranch. Come spring, I'll be returning to reunite with the Wild West in Marseilles. Before then, I'll need to arrange the import of bronchos to replace those lost this year.

You should know that I have resolved to lead the good life. While I have never been much on religion, perhaps it is time for reconsideration. Despite the circumstances of my mother's life—raising children, the loss of my father, and her consumption—her daily strength came from faith, although it did always put much on the supper table. I resolve to be good, and not allow those around me to swear or abuse drink.

My best wishes to you, and hope things are better.

Sincerely,

Will

"I continue somewhat at odds with my medical colleagues."

November 23, 1905   Denver, Colorado

D ear William,
   Thank you for taking the time to write to me.
   As you might imagine, I find little about which
to be thankful this coming holiday.

I continue at odds with my medical colleagues. Many appear unsympathetic to my recent loss; although, I do appreciate that all physicians in the city have been numbed, attending the death of so many innocents. In addition, many show indifferences to my attempts to improve the general care of our patients. One recent example is the utilization of improved technology to recognize and treat disease.

Recall my mention of Dr. Cushing. I have continued in occasional correspondence with him, particularly referring young physicians to him who desired further training in surgery—particularly those with a keen interest in surgical experimentation. Two actually caught on with Dr. Cushing and Hopkins. To my surprise, I received a postal package from him that contained a Riva-Rocci apparatus. It is a cuffed device attached to a tube of mercury marked off in millimeters. A note from Dr. Cushing expressed his appreciation for the sending of student physicians.

Through my reading, I knew of the device. While Dr. Cushing was studying in Europe several years ago, he became acquainted with the Italian medical specialist Scipione Riva-Rocci, who invented the device. It is called a "sphygmomanometer." Upon his return to the United States, Dr. Cushing had several made. He utilized manometer in his discovery of the association of increase in pressure on the brain, such as in trauma patients, with rise in blood pressure, irregular breathing, and slowing of the heartbeat. The combination is known as "Cushing's Triad." Such discoveries, as well as Dr. Cushing's surgical expertise, has brought him substantial international acclaim. Along with the other medical giants of Hopkins, the usual migration of physicians to Europe in search of medical enlightenment has been reversed, and now Europeans come to America.

Also accompanying the device was a recent article by Dr. Nikolai Korotkoff. Dr. Korotkoff has shown that by listening to the artery sounds as the cuff of the sphygmomanometer and watching the fluctuation of the mercury column, one can determine a patient's maximum and minimum blood pressure. Although there is increasing scientific literature to support the importance of measuring blood pressure in patients, I have found my proposition that it become a routine part of examination of patients is greeted by the off-waving of hands. The spread of new information within the Colorado medical community appears to advance at the pace of the Rocky Mountain glaciers of the state.

Dr. Cushing is a man often of brusque, sometimes harsh, treatment of subordinates, and I feel moved by his unexpected thoughtfulness. It brought a flicker of happiness to an otherwise dark day.

Sincerely yours,

Edgar

E.Y. Davidson, M.D.

1906

"I value my privacy."

January 20, 1906   Denver, Colorado

Dear William,
        I trust you had an enjoyable and relaxing holiday.

My brother Wallace and his family visited me to celebrate Christmas and the New Year. They have recently welcomed an infant son named Mason. Following the visit, they are returning to Urbana to prepare for a move they will be making to England. Wallace has accepted a position in a Rothschild financial institution. He believes it will give him experience and connections that he can put to use in Chicago, particularly as it relates to grain and other commodity trading. Wallace is excited, but I must say that I would find dreadful waking up each day to face nothing but numbers.

I have considered the possibility of relocating to Europe, particularly to study at one of the renowned hospitals and laboratories of Germany. Dr. Osler is now "Sir William Osler," having been selected for the Regius Professor of Medicine at Oxford. It is possible that he might be able to arrange a position there or in one of the great hospitals and laboratories of Germany.

Alas, I lack the energy to make such a move, and I have decided to spend the next year devoted to my medical practice here in Denver.

I have retained my household staff.

My housekeeper, Mrs. Clark, is a woman tall for her gender, a model of cleanliness and punctuality, her dress always spotless and starched. She is ten years widowed, her husband the supervisor was killed in the Sunnyside Mine boiler explosion. Childless, she gives her Sundays to her church. When I hired her, she specifically said she neither expected, nor wanted, any vacation days. She lives in quarters above the carriage house, and is quite stern with the young chambermaid she engaged for housework.

My cook is Mrs. Kelly, a dependable woman made round

by generous diet and the birthing of seven children, three of whom still live. She goes about her duties accompanied by a cheerful *tra la* song.

So as to not turn her out, I have retained Willis' governess, Miss Ava Ryan. Expectantly, this was a good decision in that my brother planned to employee a nanny, and Miss Ryan has the necessary experience and skills. Thus, she will be joining them in moving to England. Because Miss Ryan still harbors distrust of the English, should Miss Ryan not find England satisfactory, Wallace will provide her passage back to the United States.

I have appreciated the visit of my brother and his family, but I must admit, I am ready for them to leave. Having the child around does conjure memories. Also, I value my privacy. In addition, before their visit, I had fallen into a routine of rising early, reading, then off to my clinic and seeing patients throughout the day, followed by a light supper with wine, and then retreating to my study for more reading before retiring for the evening. I have found that this regularity keeps my mind from wandering into sad thoughts and on to bitterness.

With appreciation for your correspondence, and I hope you have a successful season on the continent.

Sincerely,

Edgar

E.Y Davidson, M.D.

"I must focus on the future and march forward."

February 20, 1906   New York City

Dear Edgar,

We're gathering up in New York to head back to Europe and reunite with the Wild West. The show wintered over in Marseilles, France. We'll open there, and then start a run into Italy.

I do not look forward to the ocean voyage ahead of me, as I usually spend the first day at the ship's rail, "feeding the fishes." On each crossing I have made, I know I have gotten my sea legs when I can enjoy the traditional breakfast of bullion and ham paste sandwiches. There is the constant thrumming and vibration of the great beast as it makes its way over the ocean. I sleep, but frequently awake. The debt I've taken on to replace animals and equipment is heavy, and it is on top of what I need to just keep my ranches and Wyoming mountain enterprises running. In addition, the Arizona mines have muscled their way in as well. The worry burns off some when the early light of the sun seeps into my cabin, but I cannot say I arise refreshed. I do enjoy a morning lap around the deck, and I am able to nap after lunch.

I have had you on my mind as I know you struggle with your sorrow. I have found the holiday period to be difficult, particularly as I see families unite and the excitement of children. When I start slipping into the past, I remind myself that there is nothing I can do to change it, but rather I must focus on the future and march toward the goals I have set for myself both in business and in making my show even better. For instance, I have added "A Holiday at the T E Ranch" to the end. It starts with the Indians attacking the ranch house, but then being repulsed by the cowboys. At the end of the scene, Red and White join together in friendship, and they close the show by saluting the audience. It is a sparkle!

Please remember that Bill thinks of you.

William

William F. Cody

"Buffalo Bill"

"Greetings from France."

March 5, 1906   Marseilles, France

Dear Edgar,

The start of a new season is the most exciting time! I've reunited with my cowboys, and they all promise they have not broken the bank in Monte Carlo over the winter. They are hard at work with the new bronchos I have imported. I have lots of challenges filling in the big old hole of debts.

I was particularly glad to see that Charles Griffin wintered well. Griffin is a Hawkeye like me, having been born in Iowa. Griffin is an experienced showman with a talent for magic, who has also proven to be a dependable manager. He can also turn a nifty phrase, one of my favorites being, "Cody, a golden rule in French pronunciation: say a word any old way except how it's spelled."

Griffin tells me he thinks he'll write a book about his time in Europe with my Wild West. Being a successful author myself, I told him, "Be careful what you write; people may starts to believe you."

Helping me manage this press this year is Frank Small. Frank is almost seven feet tall. Griffin says, "Frank is the biggest small you will ever meet." Hah!

We have already been told that when we are in Italy, both the King and Queen will attend the Wild West. Everyone, rich and poor, common or royal, loves my Wild West.

Doctor, I hope your life goes better, and I look forward to hearing from you.

Your friend,

Bill

"What is money without health?"

March 24, 1906   Rome, Italy

Dear Edgar,

I write to you from the road and from Rome, as our happy, but weary troupe moves on to its next stand. Business is spectacular. I am making as much as $40,000 a week. This is unheard of in this business.

But what is money without health? I am recovering from the grippe. Thousands come to see me and my Wild West, and it seems that it takes only a few with catarrh and bark to set up coughing, sneezing, and fever that spreads through my troupe like a prairie fire.

I am exhausted, and my nerves are horrible. Where once

my heart thundered with excitement during our most chaotic choreographed acts, I now find myself dreading the roar of guns and exertion of concentration to meet the cheers of the audience. Just yesterday I caught the pop of a shotgun just so in my ear that I could have sworn I blacked out, and found myself retiring to the arena side, dizzier than a spinning windmill. Hopefully the audience took this for stoicism and not my unraveling.

Powell recommends a daily bromide to calm my nerves. Do you, Doctor, agree with this?

How quickly good thoughts escape my mind, but if I'm patient, they may come back. I have also lately tried reading the Holy Bible, but my mind wanders and I lose the trail and its meanings.

I hope to see you soon, as I cannot continue like this, and I long for the T E Ranch. Even though our ticket sales are grand and many of the shows are turn-away, because of last year's glanders, I am financially very strapped and had to mortgage just about everything I own just to keep going. Having to kill over 200 of our horses and burn all their gear and tack presented a great financial loss to me. I estimate my loss to be over $300,000.

Exhaustedly,
Wm. F. Cody

*"Fresh air and exercise, combined with suffi-
cient rest, are better than any tonic."*

April 22, 1906   Denver, Colorado

Dear Cody,
As I write this, news continues to come in about the earthquake in San Francisco. Fires continue to burn, and it is estimated over 3,000 people have died. Over three-quarters of the city has been destroyed. The many dairy herds in the region south of the city are being slaughtered to provide food for the city's survivors.

I appreciate the opportunity to provide advice, and I advise against bromide.

I caution you that you are at risk for nervous exhaustion, which, at its worse may result in neuroasthenia. Such circumstances should never be treated with drugs, but rather removal from the offending circumstances. To this end, your longing for the T E should turn into action. Dr. William Osler was clear in his recommendations that business men who develop problems with their nerves due to overwork should enjoin absolute rest with a change of scene and diet. The longer the condition has lasted, and the more intense the symptoms have been, the longer the time for restoration of health. Shorter periods may of course be of benefit. However, as a rule, relief will be only temporary.

A sojourn to the woods, mountains, or lakeshore I have found to be very helpful. Fresh air and exercise, combined with sufficient rest, are better than any tonic. And in this regard, I must warn against the use of bromides. While they may have a salutary effect at first, those who fall into their routine use run the real risk of chronic bromism—a condition with its own undesirable consequences including confusion, weakness, and irruptions, and sometimes eroding and pustular irruptions of the skin.

I urge you to seek rest and relaxation, but having said this, I realize that you have obligations to your "happy, but weary troupe," as you so nicely put it. Unfortunately, I cannot help but relate to this, as this is a circumstance I, as a physician, too have experienced: the necessity to set my personal needs, sometimes at the risk of health, in service to patients. I remember one circumstance when attending to a man with hemorrhage from his stomach. It was Christmas Eve of my first year in Denver, and his family waited outside the bedroom door. Although I had been up the night before attending to a young girl with a complicated delivery of a child, I spent the day into the night constantly irrigating his stomach with ice water, but to no avail. I gave him an injection of morphine, and sighed, "all bleeding stops...eventually."

I hope that circumstances upon your return to America do allow you a period of respite at the T E Ranch. Should this occur, I caution you that when removed from the day-to-day stress, you may first experience some feelings that you are abandoning responsibility and the productive life. This is both normal and irrational. It has been my experience that such feelings will melt away, and once you have recreated yourself, you will return to work more productive and certainly healthier. To repeat your own words, "what is money without health?"

Sincerely,

Edgar

E.Y. Davidson, M.D.

"Life continues to conspire against Buffalo Bill."

June 18, 1906   Budapest, Hungary

Dear Edgar,

I write to you from the great Hungarian Empire, the horse capital of Europe. The horses are tall brutes meant for war or work. I wager that my little American bronchos could easily outrun or out last them. These fancy horses would tremble at the sight of a longhorn herd, but mine cowboy creatures would wade right in. If a cow don't move, the good pony bites 'em!

As always, thank you for your guidance. Powell and I have history, but part of this history is that I've learned to hear him, but not listen, when he starts in giving advice.

Life continues to conspire against Buffalo Bill. My partner, James Bailey, died in Mount Vernon, New York, in April. He contracted erysipelas. Evidentially, the infective affliction started on his face, but spread to his blood stream, causing his death from sepsis.

I am left without a partner.

I must tell you I had started to suspect that the old ringmaster was keeping the Wild West and me in Europe so as to not compete with his Barnum & Bailey Circus in America.

In addition to dealing with Bailey's loss, after the San Francisco earthquake, the earth has continued angry. We had to adjust our Italy schedule due to the irruption of Mt. Vesuvius. Along with the flows of lava, there was a rain of rocks, cinders, and ashes that caused much destruction in the Naples area. I am told that the churches were flooded with people praying for deliverance from gases and earthquakes. I decided to make my own penance in the form of sending a portion of our gate receipts to aid in the recovery.

Once again, thank you for your direction, which I shall faithfully heed. I do wish Griffin the magician could wave a wand, chant an abracadabra, and make me appear back at the old T E Ranch.

How are things with you?

With sincere thanks,

Bill

William F. Cody

"Buffalo Bill"

"My practice flourishes."

July 5, 1906   Denver, Colorado

Dear Bill,

Yesterday Denver dedicated an arch in front of Union Station. It stands as tall as the floors of two buildings and bears the word "Mizpah" on the top. Mizpah is a Hebrew name that connotes the emotional bond between people left behind and those departing Denver via train. Speaking of emotions, you would find it of interest that the Denver police have banned kissing on the train platforms. They believe such embraces impede the timely departure of trains. In your words, "Hah!"

My practice flourishes. My patients come to me by word-of-mouth, perhaps because I have a reputation of keeping my word and my mouth shut. I live by the code that the bond between patient and doctor is sacred. This success has given me the time and resources to volunteer my services to the Florence Crittenton Mission. This institution provides shelter and safety for young women in unfortunate circumstances. During their time of confinement, they are treated with dignity. After delivery of the child, assistance is provided in helping them find placement of the infant, as well as aid in their own transition back into society.

I have also instructed Mrs. Clark and Mrs. Kelly to prepare hot meals to be taken to the poor souls camped under the Colfax bridge across Cherry Creek. At first, they were reluctant to do so, expressing concern about their safety. Initially, I accompanied them, but after the first few trips, they no longer ask my escort. They find the people humble and grateful, although often expressing embarrassment about their circumstances. I have walked the slums of Baltimore, often experiencing friendlier greeting than when I attended my first medical society meeting in Denver.

Your acquaintance Samuel Clemmons would approve of my service to the citizens of Denver's Chinatown. Colorado, along with other western cities, at first favored the Chinese for their labor, including on the railroads. Unfortunately, sentiment arose against them, and the Chinese have been subject to exclusion laws, both in immigration to this country, and also an outright ban in many Colorado towns, particularly in the mining areas. Denver has not been innocent in this regard, having experienced a riot against them in 1880 that destroyed most of their homes and businesses and left one Chinese man dead. I find it ironic that it was the white gamblers and prostitutes in the area of Chinatown that came to the rescue of so many Chinese against their fellow Denver citizens. The Chinese are resilient, and they operate successful businesses, such as laundries, that they essentially monopolize in Denver. Some are starting restaurants. In fairness, I should mention that opium dens are still to be found, especially in Hop Alley. It has been my observation that the majority of their customers are white. While the Chinese favor their traditional treatments, they do allow me to provide some care to them, particularly as it relates to consumption and certain other acquired infections. I do have curiosity about how they find placement of small needles seem to affect particular areas of the body and associated complaints.

In summary, my life feels less chaotic, and though sorrow still seeps up out of the depth of my mind, I feel I have a purpose, and that makes it easier to arise each day.

Your friend,

Edgar

"Evidently money and printer's ink cannot buy every elected office."

November 7, 1906   Denver, Colorado

Dear Bill,

I thought you would find it of interest that Annie Oakley's nemeses, William Randolph Hearst, was defeated in this week's election for Governor of New York. Evidently money and printer's ink cannot buy every elected office.

It also appears his style of yellow journalism has run up against a formable foe in the form of Annie Oakley. She has been consistently successful so far in her lawsuits against the newspapers who picked up and published the erroneous article defaming her character. It is affirming to see good triumph over evil, but I also believe having a strong soul and sharpshooter behind the process favors the outcome.

I hope all is well with you, and you are either returned from Europe or on your way across the ocean.

Best regards,

Edgar

E.Y. Davidson, M.D.

1907

"It's been quite some time since I have heard from you."

February 20, 1907   Denver, Colorado

Dear Mr. Cody,
    It's been quite some time since I have heard from you. I trust all is well. It is my understanding that you have returned from Europe. I stay busy with my work.

Sincerely,
Edgar
E.Y. Davidson

"Work I must."

February 28, 1907 En route East via rail from Wyoming

Dear Dr. Davidson,
    It was my delight to find your letter waiting for me in Cody before boarding the train this afternoon. I apologize for being remiss in writing to you.

I write to you from a George Pullman private car that I have engaged for the trip east to start the show season. It is quite acceptable with nicely polished wood from Cuba, brass fixtures, deep chairs, and carpets that soften the swaying of the train. The parlor area includes the desk at which I now sit. There are four bedrooms, though I travel alone. The dining room is supported by a chef in the kitchen and a steward who serves and cleans. The bathroom has a shower and a porcelain sink and throne, although, I'm always somewhat taken aback when I flush the thing and see the railroad bed passing below. I do not anticipate availing myself of the observation deck at the back since it is winter, and the cold is not good for my bones.

I apologize if my writing is a herky-jerky. But it's better than the letter I write while riding a horse!

I enjoy good health, and the news is also good.

The European tours for the past four years were quite the success. In addition to the British Island, we toured many countries. The reception in Italy was wonderful, and in spite of my own financial situation, I gave substantial financial gifts to the victims of that volcano Vesuvius erupting and the earthquake in San Francisco. Doctor, call it what critics will, but my natural inclination is to help anyone in need. Perhaps I can call myself Christian yet. Haw!

We moved on up into the Crimean region, all the way thrilling people with my animals and Indians. I finished the Stoker book and made sure I posted lookouts for evildoers coming out of the mountains of Transylvania. I always slept with my revolver and 32-caliber automatic pearl-handled pistol close at hand, so I was ready. Even so, I always kept the window open or the tent flap up. No winged count can make this two-fisted old scout change his ways.

Following partner Bailey's death, since my return to this country, I have had to run this whole damned thing. In addition, the Bailey heirs have found a note for $12,000 that I am certain I paid. Nevertheless, they hound me.

The crowds have been good, and I fill up the treasure box, but everyone is constantly after me for money. When the money gets tight, it makes me ill, and I have to take to bed. Some ask if I am retiring. What folly. Work I must.

Through all this, I've done my best to keep the show fresh and entertaining. My show now has polo played with automobiles, the hold up of a train, and cowboys and Indians going against one another in a game of horseback football. By the way, I read that the forward pass has been made legal in American football. Well, Doctor, my cowboys and Indians have been doing this for years! I should also mention that I saw my first automobile at the Chicago World's Fair, Now, fourteen years later one is in the show ring with horses, buffalo, and the good old Deadwood stagecoach. Such is progress!

In the coming season, I plan to dress each day for the show in my buckskins and boots. My clothes still fit me rather well. I may have told you this already, but at Major Burke's urging, I agreed to wear a wig. A while back when I visited Jules Sandoz at his Nebraska Sand Hills ranch to discuss my Wyoming irrigation, I left it on the bedpost while I went hunting. Evidently his daughter Marie peeked in my bedroom and saw it and ran screaming from the house. Also, one day I rode into the Wild West arena and did my usual salute to the audience with a sweep of my Stetson hat. Well, that damnable wig came off, much to my embarrassment.

My Indians greatly enjoyed my self-scalping.

I no longer wear the wig—who could tolerate something that is a source of humiliation and terrifies small children?

Well, old friend, best I close.

I hope to see you sometime in Denver. I am working on a capital new idea and hope to be able to share it with you.

Your friend,
Bill
William F. Cody
"Buffalo Bill"

"But I am a bit low."

April 27, 1907   New York, New York

Dear Dr. Davidson,

First the good news. We have had another splendid run in Madison Square Garden. It started with the opening night in March when I rode a magnificent Arabian stallion, "Muson," into the arena to start the show. President Teddy Roosevelt was in attendance, and he greeted me with standing applause.

I've added the Battle of Summit Springs to the end of the show. General Carr absolutely loves it, and has willingly gone on record that I am the one that killed the Indian chief Tall Bull. I was fortunate to have been at the right place at the right time, and damn those people who think otherwise. I had the chief's horse and named him "Tall Bull." He was fast as lightening, and I picked a few pockets in match races. Unfortunately, one night I got a bit into my cups, lost a wager and the horse.

I am some better from the grippe, except I continue to cough. I've cut back on smoking, and that helped a bit. I do not know if it is due to the damnable cough that continues to remind me of my frail health, but I must admit that I fight moments of great sadness over the state of my life, and my fellow man. In addition, today I was informed of the death of my longtime friend, Dr. Powell. Frank and I go all the way back to my early years as chief of the army scouts on the plains. We have done much business together, and he greatly assisted me in my Cody, Wyoming, enterprises. He died of heart trouble on the train while returning from Los Angeles. *The New York Times* has contacted me about receiving more information about his life and dealings with me, so great was his repute.

Powell was in Los Angeles investigating for me motion pictures and how I might use them to tell the story of the West and my deeds. This is my new idea! Have you seen one in Denver? I believe I've mentioned seeing the one called "The Great Train Robbery." I have seen some of these things that are called "nickelodeons," because it costs only a nickel to get in. The audience lined up around the block to see the one I saw. They seem to be a combination of vaudeville followed by a short film. To my eye, the audience is much more engaged in the film —I saw them rudely clap in anticipation of the film while the poor performer was still on stage. This may be good thing for me to get into business given my expertness in both showbiz and business. I can throw a double loop and rope in twice the money.

But I am a bit low,
Your friend,
Bill
Wm. F. Cody

*"That you are so afflicted simply confirms
that you have a conscience."*

May 15, 1907   Denver, Colorado

Dear William,
          Congratulations on your success. I have attended many shows, and no doubt yours is the

only that both educates and entertains. Bravo.

Motion pictures—or as I'm hearing them called, "movies"—are a potentially important new means of informing and educating the public. I recently viewed a movie showing the effects of the San Francisco earthquake. The devastation shown in the film greatly exceeded the descriptions in newspapers; it made my heart sink when I saw the areas I enjoy visiting on my trips to the city.

I should also tell you that many people recovering from the grippe complain of continued nettlesome cough. It usually wanes over time and quitting or minimizing smoking is a wise decision.

Depression of spirits and feelings of sadness are some of the most unpleasant and obstinate features of the condition. Circumstances such as this are bound to bring out remembrances and feelings of regret. That you are so afflicted simply confirms that you have a conscience.

Some members of the medical profession are starting to use "depression" to describe melancholy. It is derived by the work of the German psychiatrist Dr. Emil Kraepelin to "depressive states" of human mood disorders.

Osler, a student of all things medical and close follower of the medical literature, only uses the term "depression" as a description, not a diagnosis. In his latest publication of *The Principles and Practices of Medicine* in the section "Morphia Habit," he describes the morphine addict: "The sleep is disturbed, the appetite and digestion are deranged and except when directly under the influence of the drug, the mental condition one of depression." What Kraepelin would now consider "depression," Osler still uses other terms. Examples include "hysteria," which he depicts as "a state in which ideas control the body and produce marked changes in its function." He also writes of "neurasthenia," which he characterizes as "a condition of weakness or exhaustion of the nervous system," and goes on to describe patients as suffering from loss of weight, often confined to bed, lacking the ability to perform normal mental work, sleeplessness, and suffering from moody, irrit-able, and depressed behavior. Again, depression is used to de-scribe appearance of the patient, not brand the condition.

As I read on in Osler's *Principles and Practices,* I found a familiar condition described under the heading, "Traumatic Neurosis." This condition occurs following an accident with injury, or as Osler put it, "severe mental strain combined with a bodily exposure." It could occur from a variety of accidents—Osler recounts the case of a naval officer who de-veloped traumatic neurosis following being trapped for a day in the rigging of his ship during a violent storm—but the most common cause was railroad accidents. Osler has sub-headings dealing with "Railroad Brain" and "Railroad Spine." After an accident, the patient complaints included headache, fatigue, weight loss, irritability, and inability to concentrate. Sufferers experienced episodes of freight and terror, some-times with violent tremor, particularly as they recounted the accident in their minds. Osler also notes that the symptoms of traumatic neurosis are particularly prominent while an ac-cident is under litigation, but "settlement is often the starting point of a speedy and perfect recovery."

I recall your telling me about the prolonged recovery of Annie Oakley after the rail accident a few years ago. I know she required surgery for her wounds. She also suffered terrible injury when left too long in a Hot Springs therapy bath. I won-der if due to the delicate nature of the female and susceptibil-ity to emotional anguish, if such depression may have affected her as well. If this is the case, the nasty business with Hearst and his newspapers could only have made things worse. The positive is, she certainly did not lack the essential energy to fight back and reclaim her reputation.

Osler explained various possible treatments for hys-teria and neurasthenia symptoms, including "hydrotherapy"; "massage"; tonics of salt, ammonium, and potassium; and the drug, antipyrine. Osler feels strongly that drugs should be of last resort in treating sleeplessness and other symptoms of neuroasthenia. Opium might be necessary for treatment of acute anxiety, but "prolonged treatment with opium is, however, never necessary in neuroasthenia." Osler even included a section on the role of "faith healing," one of the key elements of which was a patient's faith in the physician. To this, I personally place little value, but I do think patients do respond to having trust in their physicians to be prudent, respectful, and avoid the many nostrums of the quack.

He is greatly missed in this country. He did create a stir before he left for Europe. In a farewell address given in Baltimore, he commented on the "the energy of youth and the uselessness of old age." Osler then made reference to a novel by Trollope that proposed forced retirement at age 60 and "a year of contemplation before a peaceful departure by chloroform." Well, the next day, the newspaper headlines screamed out, "Osler recommends euthanasia." Although he maintained his statement was facetious, a new verb has appeared associated with euthanasia, "To Oslerize."

I believe the lesson is to take care in the presence of a headline-hungry press.

With best wishes,
Edgar
E.Y. Davidson, M.D.

"I still want to believe in a brotherhood of man."
May 26, 1907   Poughkeepsie, New York

Dear Edgar,
Thank you for your reply to my letter. I must admit that I have had to read it over and over to take in all the information you kindly provided. I read trails real good, and you leave lots of signs.

I appreciate your understanding about my situations and their impact on my health. I assure you that I am not yet ready to be Oslerized.

God's not ready, and the devil's afraid of me.

I continue to stew about decisions made or forced upon

me in my past. My family and financial situations are always with me, but this has been my life, starting with the death of my father. When I was but a boy, I stood by my father's side when he suffered the wound that would eventually kill him. We were in a store, and men began to argue about bringing slaves into Kansas. A man of principle and passion, Father bravely joined the argument and condemned the evil of slavery. One of the men pulled a knife and deeply stabbed Father. It did not kill him then, but he suffered for weeks, was barely able to walk, and finally died from the injury and an infection of his lungs. I later rode on raids against those in Missouri that would defend the keeping of slaves and tried to force that wickedness on Kansas. People spoke and wrote about "bloody Kansas," but the first blood was of my father.

With my father's death, my childhood ended. I worked carrying messages back and forth for the freight-hauling firm Russell, Majors, and Waddell. What money I made went to support my mother and sisters. I scouted, provided meat for the railroad, and even took a shot at the hotel and land business before hitting on the stage and Wild West.

I am not just a silly showman. I believe I told you about how much Nate Salsbury and I worked and spent money to bring to the world the stories and entertainment of the American Negro. It saddens me to this day that we failed to do so. I miss Nate and wish that circumstances had allowed us to part ways on better terms.

So, this is my secret, Doctor: I still want to believe in a brotherhood of man, particularly with the Indian.

I have tried to do the right thing as regards the Indian. There are things in my youth of which I am no longer proud and work hard to charge off to the time and circumstances of the day. In addition, I have come to appreciate the circumstances that have so unfairly worked against Indians and have tried to use the Wild West to educate the people of the world as to their equality and nobility of race. I'm not sure when this change of heart occurred, but I do remember visiting the

Columbian Exposition next to which we set the Wild West in Chicago in 1893. Acre for acre, we cleaned those Chicago boys' clock for the number of visitors and money in the ticket wagon. I know we gave a better show. However, I did have occasion to visit the Exposition and was much impressed by the displays depicting the lives of Indians of the Northwest. Like the Indians in my show, their virtues and pride of race were well presented with none of the bloodthirsty savage stuff that other shows and presentations have laid on nickel audiences. Inside the Indian display, marked by a queer sign "Anthropology," I met the young man in charge of a display of Northwest Indians. In spite of his rather thick German accent, we swapped a few stories—particularly about our various scars. I got mine from fighting and he got his from dueling.

Having said what I said, I got holy hell from all sides because of the Indians in my show. The missionaries said I was keeping Indians in their primitive condition and preventing them from receiving redemption. Many in the military said I encouraged those among the Indians who are still reluctant to accept the civilizing influence of reservation life. Still, I believe it is important that their spirit and traditions be kept alive.

I have seen more fairness and kindness from Indians than any one of my creditors.

Anyway, we all look pretty much the same with our skins off.

I should also tell you that while in New York, I met with Bessie Isbell, the young woman you so kindly examined in Denver and arranged for accommodation in a sanitarium after finding that she suffered from consumption. Bessie made a splendid recovery and thus was able to travel. She plans to visit Italy. As a favor to her, I had my personal attorney arrange to sell the Wyoming land I provided to her and then send on the proceeds to her mother in Denver.

This is a superior outcome to that of Miss Katherine Clemmons, who so aggravated Louisa. I assisted Clemmons on the stage. I was forced to sue her to try to recover such funds, and the whole relationship was portrayed as sinful during my Wyoming trial. Miss Clemmons went on to marry the son of the financier Jay Gould, who, after trial of marriage, found her to be a philanderer and drunkard—a behavior usually reserved for men. In Gould's suit for divorce, I was offered $50,000 to testify as to her character. Even though I sorely needed the money at the time, Buffalo Bill does not trade on the honor of women, and I refused.

The divorce went through, and younger Gould agreed to pay her $34,000 each year in alimony—an unheard-of sum. In an article I saw, Clemmons commented, "It's hard to dress well on less than $40,000 a year in Manhattan." I roared, and again wished her good riddance.

Again, thank you for your letter. I must close as the train to which my car is attached is preparing to leave, and I wish to give it to the young man who collects mail to post from the Wild West before we depart.

With best wishes,
Will
Wm F. Cody
"Buffalo Bill"

"Wherever I have gone, issues of race have confounded my own sense of justice and humanity."

June 13, 1907   Denver, Colorado

Dear Buffalo Bill,
I found your brief, but moving, letter very touching. As you know, I have followed your career ever since I was but a stripling.

I must tell you that you have not gotten enough credit for your relationship among the races. I recall that those attempting to bring the red man into our Christian society criticized your use of Indians in the Wild West and characterized it in the newspapers as exploitive and harmful to them as a people. I, on the other hand, believe you provided them not just honest labor, but a chance to share, perhaps even retain, their lifestyle.

I believe the young man you met at the Columbian Exposition was Franz Boas. He is a very vocal opponent of racial prejudice and believes the scientific study of cultures must be used for the benefit of society. These studies he terms, "anthropology," a somewhat clunky term, and I question whether or not it will catch on.

Boas holds that the culture of any group must be scientifically studied to determine those factors of history and environment that determine behaviors, and to this end, there are no inferior races, just differences in culture. As you might imagine, this position is not embraced widely, particularly in those quarters who believe Europeans in general, but particularly those of northern, non-Irish, birth to be superior to other races. The true agenda of those that criticized you was your thwarting their efforts at Indian assimilation and Christianization. To them, the only true culture is that of European civilization. I wish such people believed in a broader brotherhood, as I believe do you.

Wherever I have gone, issues of race have confounded my own sense of justice and humanity. For instance, Johns Hopkins, where I trained in medicine, did not turn anyone away. Some Negro patients had would have to come from many miles away, often under great hardship, and some dying in route. Yet, when they arrived, they had to use separate entrances and facilities.

I have witnessed further, fouler, examples of injustice. When I first came to Denver, a 16-year-old black boy was accused in the sexual assault of a young white woman. I had occasion to examine him, found him feebleminded, and suspected he was luetic. A mob seized him and a "confession" extracted under coercion. The poor boy was chained to a railroad overpass, and a bonfire was built under him as he pleaded for mercy. It took almost twenty minutes for him to die. At the end, he beseeched heaven for the forgiveness of his murders, something I cannot do. It is a continued blight on the history of Colorado.

Today I read of the race riots in Atlanta, a southern city previously known for its prosperity and accommodation of the races. The lives lost from both sides, and the necessity to call in the state militia, has led to a rising element in the Negro community frustrated with their own leadership and now looking for a more aggressive approach to obtaining racial justice. I can only hope that leaders emerge on both sides that will put aside prejudice and find harmony among the races. Alas, I remain skeptical as it seems people are more inclined to violence and fear. That hooded order of beasts known as the Ku Klux Klan, first born in the South, has now spread to Colorado. I have been told of a burning cross seen on Table Mountain west of town, near Lookout Mountain.

The overall situation gives little comfort to one who wants to believe in the charity, tolerance, and so-called Christianity of white men.

With sincere best wishes,
Edgar
E.Y. Davidson, M.D.

"In all my enterprises, the most difficult challenge is people."
August 29, 1907   Dayton, Ohio

Dear E.Y.,
I sit at my desk in my personal tent. I have a good light from the electrical dynamo that provides far superior illumination, and without the oily smell and watering eyes from the fumes of kerosene. I have so enjoyed watching the modern evolution of my world. I am actually trying out another one of these new repeating pistols that is self-loading and cocking. Leave it to the Germans to come up with the idea, but the one I have was made by a fellow American, John Browning. It is a dandy. I bought it in Belgium. I am working on how I might include shooting demonstrations with it in my show.

So far, the Wild West has bested "The Greatest Show on Earth" in attendance and receipts. The Wild West makes the audience's heart race. We blaze guns, save a damsel in her burning cabin from Indian attack, arrive almost in time to save Georgie Custer, hunt buffalo, recreate the days of the Pony Express, and race my Deadwood Stage around the arena. I give a grand demonstration of fine shooting. We even have a tornado! The Congress of Rough Riders stages horse races between American cowboys, Cossacks, Mexicans, Arabs, and Indians. We provide demonstrations by Syrian and Arabian horsemen, bolas throwing exhibitions by Argentine gauchos, and Mexicans performing feats of horsemanship and roping. Unlike the circus, we have no candy butchers, snake charmers, dwarfs, contortionists, and pickpockets. Our stock-in-trade is action and education.

Dr. Davidson, your letters have caused me reflection, particularly as they relate to people and business.

Although it's been difficult to come to my own personal terms with the decisions I have been forced to make and conflicts into which I have been thrown, I must admit that the night is the worst time. While I fall asleep easily, about two hours later I awake and cannot get back to the escape of sleep. On the prairies, the wolf and coyote were creatures of the night. If they got too close, I'd just throw another log on the campfire, grip my rifle a bit tighter, roll over, and go to sleep. Not so with the worries that now plague me.

One thing that causes me to fret at night, as well as sometimes even pound my pillow in frustration, is thoughts of betrayal. I have fed too much rope to those who would take advantage of my goodwill and charity. I should remember to take a few dallies around the saddle horn, trip the boogers, and give them a talking-to about right and wrong. They should be the ones having trouble sleeping, not me.

I do admit fault in not having been more questioning, and I also have gotten involved in enterprises more to the liking of my gut, not my head. I was also making so much money, and opportunity was just there for the picking. I felt the best way to assure my continued fortune and financial safety was to diversify into several areas, such as cattle, land, and even the enterprises with Dr. Powell. I've gotten deep into mining in Arizona.

In all my enterprises, the most difficult challenge is people. The perfect business would be one in which the only people are customers.

Once I knew I had to discharge a young man because of his love of the bottle, and when so imbibed, he played at rumps-kuttle. As a result, when he could not report for work, others had to take on his duties, and there was increasing grumbling. When I confronted him, he said, "Colonel Cody, you can't fire me; it will destroy my marriage. I give you my word that I will reform." Well, I relented, and gave him a stern lecture and a second chance. The grumbling started around the camp that the Hon. Cody was a soft touch. This I did not like. While I enjoy my veneration by others, I also want to be seen as having a stern side that lets people know that Buffalo Bill does not tolerate fools. When the man failed and again embraced the bottle and Venus, I booted him, vowing to not trust a drunkard. He became a reminder to me that those who will break their marriage vow will think nothing of breaking their word to me.

When you're dealing with 600 souls, it is amazing the mischief they find.

And, wives are the worst.

Within our group we had some very attractive young single women, and woe to the cowboy or Cossack who lets his eye wander in the presence of his wife. But worse is the wife that becomes ill with another wife. Not only do they battle with each other, but they also drag husbands, children, and friends to the fray. Before I know it, the back of the Wild West is its own little arena, as they scream, threaten, and throw. Good old Nate Salsbury. He was so good at knocking heads together and restoring order to the troupe.

Best wishes for your happiness,
Wm
William F. Cody
"Buffalo Bill"

1908

Chil Scoggin

"We've never been a family that has showed our emotions."
May 20, 1908   Denver, Colorado

Dear Bill,
    I know you are on the road, so feel no obligation to respond to me.

I have just returned from Chicago. The American Medical Association is finally recognizing the problem we have with the education of doctors in this country. As I have written and discussed with you, you don't even need a college degree to attend a medical school, and most schools themselves are little more than a short time in the anatomy lab, some lectures on apothecary, tutorials on the microscope, and a few other courses that are pure bunk, such as the electricity and magnetism of the human body. Furthermore, there are some schools that will award a medical degree without a student ever having examined a patient. This is in contrast with the fine European schools that require rigorous course work in science and mandatory clerkships in clinic and hospital wards.

While I am not much on joining organizations, I do applaud the AMA for taking on the task of addressing this shameful educational situation.

You might ask why a doctor in the hinterlands of Denver was asked join the AMA Council on Medical Education (CME). First, I know they received a recommendation from my father, and second, my being a product of Johns Hopkins also played a role. JH has been the leader in developing a rigorous, science-based medical education curriculum as well as an unfailing advocate that medicine is learned at the bedside.

It proved to be a surprisingly constructive meeting, and we made the recommendation that the first step in reform is a national survey of medical education. To this end, the CME intends to engage the services of the Carnegie Foundation for the Advancement of Teaching.

While in Chicago, I spent some time with my father. He greeted me at the door in his dressing gown, and asked that we sit in the kitchen. On the way there I noted his bed was not yet made. In the kitchen, the sink was empty, and there was the odor of a pan left on the stove too long. He assured me that he took most of his meals at a nearby restaurant, but a woman came in each day to tidy up and cook his breakfast. He made me tea using a bag and poured the boiling water into his own cup over already soggy leaves in the maker over his cup. He brushed away graham cracker crumbs on the table before asking me about the medical committee meeting. When I excused myself to use the bathroom, I noted there were copies of both *Boston Medical and Surgical Journal* and *Police Gazette* next to the toilet stool.

We met for about two hours.

Father told me of what was happening in his neighborhood: the wife whose husband had left him for his secretary, the teenage boy who favored dressing as a girl, and a general run-down of Father's take on the financial situation of several people. I sat quietly, but inside felt unease in his judgment of other people.

When needed to change the subject, I inquired about the Whitechapel Club. Father took this bait and ran with it, telling me in detail about the ongoing examination of the motives and activity of Dr. Henry Howard Holmes and his Murder Castle in nearby Englewood. "It is now estimated he killed over 200 people," Father told me. "I petitioned the Philadelphia authorities to allow me to examine his brain for peculiarities after his execution, but they refused." Father went on to tell me that the "long drop" method of hanging was used, which assured instantaneous death due to the neck being snapped. This was in contrast to other methods in which the executed succumbs to the effects of strangulation and asphyxiation. I judged father to be rather encyclopedic in his knowledge of hanging, as he recounted other consequence on the human body, including erection of the penis, or so-called "angel lust." I felt gladness when we finally moved away from this subject; it was gruesome, but at least it wasn't gossip.

At the end of our meeting, he did inquire about me in a general way. He lowered his voice and looked away when he did so. When I asked after my brother and his family, his gaze returned to mine, with forthcoming details about Wallace's business. When I asked if Miss Ryan was still in employee, Father said he did not know.

I did take the liberty of telling Father that we are in correspondence, but his only reply was "That is nice."

As I left, I shook his hand, and as I moved to give him a hug, he said, "We've never been a family that has showed our emotions, but that does not mean we do not love one another." I agreed. When I looked back before walking to a waiting taxi, I saw the curtain in his parlor pulled aside and him looking out at me.

After finishing this letter to you, I plan to pen one to father, extending an invitation that he visit me in Denver.

Bill, the hour is late. I am tempted to open another bottle of wine, but prudence dictates that I finish my correspondence and prepare a list of tasks for the morrow.

With friendship,

E.Y.

"But in the end, there is only Buffalo Bill to solve problems."
September 7, 1908   Grand Junction, Colorado

Dear Dr. Davidson,
I write from the other side of your Rocky Mountains.

As you anticipated, the challenges of having to manage the Wild West without a partner have stolen my time and sapped my energy. What little time I have had for correspondence has be sucked up by dealing with creditors.

And on the positive, I have a happy company because there is little chance of rain, and they are already enjoying the sweet peaches and pears for which this part of Colorado country is so famous. The river bottom is fertile, but hills and mountains that surround it are deserts that will never welcome the plow.

But what a melancholy view have I. We have a fine camp on Pitkin Avenue adjoining the railroad yard, but sadly, overlooking us to the northeast is a large mesa, Mount Garfield. It is named for the assassinated President. Garfield would have been such a fine leader of this land—a fact too few now know. He was a man who might have healed the South and the North.

I remember the defense of the madman who murdered him: "Yes, I shot the President, but his doctors killed him."

We are here but one night with the show scheduled for 11 a.m. tomorrow. I surveyed the building of the camp and the pitching of tents from my automobile. Doctor, after riding in your little electric buggy when we first met, I've been interested in automobiles. I not only ride in them in my show, but I'm going to get a fleet of White steamers to carry hunters to my Cody camp. I insist on big cars, because what would people think if they saw Buffalo Bill riding around in a little dinky thing?

Everywhere the Wild West goes, we provide a boon for the locals in that hay, grain, and straw must be procured for our beasts. Also, we must purchase food and other supplies for the cast and workers. When Buffalo Bill comes to town, he leaves happy faces and lots of money. Little do people know how I worry about things being done right, and how to keep paying for it all. I am always the first to appear, and last one to get paid.

Major Burke tells me today the show is already sold out with 10,000 souls and will be the largest gathering ever seen on the West Slope of the Colorado Rockies. We'll present the great dramas of civilization, including the Battle of Summit Springs, a train holdup, holiday at the T E Ranch, equine demonstrations, and Johnny Baker's demonstration of trick shooting. I particularly like his shots taken while he stands on his head.

My Congress of International Rough Riders of the World now includes Royal Irish Dragoons, Japanese warriors, Mexican masters of the rope, South American gauchos, Russian

Cossacks, the American volunteer cavalry, and demonstration soldiers firing field artillery. Of course, there are cowboys and cowgirls of the Wild West.

I currently have over 100 Indians who put on aboriginal dances and present their customs. They are a consistent source of curiosity for visitors to the camp.

This season the show has gone well, although I must constantly be on guard to make sure each day's operation comes off on schedule. I appear at each performance no matter the weather. Johnny Baker is a willing helper, and Major Burke promotes us so well, but in the end, there is only Buffalo Bill to solve problems. Having a business partner so helps in sharing risk and daily burdens. How I miss Salsbury, and even Bailey.

My new book, *True Tales of the Plains,* sells well, and I am appreciative of all the help I had in putting it together; although, at their request they remain nameless. In the book I provide my eyewitness accounts and experiences in the West and Civil War, including famous people who have sought my friendship. Sam Clemens will rip me for the first chapter, "How I killed my first Indian," but the publisher wanted it because it was such a grabber. I'm a good storyteller, and I do get wrapped up in enthusiasm when I recall and write. There have been those who say I'm short on truth and tall on tales, but they're just jealous. They said the same thing with the Wild West, and I just told these critics, "You can't teach people if you don't get their backsides in seats." And I laughed when I looked in each day's cash box. This whole writing deal was a challenge when I started since periods, commas, capitals, and such were not my strongest skill. But like everything I've taken on in life, with hard work and determination I've made it work. Reading the book is like attending the Wild West but enjoying it from the comfort and safety of the own fireside chair or bed. Some have said I tend to sometimes come up a little short of the truth, but I've never been accused of not providing entertainment. I appreciate that people reach into their purse for the latter; the former, not so much.

Well, my friend, I must close and seek sleep. After the show tomorrow, everything will be packed on the trains, and we will be off to Salt Lake City that same day.

Perhaps I will see you in Denver when I return home at season close next month.

With sincerity and hopefulness,

Will

William F. Cody

"Buffalo Bill"

"I first thought it was you, knowing your taste for adventure and innovation."

November 19, 1908   Denver, Colorado

Dear Bill,

I read the following article in *The Denver Post* today, headlined, "Cody makes first aeroplane flight in England." Of course, I first thought it was you, knowing your taste for adventure and innovation. To quote you, "Haw!" It was an American also named "Cody," who has been building manned kites for the British Army.

I have enclosed a clipping of the article.

Every best wish,

Edgar

"I feel such relief."

December 27, 1908   Cody, Wyoming

Dear Dr. Davidson,

This Cody in an aeroplane? Hah! I know well the rascal Samuel Franklin Cowdery. The only thing we have in common is we were both born in Iowa. For years he has been going around claiming to be a cowboy, and like me, giving shooting demonstrations and acting on the stage. He even stole my name, "Cody." While in Europe, I read newspaper accounts of his development of kites and manned airships for the British Army. I did not know that he was also trying to make heavier-than-air machines. Just so you know, there is no worry that the real Bill Cody would ever get in an aeroplane. People have tried to get me to go on balloon rides. I have told them, "Buffalo Bill may climb on a horse or a stage, but otherwise his boots stay on the ground."

Edgar, when I was in Denver earlier this month, I called at your home but was told that you were on your annual sojourn to San Francisco. I trust you received my calling card. Your housekeeper was rather curt, but I did soften her a bit with the Cody charm. I'd hope to share good news with you in person.

I am off to visit my Arizona mines. My partner is Daniel Burns Dyer. Like me, Colonel Dyer is an old Indian fighter. After leaving the army he has made a substantial fortune in real estate and electric trolley cars. Our enterprise in known as the Cody-Dyer Mining and Milling Company, and I predict it will find future fame as one of America's most successful ventures. As you can see, I am quite busy. It is a chore just to remember where my money goes, as well as deal with those who demand various payments.

My having to manage the Wild West and International Congress of Rough Riders, as well as my many business ventures, places a great strain on me. Providence must have taken pity on me and sent me a solution in the form of an old-time acquaintance, Gordon Lillie, or "Pawnee Bill" as he is also known. He gives great promise as I've struggled with the absence of Bailey to share in the issues and costs of the Wild West.

I first met Lillie in 1883 when I first put together the Wild West. I needed an interpreter for my Indians. Gordon grew up next to the Pawnee nation and was fluent in the tongues of the Indians of the West. He took to the life of show business and started his own show with some success. I never saw his "Pawnee Bill's Historic Wild West" as competition to my Wild West, and he just about bit the dust his first year touring. To Lillie's credit, he picked himself up, worked on his show, and came back out as "Pawnee Bill's Historical Wild West Indian Museum and Encampment Show." Well that worked, and Bill's been doing well ever since, even lighting things up in Europe. Two years ago, he came up with a nice twist, adding Mexican cowboys, Japanese acrobats, and even Arab jugglers. He called it "Pawnee Bill's Wild West and Far East Show."

Here is the good news. At the end of this year's season, Lillie approached me about buying into the Wild West and combining our two shows. I feel such relief. Joy quickens the circulation.

Excitedly,
Bill
William F. Cody

1909

"I have come to appreciate that the holiday season brings out behaviors in humans that at best, they regret, and at worse, require my medical attention."

March 10, 1909   Denver, Colorado

Dear William,

I have been remiss in writing to you.

By way of explanation, but not excuse, I have been busy with my practice. I have come to appreciate that the holiday season brings out behaviors in humans that at best, they regret, and at worse, require my medical attention. This is certainly true when it comes to ingestion of spirits and attendant the softening of inhibitions—particularly those related to the perpetuation of the species. Too often I have witnessed the results captured in the wise words of Seneca: "Drunkenness is nothing but voluntary madness."

I recall the less eloquent words of one of my patients: "Doctor, the more I drink, the lower became both my standards and then my pants."

After the holidays come the darkness of January and the rebirth of spring and Easter too far away to blunt the effect of short days and dark nights. I have come to hate the dark but am loath to seek what I see to be the false warmth of taverns and inebriates. Furthermore, my professional position is such I dare not be associated with such establishments. Doctors who gain reputations as "jolly good fellows" endanger both their reputations and respect.

William, I do not wish to sound sanctimonious. I would be less than truthful if I did not admit that partaking of a good spirit helps me come down from the stress of the day. That said, I am mindful of the observation of Oscar Wilde with whom you once took tea: "There can be nothing more frequent than an occasional drink."

I trust the New Year is treating you well.

Respectfully,

Edgar

E.Y. Davidson, M.D.

"I will pay back my debts, and be on easy avenue."

May 27, 1909   Brooklyn, New York

Dear Dr. Davidson,
        I also must once again apologize for my lack of writing to you.

I can tell you that "Buffalo Bill's Wild West" combined with "Pawnee Bill's Great Far East" has ripped it up. We've added camels and even more elephants. Our train has 70 cars, and we have 170 big draft animals to help in making and breaking camp. The Two Bill's sold out Madison Square for two weeks, and we made $60,000 in Philadelphia.

This is no circus, my friend. We're honoring the West and putting equal with other exciting places in the world. The audience just sits in the seats, and I bring to them cowboys and cowgirls, along with a few other guests from Africa and the Orient with whooping, hollering, and shooting. No one has ever asked for his money back. Bill Cody delivers and never disappoints.

I'm minting money, but everyone still has his hand out. Sometimes I feel like my finances are a runaway wagon team on a bad mountain road. The good news is that partner Lillie bought the Bailey share of the show. He also paid off the Bailey loan. This has been a stone in my boot for quite some time as I am sure I satisfied the note, but the Bailey heirs claimed otherwise. Lillie came up with a plan whereby I can buy half of our combined show from my share of the proceeds. It will mean hard work, but if I live to a good old age, it also means I won't have to worry for money.

I found Lillie's plan a capital idea. I told him that this could start after I settled some outstanding obligations to a few people who had advanced me a little capital to help me tide over a rough patch or two. Lillie seemed a bit taken aback and surprised about these additional liabilities. Lillie said, "Pay off and move on. You'll just chew up time and make lawyers rich by continuing to fight creditors." Good old Pawnee Bill.

Speaking of fights, we're in a big circus fight with Barnum & Bailey, Ringling Brothers, Sells Floto, Hagenbeck Wallace, and Miller Brothers 101. So far, we're the only one that makes money. As the money comes in, I will pay back my debts, and be on easy avenue. I have written my bankers with the good news.

With wishes for good health and happiness.

Bill

William F. Cody

P.S. I have noodled on your last letter to me. Doctor, I am not good at reading rocky trails or between lines, but I wonder if, from topic and tone, you might be giving me sign that your loss, grief, and perhaps loneliness, cause you to seek relief in spirits? I find it dangerous to be this forward, but having fought that particular battle, I know its grip. If I am off the mark, forgive me. Sometimes my sensitivities take command of my judgment.

"I have no problem than I cannot handle with the tonics of hard work, professional behavior, good books, and the occasional adventure."

June 30, 1909   Denver, Colorado

Dear Friend Bill,
I thank you for your last letter. I appreciate your forthrightness in the post script.

I have reconciled in my mind the reality of the loss of loved ones. While it has caused me to re-examine my faith, and despite the pestering of an episcopal priest, I seek not formality of worship. Furthermore, I think the priest may have a secondary motive of trying to get into my pocket to help with the construction of the new cathedral to replace the one that burned down. Believe me, I am more suspicious than simply cynical. In my occasional care of the Chinese of Denver, I have come to admire their appreciation of nature, ancestors, and importance of rational order in things. This has helped me

195

more than anything in trying to turn away from the darkness, bitterness, and anger that can come about from the chaos that is life. Do I not check these feelings, I fear what I might do, and that, William, is a place I dare not go. I think this might be an important part of being a human being. We all harbor terrible thoughts and temptations that might translate into the most loathsome and cruel of behaviors.

Again, thank you for your concern, but I assure you, I have no problem than I cannot handle with the tonics of hard work, professional behavior, good books, and the occasional adventure.

All best regards,

E.Y.

1910

"There are two jackasses in this picture."

February 20, 1910 Oracle, Arizona

Dear Edgar,

I have finished up my business at the mines and prepare to return to the road for yet another season.

The winter in Arizona has been good for my bones. I have continued to prospect and add claims.

I thought you might enjoy the photograph I have enclosed. It is of me mounted and moving out to look for minerals. These burros are surefooted and strong. When they see a diamondbacked rattlesnake, they merely step away, as compared to a horse which either doesn't see it or hear it, and if it does, it either sticks its nose down to investigate (with associated nasty consequences) or presents its rider with a moment to experience the consequences of a man's sudden meeting of ground.

Take a good look, Doctor; there are two jackasses in this picture. Can you find which one I am? Hah!

Your ever-optimistic friend,

William

"I fear my Denver colleagues…will not be happy with me."

March 5, 1910 Denver, Colorado

Dear William,

I think things are going to get hot for me in the Denver medical community.

I believe I wrote to you about being asked to attend a meeting in Chicago with the AMA Council on Medical Education. After the meeting, they did engage the Carnegie Foundation for the Advancement of Teaching to do an assessment of medical education in North America. Somewhat to my surprise, I was contacted last fall by a man named Abraham Flexner. Although not a physician, in 1908, while at Princeton, Flexner wrote a critique of medical education. The head of the Carnegie Foundation read this, and he selected Flexner to carry out the research requested by the AMA. In his tour of the 155 medical schools in the United States and Canada, Mr. Flexner requested a Denver meeting with me, having gotten my name from the AMA.

Mr. Flexner and I met for two days last September. Flexner did not like what he saw in Colorado. We have two medical schools, the Denver and Gross College of Medicine and the struggling little University of Colorado. Flexner found no full-time teaching faculty at Denver and Gross, and "a total lack of scientific activity." When the dean of Denver and Gross heard this, in a fit of harrumph, he said, "I had never heard of Mr. Flexner and didn't know of his importance in the world, or if he was a prophet, the son of a profit, or the son of anything else."

Flexner's report is coming out soon, and he has privileged me by sending me a draft. In it he recommends reducing the number of medical schools in North America from 155 to 31 (!) including closing the Denver and Gross. He feels that all medical education should be under the umbrella of a university, and to this end, only the Colorado medial school would be that of the University of Colorado. There is ongoing hostility to this idea from the medical establishment, dating back to its founding up in Boulder when the editor of the *Denver Medical Times* wrote in 1885, "The Editor finds it comical and absurd to see this Colorado pygmy try to hold its head up among the national giants...we will exert every effort to kill this jackass incubator and thus rid the state of a flyblown excrescences which cannot be other than a noxious nuisance to every medical man within borders."

Knowing I hosted Flexner, I fear my Denver colleagues—and I use the term "colleague" guardedly—will not be happy with me. But having read the draft report, I side with Flexner. Medical education demands great reform. Wonderful models exist in Cleveland and Wake Forest, and particularly in Baltimore.

Cody, I must also tell you that I was not particularly taken by Flexner. I find hypocritical the fact that he operates a for-profit educational institution in Louisville, Kentucky, and at the same time criticizes medical schools operated similarly. What bothers me more is Flexner's attitude toward black Americans. Over dinner, he told me that he felt that the practice of the Negro doctor should be limited to his own race. Remembering my experiences in Baltimore, and now my ministration to Mexicans, Indians, Chinese, and the few Blacks in Denver, I know that disease resides in circumstance, not blood. Intellect and integrity reside with the individual and are not a consequence of race. I left my meals and meetings with Flexner more excited by his mission, but with measured reservations about the man.

I close with hopes that your new relationship with Lillie proves to be satisfying for you personally and financially.

Your friend,

Edgar

"My cousin in Canada has been sending me some little powders."

June 23, 1910 — Orleans, New York

Dear Dr. Davidson,

The spring has brought clouds, sunny weather, dry camps, and big smiles when we look in the cashbox in the ticket wagon.

All the papers I read are headlining the coming passing through the tail of Halley's comet. Some people worry that it might bring the end of the world. Not this scout. I've escaped more danger than the doorman in a twenty-five cent French brothel. I am thinking about how to work the comet into the Wild West. Our prairie cyclone has been such a great hit. Crowds like to see the telling of current events. Having said that, as I told you a while back, I missed the mark with Mark Twain and the China Boxer Rebellion. One article I read told of Mark being born in 1835 when the comet last passed over, and last year predicting he would die when it reappeared. Well, old Mark got that one right when he died last month.

The Two Bills continues to flourish. We are finishing again in Madison Square Garden before starting to hit the road. We will travel, pack up, set up, put on the show, then start all over again. All this wears on me. I am constantly in costume. When I am not running the back part of the show, I have to help Lillie and attend to my business matters, and sometimes this takes us into the night. Lillie has been excellent in taking care of the front of the show. He chides me about the payments the show had made because of my hotel bills. I told him that I had appearances to keep up and tried to be frugal in accommodations. I must admit, I too was a bit surprised that a week in the Waldorf had built up to over $1,200 in charges.

It's all I can do to keep ahead and assure those who hold my paper when I fall behind. Buffalo Bill always pays his debts, but sometimes it takes time.

My business expenses continue to grind me. I have the cost of opening and running my mountain hotels, buying automobiles to carry tourists and hunters, paying Mrs. Cody's debts, and then I had to buy several thousand sheep to eat up the crops of Scout's Rest Ranch. I am not a fan of these woolies, or as brother-in-law Al calls them, "Wyoming range maggots."

The news from my mines in Arizona continues to be good. I have received word of rich veins of tungsten and gold. Yesterday, I told Lillie that I have always wanted a gold mine. I told him, "Gold is the best kind of business. When you need more money, all you have to do is send down miners and they will come up with as much gold as you need."

Lillie laughed, and said back, "Bill you have been sitting on a gold mine all along. If we play it right, this show can give us both all the gold we shall ever need."

Well, he might be right, but it don't rain in a gold mine, and you don't have to do the diggin' yourself. You send down miners to get it, and you don't have crawl up on horse twice a day and gallop in the dirt, no matter how your old bones hurt. The biggest chore in owning a gold mine is countin' the money and sending creditors packing. The toughest ride you have is

Chil Scoggin

on the front porch rocking chair.

My bones do hurt, but my cousin in Canada has been sending me some little powders that have also proven to be a godsend for my aches and pains. As they are not available here, I will bring some for you to see. I greatly appreciate my cousin's concern and help. Family is so important. As you know, the reaper has called upon me frequently. Only two of my six brothers and sisters still live. Of my own children, only my dear daughter Irma is with me. My sore heart aches in lonesomeness for little Kitty, Orra, and Arta, all having gone on to a better place.

Oh, Doctor, how cruel is this thing called age. As I look in the mirror, I do not recognize the person I see. I know that changes of the body are expected and I can do nothing to reverse them. I worry though that when others see me, they do not see the man I truly am. It is a shame to die without the world knowing me. I have my weaknesses, and regret often flows downstream from it.

Well, enough of bellyaching.

I should also tell you that when I last traveled through North Platte, the town welcomed me with enthusiasm and sincerity. It made this heart feel so good. Unfortunately, I called up Louisa. She was in her bedroom. I rapped upon her door asking that she come out and see me. She would not. I had every intent of reconciliation. With divorce not being an option, civility was. In addition, we shared financial challenges. My pride kept me from also admitting to my age and loneliness, and I said, "If not for us, we should do this for Irma." Our poor daughter Irma was so distraught, but at least she knew her Pa tried to retie the matrimonial knot.

I look for appreciations for what I have done, and encouragement for what I have yet to do.

With lament,
Colonel

"I understand the bond between weakness and regret."

July 1, 1910   Denver, Colorado

Dear William,

It is good that you are enjoying success, even though, as you point out, it comes with such hard work and the burdens of travel.

Fear not about appreciation. You are "Buffalo Bill." As we have discussed, you have such international fame that it does serve to overshadow the private person. I have had the opportunity to make the acquaintance of many men, some of great note and popularity. For instance, a young aspiring actor like you was referred to me for an interesting problem I must keep confidential. His name was Lon Chaney, and he was born in Colorado Springs. With my diagnosis and assurances, he has moved on, and I personally predict he will experience a highly satisfactory career, particularly in these moving pictures where there is no sound, and the actor has to find gestures and other forms of expression to engage the audience in the show. He has a true gift for pantomime since both of his parents were born deaf (they met and married at the Colorado School for the Deaf and Blind).

Five years ago, I was called to the Brown Palace. President Theodore Roosevelt stayed there on a whirlwind tour of the West. He had given a hundred speeches over the course of three weeks. T.R. Brown had arranged a banquet in his honor in which over 1,500 cigars were said to have been smoked over the course of the evening. That, the almost 100 speeches he had given over three weeks of visits to various western cities, and the dry Denver air had robbed Roosevelt of speech. I prescribed menthol vapors and ice for his throat. He recovered quite nicely; however, there are those on the opposite side of his politics who feel I did the country no favor.

Of course, at Hopkins I met giants. Halstead was the head of surgery and pioneered new techniques for keeping the operative site free of germs. Surgeons now most always use sterile gloves, but Dr. Halstead invented them to protect the hands of his nurse from the effects of caustic acid. He was a remarkably fast, but meticulous, surgeon, but when a case lingered, I recall him leaving the operative theatre, but then coming back shortly later, renewed and full of new-found energy. I must say I was both surprised and curious as to how but a brief respite might lead to such a remarkable renewal.

In my encounters with the famous, I have detected that fame presents a particular burden. Daily the bearer must live up to the image bestowed upon them.

So, take heart. I continue to hope that you find satisfaction in the good that you have done. We all must witness the changes reflected in the mirror, as well as the pointed pain in loss of loved ones. I have come to feel that I must embrace only those things I can effect, and control the demons of remorse that work so hard to crawl into my mind and weaken the spirit. I must tell you that I understand the bond between weakness and regret, and how it can cool the warmth of fond remembrance. When I have thought of Jane, sometimes I question whether I did the right thing in bringing her to Denver and continuing the pregnancy. Then I remember her happiness in becoming a mother, and the pride I feel in having our fine son.

Bill, I close with the words of Cicero: "*Fortis vero, dolorem summum malum judicans; aut temperans, voluptatem summum bonum statues, esse certe nullo modo potest*—No man can be brave who thinks pain the greatest evil; nor temperate, who considers pleasure the highest god."

Your friend,
Edgar
E. Y. Davidson

"I wish my mood were as sunny as this place."

September 25, 1910   Santa Rosa, California

Dear Dr. Davidson,
          I write to you from California where our show experiences great success in the warm, and thankfully dry, climes of this region. We're packing them in and

turning them away.

I wish my mood were as sunny as this place.

I fear I must once again turn to you for solace. I know there is nothing you can do about my damned financial problems, but somehow it just helps being able to write them out and share with someone who I know will treat them with the greatest of confidence.

Even though Louisa and I don't speak, we share a common purse, as well as the curse of indebtedness. This is not to say that we are not without resources. We have the Scout's Rest Ranch, her "Welcome Wigwam" home in North Platte, and the Wyoming T E Ranch, as well as some other nearby ranches I have purchased. Unfortunately, the Big Horn Valley ventures in Wyoming, have not worked out as I have hoped, and it now looks like I am in competition with the federal government for water. Even the Irma Hotel, as fine as it is, is losing almost $500 per month. It just appears to be too big for the Cody town.

The Arizona mine is a particular worry. When I discovered gold at Campo Bonito, I thought my retirement was safe. Since that time, I have had nothing but frustration, shoveling money into the mine, and taking but little out. In fact, tungsten now appears more promising than gold. It is key to making these new electric lights work. I continue to have high hopes, depending on which way the cat jumps.

The mine manager, Getchell, grieves me. He positively refuses to answer my letters or telegrams when I am straining my heart's blood to raise money for him to make a success of our enterprise. All this delay and many things he has done without consulting me. No answer to three telegrams. Why is it?

The mine's mill still does not work. I telegraphed Getchell from here in Santa Rosa telling him that a year had transpired and that I was nearly out of cash but heard nothing back. If there is no word, by the time we get to Santa Barbara I will again write to him about how my letters and telegrams were being met with silent contempt on his part. He is the first man I have ever done business with who will not acknowledge receipt of money. It is a new experience. I never know whether he receives my money or not. Dr. Davidson, I am not cranky when I am kept posted.

I am not at all well, and it is all I can do to get on a horse.

Although there are hundreds in my cast, as my health declines, I feel loneliness. I have taken the step of writing to Louisa, in hopes that she might join back up with me. I have assured her that I will respect the importance of a loose rein and allowing the tincture of time to heal our marriage.

Your sick and tired friend,

Cody

"It greatly saddens me to hear of your difficulties."

October 6, 1910   Denver, Colorado

Dear Cody,
           I have just returned to my home and I found your letter waiting for me.

It greatly saddens me to hear of your difficulties, particularly given the irony that I was in San Francisco, and had I known you were nearby, we might have met. Perhaps there was mention in the newspaper, but if so, I failed to notice. I yearly visit San Francisco. In particular, I spend time with Dr. Julius Rosenstirn. Dr. Rosenstirn played a key role establishing San Francisco's Mt. Zion hospital, the first Jewish hospital in the western United States, two years ahead of our Denver National Jewish Hospital. As part of this he donated his private twelve-bed hospital. Dr. Rosenstirn lives to a charge from the Talmud: "If I am only for myself, what am I?"

Similar to National Jewish, Mt. Zion's founding purpose was "aiding the indigent sick without regard to race or creed, to be supported by the Jewish community." Mt. Zion has become the most modern hospital in San Francisco.

I also find San Francisco be a most enjoyable city. It has good restaurants and a fine opera. Dr. Rosenstirn has also introduced me to various intriguing parts of the city, particularly China Town. It is substantially larger than its counterpart in Denver, and as such, as many more opportunities to learn about the Chinese culture and medical practice. I have found speaking with Chinese physicians to provide substantially more stimulation than most of my Denver contemporaries. I even have a chart of the human body identifying specific areas that the Chinese feel can be therapeutically benefit from the application of pressure and even small needles. I am cautiously exploring its use in my practice, particularly for patients with low back pain or who suffer from complaints of the upper bowel. It certainly can be worse than the so-called remedies I see poured down the gullets of patients by traditional doctors.

I hope you are able to come understanding with the fellow managing your mines. I don't have to tell you mining certainly attracts those who swindle. There is still talk in Colorado about the great diamond fields of northwestern Colorado. Promoters salted them in and escaped with a small fortune before their deed was discovered. Of course, all the gold and silver mining towns of Colorado have their own tales of scams. I believe it was your acquaintance Samuel Clemmons who said, "A mine is a hole in the ground with a liar on top."

I applaud your decision and courage to try to again seek reconciliation with your wife. Perhaps enough time has transpired to unburden both of you from the pains of the past and take you to a peaceful future. That might prove a great tonic against loneliness, and perhaps improve the strength of your soma. I look forward to hearing of a positive outcome.

Your friend,
Edgar

"I am full of Arizona sunshine and enthusiasm."
November 1, 1910   Campo Bonito, Arizona

Dear Edgar,

I write to you from my mines. I became so frustrated with Getchell that after I closed down the Wild West for the season, I moved to Oracle. Louisa agreed to join me because she thought a winter in the Arizona sun would be more than superior to yet another in Nebraska. So far this has worked out, but she spends her time at the Mountain View Hotel and I am mostly out at the mines or prospecting. We're both being cautious, I think. She likes to knit; I like to get out and explore and look for new finds. Should you need to correspond with me, please feel free to send it to the hotel as I check my mail several times a week.

After I see all the activity and the promises of those involved in the mines, I am full of Arizona sunshine and enthusiasm. There are now others who want to put in money, now that they see a sure thing. I'm holding them off as I have taken all the risks.

I plan to get out and do some prospecting on my own. I will build a fortune in claims and spend my old age handing out advice and twenty-dollar gold pieces.

I trust you will have a wonderful Thanksgiving and the merriest of Christmases.

With Oracle optimism,

Will

1911

*"Every good actor should know when and
how to get off the stage."*

March 18, 1911   North Platte, Nebraska

Dear Dr. Davidson,

I write to you with good news.

First, there are now three wells producing oil in Cody. It is as good as anything from Pennsylvania. I also had a good winter in Oracle and have great hope for my mines.

Louisa is so happy with our reconciliation. She missed her Willie, but it's been a drain on both of us to feed our financial obligations. She sees putting them under one tent is duck soup and cherry pie. We put the blanket back together and grow old and fatter. In addition, we have both decided that it will prove prudent to accept Pawnee Bill's offer to buy the Scout's Rest Ranch. It will provide us much-needed funds, and Bill has graciously allowed us to use it as our Nebraska residence. It is so good to have a friend willing to help, not looking for a handout.

While we have enjoyed the ranch's 4,000 acres, salubrious location of the North Platte River, and home to my fine horses and cattle, it is time we consolidate our many holdings, and plan to move to our golden years. In addition, I told Pawnee Bill that I knew how we could make a million dollars. We are going to promote this three-year journey as my farewell tour. I told him that there are people who have come to see me for forty years, and they'll want one last gander at the Scout and they'll bring their families with them. Also, there are those that have yet to see me, and this will be their chance. Lillie and Major Burke agreed, although I'm not sure they totally agreed with my math. We're getting competition from the other shows and circuses, and people are falling over themselves to watch baseball. Moving pictures have caught on, and there was even a color one in our old Madison Square stomping grounds.

The cities that we plan to visit may be assured that Buffalo Bill has no plans to ever perform in them again. I must admit that this make the old scout a bit on the sad side, but even the best of things come to an end, and every good actor should know when and how to get off the stage.

I am giving consideration to running for the United States Senate from Arizona now that it is on its way to statehood. How about that? Senator William Fredrick Cody. It has a nice ring, doesn't it?

With hope and better health,
Col. William F. Cody
"Buffalo Bill"

"This is good for both of you since lone-liness can be so deadly."

March 25, 1911   Denver, Colorado

My Dear Buffalo Bill,
        This letter came with words of wonderful surprise. Your time together in Arizona appears to have set the healing tone in time to come.

I congratulate Mrs. Cody and you for the wise decision of reunion and wish you the best for your future. This is good for both of you since loneliness can be so deadly.

Some unsolicited advice to you both: Dr. Halstead, my teacher of surgery at Johns Hopkins, emphasized that great care must be exercised in the treatment of wounds to promote successful healing. The fragile tissues that surround them must only handled with delicacy, and it is critical that suture tension avoided when closing wounds. Even a small gash that appears to be healing if subject to constant strain may be deprived of vitality and then fester and rupture back into a tear that cannot be brought back to closure. So it is too with human relationships—grudges and remembered small slights being a major source of tension when trying to bring people back together with one another.

William, you are a fortunate man to have a second chance at marriage. I so miss my wife. When I think of her, I do find a small bit of peace knowing I was able to care for her during her illness. She did not die alone, and that is perhaps the best gift one can give to another human being.

Please keep me apprised of your political plans. I must say they came as a great, and unexpected, surprise.

With sincerity,

Edgar

E.Y. Davidson, M.D.

"I don't trust happiness."

September 12, 1911   Iola, Kansas

Dear Dr. Davidson,

     I know I have not written to you or had occasion to visit Denver for quite some while. The Two Bills show has been back on the road.

I don't trust happiness. Last night a cyclone tore my outfit to pieces. Every damned thing blown to tatters.

In addition, Getchell at the mine is back to his old tricks. He writes to me of rich new strikes of ore, then a few weeks later come the urgent telegraphs demanding more funds to support the operation.

Altogether, I fear I am boarding on nervous prostration.

No need to write back, as I must travel even more, and lately have not been receiving my mail.

Sick and nervous,

Bill

William F. Cody

"I realized my long-standing ambition to visit Summit Springs."

October 1, 1911   Denver, Colorado

Dear Bill,

     It troubled me to read your letter about the troubles with the show, as well as the difficulties with your mining venture. You are much more experienced in business, but if you can't trust someone, do you really think you can consider them a partner? I know it's a banality, but there is the old saying about throwing good money after bad, and watching the ups and downs of Colorado, I can think of no bigger hole in which to throw money than a mine shaft.

On a positive note, I realized my long-standing ambition to visit Summit Springs, the site of your famous battle with Tall Bull and his band of Dog Soldiers. I have recently purchased the touring model of Henry Ford's Model T. It has four cylinders, not two; metal side panels, not wood; and is built for taking to roads, not just streets. I think you will approve. A trip out to Sterling and the nearby Summit Springs allowed me to test out the automobile high-stepping down gravel roads and the occasional shortcut across a pasture.

In Sterling, I was given directions to the battle site by a clerk of the Logan County courthouse. She featured herself quite the historian, and I had to politely rein her in when she veered into a story about George Bent and his Indian raids along the South Platte River.

The gravel road south out of sterling was sorely in need of a team with a road grader. Fourteen miles later, I came to a dead end, but a single-track road ran off to the right. It ended at a barbed-wire fence with a single stone marker that lacked inscription. I pulled next to a windmill that spun casually in the prairie breeze, and I disengaged the Ford's ignition.

I stepped carefully over the three-strand barbed wire and into the tall prairie grass.

Good rattlesnake country, I thought, and twenty feet in, my assessment was validated by a small creature who sang briefly to me with his tail.

We agreed to go our separate ways.

The ground was moist, even in October. Of course, this was Summit Springs, and somewhere the last summer vestiges of White Butte Creek ran. Looking first for reptiles, I picked up a small white rock and placed it in my trouser pocket. It would be my memory of this visit.

As you so well know, at this spot more than forty-two years before on July 11, 1889, the Southern Cheyenne, fleeing from the United States Army after attacking western Kansas homesteads, had camped here. There was water and grass for their horses. The women and children were tired, and the leader, Tall Bull, knew they had to rest before crossing the Platte River and escaping to the north.

He did not know the 244 army officers and men of the 5th Cavalry, with you as scout, along with 50 Pawnee scouts, was only a few miles away.

From where I now was, it would have been hard to see them until they were on the camp. The afternoon wind would cover the sound of their approach. General Carr, leading his men, sent part of the column to the right, another two the left to cut-off escape, while the remainder charged into the village —a classic "high diddle-diddle, right up the middle."

Standing in the grass, I looked for sign of the grave of Susanna Alderdice, the woman captive from Kansas killed by the Indians during the battle. I saw no evidence of the burial, or of the burning site when General Carr ordered everything of use to the Indians, including 84 teepee lodges, burned. I turned to my right and looked at the gullies cut into a hillside to the right running up to the White Buttes. I walked up to the largest. This must have been where the Dog Soldier leader, Tall Bull, plunged a knife into the heart of his horse to form a redoubt, staked his ceremonial dog-rope into the ground, and fought to the death a delaying action to allow his wife and other people to escape up the gully.

I felt your presence Bill. I imaged you capturing Tall Bull's horse. I wondered how you felt after the battle. What did you think about Carr's lack of control of the Pawnee scouts as they fell upon the Cheyenne women and children—shooting, stabbing, and worse? Did you see the body of the Indian herdsboy who saw the troops coming and rode to give alarm by stampeding the Indian ponies through the camp? After the battle, an army scout, Luther North, wrote of the boy, "No braver man ever lived."

I walked back to my auto, climbed over the fence. On the

ground around the single stone that marked this spot, I saw that some had placed offerings of dream-catchers, tobacco, pieces of horn, and bundles of sage and tobacco. I know you take pride in the recreation of the Battle of Summit Springs in the Wild West. I wondered if you had ever returned to the actual battle site.

I reached into the pocket of my trousers and took out the rock. I put it on the monument, walked back to my Ford, and started the drive back to Denver. Where the single track joined the gravel road, I looked back and I saw through the dust the place of the last major Colorado battle between whites and Indians.

There you have it, Cody. Dr. Davidson's Buffalo Bill Adventure. Oh yes, my new car proved a jewel, and I only had one blowout tire.

With remembrance,

Edgar

E.Y. Davidson, M.D.

1912

"Alas, I also think I have played Santa far too long for far less appreciative people."

March 15, 1912   Onboard Southern Pacific Railroad

Dear Edgar,

I wintered at Campo Bonito. I write this letter to you as I travel back to New York City to prepare to start up another season of the Two Bill's Wild West show.

There were happy, but also some not-so-happy, moments in my visit to Campo Bonito. The happy moments were seeing my fine little sleeping teepee with some many memorabilia of my adventures and travel in the world.

I disposed of the Indian scalp I took in revenge of Custer.

I also arranged to play Santa Claus for the children throughout the region. Oh, how it gladdened the little tykes' hearts to sit on the lap of Buffalo Bill and receive the gifts I had for them. It made me long for the childhood I never had when Father died, and I had to step into his place.

Alas, I also think I have played Santa far too long for far less appreciative people. There is growing suspicion that Getchell and his son have been misleading me. My partner, Colonel Dyer, engaged a mining engineer to assess the operations. He is preparing a detailed report, but before I left, he said to me, "Colonel Cody, I'm working hard to prepare and honest assessment, but you should be prepared to read of some things you will not like." Doctor, I have so many worries already on my mind that I could not bring myself to ask then and there for details. I want to get back to the show and start seeing some cash. I also wanted to hold out hope that the news about the mines and mill might be like fine wine and improve with age.

I look forward to hearing from you soon. It is a good day when I open a letter from Davidson.

With sincerity,
Will

"I feel a part of my life has again been torn away."

April 30, 1912   Denver, Colorado

Dear Cody,
  I have been revisited by death. Three weeks ago, I opened my copy of *The Denver Post* to see the headline, *April 16, 1912: 1,300 perish when Titanic sinks; 866 known to be rescued.*

I immediately telephoned my father as I knew my brother and his family were returning to the United States, but I knew not how. I asked the operator to start the process of connecting me to my father's number in Chicago. A few minutes later, she called me back, telling me my father was on the line. His voice shook as he confirmed my fears. On April 10th he had received a telegram from Wallace informing that his family and he had boarded the Titanic in Southampton. They expected to reach New York City on April 17.

Because the survivors picked up by the RMS Carpathia were not expected to reach New York for at least two days, he had no idea if they had survived. The next 48 hours had little sleep for me. Father and I spoke on the telephone each day, but neither one of us had news to share. Then at 8 a.m. on the 19th, a telegram messenger boy appeared at my door. The telegraph was from Mrs. J.J. Brown, a neighbor, and it was sent from New York City. It read:

> *Dr. Davidson, Survived sinking. Your nephew and his governess with me. Parents appear to have been lost. Staying at Ritz-Carlton hotel. Margaret.*

I immediately contacted Father. I telegraphed Mrs. Brown advising her that I was on my way to New York via the first available railroad train. In an attempt to quiet my mind and get some sleep on the train, I took several doses of chloral hydrate. I arrived in New York weak with worry.

In the lobby of the hotel, I met Mrs. Brown. She told me she was on the Titanic after a tour of Europe and Egypt. When the ship was being abandoned, she was pushed into a lifeboat where she found my nephew Mason and Miss Ryan. Mrs. Brown is a formable woman and had enlisted my medical services in caring for miners she feed from the various soup kitchens she sponsored. Her leadership skills quickly went to work as she organized the care for survivors, both onboard the rescue vessel and upon their arrival in New York. The papers have taken to calling her "unsinkable." I also note that the Denver Times quoted her estranged husband, J.J. Brown as saying, "She's too mean to sink."

I then reunited with Mason and Miss Ryan. The boy was frightfully quiet. "He's all cried out," Miss Ryan said.

I immediately arranged transportation back to Denver. Since his mother's family has all passed on over the years, Father and I are Mason's only living relatives, and I am petitioning the courts for him to become my ward. Miss Ryan is to continue as his governess, and my housekeeper, Mrs. Clark, is helping arrange suitable accommodation for her.

As I write this, the search for bodies in the North Atlantic continues. The newspapers report that some are found with articles that allow identification. These bodies are embalmed and kept onboard the ship; the others, unknown, are being buried at sea. Thus far we have not further word on my brother or his wife.

As you might imagine, the lad is quite traumatized. Each night he sobs, and Miss Ryan and I provide him comfort with warm milk and our presence until he falls asleep.

Father suffers from grief, and I have encouraged him to visit us in Denver. He has taken this under advisement.

While my brother and I differed, and I felt Father favored him, I feel a part of my life has again been torn away. I hope that the tonic of time I have experienced from my previous loss of family will soon start to help not just me, but too the child. Although she will not complain, I know Miss Ryan suffers.

The house is quiet. Mrs. Clark speaks in a low voice, and the cook does not sing. Having my wits about me, and the resources and time to respond, has allowed me to make a plan and execute on it. This has prevented the loss and associated sorrow from becoming hell.

In mourning,

Edgar

"What is now heartbreaking, I wager will prove providence."

May 6, 1912   Mount Vernon, New York

Dear Edgar,

       I struggle for words to write on this paper to express my condolences for death having once again come to your door.

I have read daily in the paper about the Titanic tragedy, how those that did not go down with the ship succumbed to the icy, cold Atlantic waters. There is also an involving controversy. It is not understandable why there were not enough lifeboats for the number of souls on board. An important question has been raised as to why the nearby S.S. California did not immediately respond to the distress signals from the Titanic. I have traversed that same sea route many times, sometimes experiencing storms and close passage to icebergs. I now feel particularly blessed to have survived.

If there is any of the silver lining to all this, it is the boy coming into your life. While I was living in North Platte a young boy, Lewis Baker, became my shadow. He would do anything I asked, whether it was running an errand or just holding the reins of my horse as I visited his father's saloon. When I first formed the Wild West, he was fourteen years old, and he begged to join me. He was so pestering and enthusiastic, I agreed. He has been with the Wild West ever since.

I took to calling him "Johnny." It just sounded better than "Lewis" or "Louie." I originally billed him as "The Cowboy Kid," as he gave demonstrations of trick riding. He was a good-looking rascal, and the girls took quite a shine to him. Annie Oakley taught him how to shoot, and we promoted "contests" between the two, but Annie always won. Johnny is now a fine man, and continues giving wonderful demonstrations of fancy shooting, including hitting targets while standing on his head. He also became my arena director. Moreover, he has truly been a son to me, and while never replacing my lost Kitty, I do find his daily presence and his appreciation for what I provide to him, similar to the satisfaction that flows between a father and a son.

What is now heartbreaking, I wager will prove providence.

With sympathy,
Bill

"I have lost a fortune and next year must return to the road."

December 15, 1912   Cody, Wyoming

D ear Friend Edgar,
I'm sorry I once again missed you in Denver, but I did not expect to see you since I know that each year during this time you visit San Francisco. I would like to hear your opinion regarding the rebuilding of that once fine city. I suspect that the collapse in the mining industry, as well as the general state of the business in the world on which it so depends, will prevent San Francisco from re-becoming what it once was when I took my stage show there. The show flourished; many the morning I woke up with a sore head and full pockets.

I met your fine nurse, Miss Adams. She impressed me with her patience and willingness to listen to both my complaints and my chest. Please extend to her my gratitude and advise me as to the charge for her attention. I offered to pay her, but she said such billing is to be done only by supervising physicians. Only private duty nurses were allowed to directly charge for their services.

The Two Bills closed out a fairly successful season. While nothing like the previous two years of my farewell tour, Lillie and I made over $126,000. That's a lot of sparkle.

I placed the Wild West and Orient show into winter pastures. To tide us over, I have secured a $12,000 loan in

Denver from a Harry Hyde Tammen. Do you know him? I first meet Harry when he was bartending at the Windsor Hotel in Denver. He is quite the entrepreneur, having built a nice business selling curios both from his downtown Denver shop and through the mails. He comes up to my shoulder, will shift his gaze a bit as he speaks, and people call him, "The Little Dutchman." And, he did have busy little mind that ran a busy little mouth.

As you know, Tammen who, along with Frederick Bonfils, purchased *The Denver Post* newspaper. While I resent that rag's wicked headlines maliciously portraying my divorce petition, they do what sells ink.

Tammen owns all or a part of many enterprises, one of which is a circus, the Sells Floto. (I am told he took the name "Floto" from that of the *Post* newspaper sports reporter because he liked the sound of it.) Given this, Mr. Tammen understands my business, and was comfortable, even anxious, to provide me funding.

Pawnee Bill is a bit put out that I struck the deal without his consent, but then again, he did not himself step forward with funds. I needed to make a decision, and I did what I thought right. I did take occasion at the completion of our signing the note and receipt of funds to tell Mr. Tammen that I predict that *The Denver Post* will not long survive if it continues to slander an internationally famous person dear in the hearts of its readership. Mr. Tammen gave me his personal apology and assurances that henceforth all the news about Buffalo Bill in the *Post* will be good news.

And, so much for the good news.

Unfortunately, I made a bitter discovery. The mining engineer Colonel Dyer and I engaged believes the mine has been salted with gold, and the prospects for financial return far less than we had been led to believe. In addition, I heard that Getchell's son has been seen parading around Columbus, New Mexico, in a fancy touring car, no doubt paid for with my money. I fear I have been swindled, and Dyer and I must decide what to do next. I am not anxious to share the news with other investors, particularly Lulu.

I have lost a fortune and next year must return to the road. Dejectedly,
Will
William F. Cody

*"I may be out of place, but felt moved to urge you
caution in your dealings with these two."*

December 29, 1912   Denver, Colorado

Dear Friend Cody,
  Although it may be unwise—or forgive me, perhaps unwanted—for me to give you any advice about your personal affairs, but I must tell you that when I read of your dealings with Harry Tammen, it set a loud bell to ringing in my head.

Tammen and Bonfils jointly own *The Denver Post,* and they have, at best, a remarkably checkered reputation. Bonfils was a land speculator and lottery operator. He was run out Kansas Territory for selling lots in Oklahoma City at a steep discount until it was found out that the lots were in Oklahoma City, *Texas.* As you pointed out, Tammen was a bartender before he went into the newspaper business. When they bought *The Evening Post,* they changed the name to *The Denver Post.* They said, "We will wean our new paper on tiger's milk." And they did. Their private office is painted flame red. We Denverites refer to it as "The Bucket of Blood" given their propensity to slander and sensationalize in the name of selling newspapers. When I learned of this, I pledged to distance myself from any dealings with the newspaper and its owners.

Tammen likes to portray himself as an affable and lovable sort, but he's a scoundrel. Believe me, I know one when I see one. His curiosity shop sells trashy goods and Indian relics of dubious authenticity. Bonfils is the dark, brooding type who believes money is power, and power is God. Together, they once perpetrated a hoax that China was going to tear down its Great Wall and would be seeking laborers in Colorado. It sold papers, and Tammen said, "The public doesn't like to be fooled, it insists upon it." An example of the attraction of the improbable, if not preposterous, to the human mind. Newspapers should report on hoaxes, not create them.

You will recall that shortly after your first visit to me in Denver, both were shot in their office by the lawyer representing Alferd Packer, "The Colorado Cannibal," after the *Post* accused him of making off with Packer's money. Later, another attorney walked into their office and severely horsewhipped both Tammen and Bonfils for slanderous accusations. But they have been undaunted. It is widely known that if a business wants mention in the paper, it first must buy advertisement therein.

They have been at war with the *Rocky Mountain News*, and the Rocky Mountains are awash in yellow journalism. They'd rather publish a purple article about a dogfight in the streets of Denver than mention a war anywhere in the world. They blackmail and smear, and spread filth through innuendo. Although I have not been the subject of their deceitful fabrications, I have several friends whose reputations have greatly suffered, particularly one who refuses to be blackmailed by this pair. A banker of great success—but who steadfastly refuses to do business with the *Post*—has been an ongoing target. The paper threatened to expose that he is a member of a Jewish cult that murders Christian children to procure blood to mix with the cult's unleavened blood for the Passover. Tammen and Bonfils thought better of it when faced with the fact that the banker is the largest individual benefactor of the Catholic Church in Colorado.

I had occasion to treat Senator Patterson, the elderly publisher of the *Rocky Mountain News*, after Bonfils had snuck up behind him and punched him repeatedly in the head. Bonfils is reported to have stood above the stricken Patterson, told him to never publish his name in the *Rocky* again, and then cruelly laughed that it was December 26—Boxing Day.

The Sells Floto Circus they own is little more than a dog-and-pony show.

Again, I may be out of place, but felt moved to urge you caution in your dealings with these two.

On a different topic: I am pleased that you met Nurse Adams. She is a highly competent Sister, with gentle ways and a fine mind. I find her helpful in many ways, including providing care to patients in my absence. She also helps assure that patients are faithful in following my recommendations. Some patients will confide things to her to which they are reluctant to share with me. Dr. Osler remarked that a talented nurse has become one of the great blessings of humanity, taking a place beside the physician and priest. Three years ago, the University of Minnesota actually started a school dedicated to the training of nurses. I smiled when I read the comment by Finely Peter Dunne who heads the editorial pages of *The Chicago Evening Post.* He remarked thusly on the ongoing controversy about Christian Science, "If Christian Scientists had more science, and doctors more Christianity, it wouldn't make any difference which you called in—if you had a good nurse."

Your friend,
Edgar
E.Y. Davidson, M.D.

1913

"Oh, what treachery!"

July 27, 1913   Denver, Colorado

Dear Dr. Davidson,

I send you this message as I suffer from distress, frustration, and embarrassment. I cannot bear the thought of looking you in the face. That short round Dutchman has horse-thiefed my show and stolen my pride.

Oh, what treachery. I believed I'd done the right thing last year at the close of the show season in securing funds from Tammen. This assured that we could get our animals, costumes, and equipment into proper winter quarters. We came back on to the road this year. The weather was not our friend. We had to deal with floods, freezing rain, and when we took our show into the South, the poor economy due to the pitiable price of cotton kept our audiences low. While we weren't going to make the million I predicted, Pawnee Bill allowed as how we would start to make hay once we made Denver.

When we got to Denver to set up our show, out of nowhere things fell apart. Just as we'd finished our afternoon show, with the audience standing, cheering, and imploring that we bring forth more, the sheriff and his deputies appeared with a piece of paper claiming that my Wild West was in seizure. They took possession of the treasury wagon that not only had all the receipts for the day, but the strong box containing our ready cash.

When Major Burke started investigation, he returned to my tent with the most awful look on his face. As it turns out, Tammen, whom I had so trusted when he offered up the loan, was at the bottom of the whole thing. He is bad medicine. To my surprise, I found he had controlling interest in the United States Printing and Lithography Company, which provided printing for the posters and programs for the Wild West. I knew we owed them $60,000 for work they had delivered, but I had every intent and means to pay them off during this year's tour. Instead, they wanted their money, and they wanted it now.

Over 500 people are now out of work. I am doing my best to find funds to help those left so destitute. Some of our performers, such as the "Armless Wonder," "Fat Woman," and "Bearded Lady," are doing individual exhibits on the streets of Denver. It broke my heart to see the troop of Boy Scouts traveling with us march away from Denver, toward their homes in Iowa. They intend to support themselves by giving marching demonstrations in the towns they travel through.

I will fight this injustice, and await word from my partner, Lillie, who has gone back East to file a lawsuit against Tammen. I have to stay here with nothing I can do until I hear from Lillie. The *Rocky Mountain News* has asked me for comment about bandito Tammen, but I consumed my smoke. Barkin' at a knot don't make it come untied.

I feel such humiliation, as I know you will read about this in tomorrow's paper. I dread having to tell Louisa.

In yet another battle,

Buffalo Bill

"Showman Cody Dead."

August 14, 1913   Denver, Colorado

Dear William,
I returned yesterday from a camping trip in the Colorado Rocky Mountains in an area known as "California Park," and much favored by our former president, Roosevelt.

When I started reviewing the newspapers delivered to my home in my absence, I was jolted by a headline, "Showman Cody Dead." My hands trembled as I read, and to my relief, I found that the article reported the death of a Samuel Cody who started his career as a showman but gained fame from inventing kites and aeroplanes in England. On August 7, one of his machines crashed, and he was killed. It was stated that over 100,000 people attended his funeral.

While momentarily relieved that the death was not yours, as I read through the papers, I came upon the reports of your show having been seized. Then I opened your letter of July 27, and my heart sank as I read your words.

Please advise as to how I might be assistance to you in what must be a most terrible time.

Distressedly,

Edgar

E.Y. Davidson, M.D.

"Now I have been caught."

September 17, 1913   Denver, Colorado

D ear Edgar,
        Thank you for your letter of last month. I have struggled to summon the strength to reply.

I am sending you this brief note, rather than suffer the shame of seeing you in face. I know there are stories in the newspapers, but given our friendship, I wanted to share with you the truth.

I feel like I should be writing this from under a rock so great is my disgrace. Since rocks are favored by snakes, I'd been in good company with Tammen and Bonfils.

I have been working to find solution to the problem of my show being seized, but to no avail. Two days ago, the sheriff held a debtor's auction in Overland Park, and everything of the Wild West was sold. Oh, the disgrace and mortification as I watched the hammer go down on everything Lillie and I had put together. Gone was the bandwagon with Columbus' landing in the New World carved on one side and Pocahontas rescuing Captain John Smith on the other. Bidders walked off with both Lillie's and my silver saddles. And gone are all our fine animals—including camels, donkeys, oxen, and my matched mules. Sold too were the circus cages, baggage and historic wagons, and automobiles.

Tammen intends that I should join his Sells Floto Circus, and by this means, meet the obligation of the note to him. I have no choice. Oh, how I wish that I'd sought better advice about the financial state of the Wild West and had the protection of a better contract. The only legal advice that's more expensive than good legal advice is bad legal advice.

I write you this letter fighting to keep my mind and my honor. My nerves are so bad that all I want to do is find relief in sleep. If I do not get better, I will climb the hill up to your house to seek your advice and treatment. If you travel, perhaps Nurse Adams can give me something to help.

I have always stayed ahead of my debts and obligations. Now I have been caught.

Despondently,
Bill
William F. Cody

P.S. That airship fellow Cody had once claimed he was my son. I had to sue him to make him stop. The only thing we had in common was being born in Iowa.

"Fatigue and lack of rest makes cowards of us all."
October 1, 1913   Denver, Colorado

Dear Bill,
   I have sent this letter c/o the T E Ranch in hopes that it will be appropriately forwarded to you.

As always, it was a pleasure being of service to you, even though you are difficult circumstances. I know you were reluctant to accept my modest offer of assistance, but I wish to assure you that I felt no imposition. Given the challenges you face, it was my honor to help you settle your obligation at the Savoy Hotel.

Please use moderation in using the chloral hydrate preparation I provided to you. It is an effective sedative and treatment for insomnia, but also has its risks. It can depress breathing and have a depressive effect on circulation. These concerns are pertinent for you because during your examination, I found evidence of both impediment of your breathing, as well as signs of circulatory strain.

I appreciate that you must travel but urge you to avoid physical exertion and mental weariness. Fatigue and lack of rest makes cowards of us all. Unresolved, this can move us from the situational sufferer to chronic invalid.

Even though I did detect the above physical issues, I wholeheartedly support your conclusion regarding "Oslerization." You will be interested to know that in the face of the firestorm occasioned by his quote of use of chloroform in old men, Osler wrote, "To one who had all his life been devoted to old men, it was not a little distressing to be placarded in a world-wide way as their sworn enemy, and to every man over sixty whose spirit I may have thus unwittingly bruised, I tender my heartfelt regrets."

I can only speculate that his earlier comment was made in jest. Sir William is himself sixty-four years old and still going strong at Oxford. He has a fine son, Edward Revere, whose middle name is taken from his maternal great, great grandfather, Paul Revere. I'm sure the enjoyment of his son provides additional motivation for Sir William wanting substantial longevity.

All the very best,

Edgar

"I feel like new money."

October 10, 1913   Cody, Wyoming

Dear Dr. Davidson,

I so appreciate your coming to my aid last month in Denver. When I heard the knock on my door and heard your comforting voice, this old heart sang. I too enjoyed our conversation. Getting things "out in the open" helped quiet my mind. The tonic you provided greatly helped me, and I was able to get the first night's sleep I have had for months. I arose the next morning with new vigor and a commitment to take on the day, open a new life chapter, and never get myself in a circumstance such as this again. I feel like new money, and my head is clear.

Better to feel young in the sixties than old in the forties!

I remind myself to stand tall and speak straight. I cock my hat, keep my shoes shined, and my collar buttoned. One of the lessons of my business that I have learned is that my capital and stock are a smiling continence and buoyant spirit.

With appreciation and resolve,

Your friend,

Bill

William F. "Buffalo Bill" Cody

"The hungry child needs attention, not the tut-tut of pity."
November 1, 1913   Denver, Colorado

Dear William,
It pleased me to read of your improvement of spirit. I have continued to reflect upon our discussion at my home.

You are a person gifted with creativity. The Wild West would not have been born if not for you vision. You have been wise to involve men such as Salsbury who blessed with organization and the ability to make your ideas degenerate into work. Your whole life you have shown you are comfortable with risk, and, if I may be so bold as to say, you saw boundaries as something to be crossed, not obeyed. I know from your experiences in mining and most lately with Tammen and Bonfils, you trust in the conscientiousness of others to treat you fairly. When this does not happen, you suffer the great cruelty of betrayal.

As a physician, I do best when I can employ logic and order so as to deal with the complexities presented to me by my patients. I do possess modest intelligence, and I regard myself as conscientious, that virtue perhaps more important in a doctor than coming up with creative explanations based on creative supposition. I find more personal satisfaction in what I discover in reading and study than what my own mind conjures up.

I have tried artistic endeavors, such as painting, but the results belong in the trash, not on walls. I enjoy music but attempting to learn to play it was an experience of deep dissatisfaction and frustration. After the death of my wife, I had her piano placed in a home for unwed mothers in hopes that one of the unfortunate girls would find pleasure, and so that it would no longer exist in the home to remind me both of her and of my ineptitude.

This does make me rather conservative, but I do balance this with compassion for others, with measurable action. The hungry child needs attention, not the tut-tut of pity.

My mind works best when solving problems. I cherish those moments when lucidity emerges as to allow me to formulate both explanation of a situation and what might be done to deal with it.

I recall a recent case of a woman to whom I attended. When her husband was found dead in bed and analysis of his blood showed high levels of arsenic, she was accused of poisoning him. Two things occurred to me. First, she did have a motive in that he was both abusive to her and was also known to seek satisfaction outside of her bedroom. Second, she was much concerned about the nature of her complexion and related to me the various creams and other potions she placed on her skin as well as ingested. I suggested to the detective investigating the case that a sample of her hair be tested for the presence of arsenic. The levels came back exceedingly high. In addition, the couple's home had recently been wallpapered, the dyes of which have been found to be notoriously high in arsenic compound.

An explanation came with clarity to my mind.

I testified in her defense, stating that over time, she had developed tolerance for the poisonous effects of arsenic, but her husband had not. In sensitivity to the wife's circumstances, I did not recount in detail to the court the luridity of the act of congress insisted upon by the husband. Suffice it to say led him to incidentally ingest the arsenic from his wife's person as well as inhale the vapors of the new enhanced environs of the home. My argument to the jury was that the cause of death was accidental. They deliberated for but thirty minutes before returning a verdict of innocence. It is my understanding that the wife is enjoying widowhood, and now puts oatmeal, not arsenic, on her face.

As I write about this to you, it occurs to me that this is a circumstance where I actually saved a life, and I did so without benefit of balm or blade.

In closing, I hope that our discussion about our differences as human beings was not too sophomoric or erudite. It has certainly caused reflection on my part.

I look forward to hearing of continued progress in bettering of your circumstances.

With sincerity,

Edgar

"We both will know what it's like to be on display."

November 21, 1913   Cody, Wyoming

Dear Edgar,
I thank you for your thoughtful letter and boost.

I appreciate your kind comments about my creativity, but it seems that when it comes to my businesses, all I create is trouble and debt. Each day, I arise and look for the shovel I can use to fill up this unfortunate hole in my finances and life. I fear that in accepting Tammen's insistence, I find myself a curiosity in a traveling circus. It looks like old Bill Cody will something more in common with his Indians—we both will know now what it's like to be on display.

I did enjoy your story about arsenic, as you know, having been victim of poisoning myself. Thankfully those days are behind Lulu and me.

Well, I must once again start to think about ways to further improve my circumstances. I hope to create something of meaning out of the chaos that has been my life for the last few months.

I close wishing you the very best for the coming holiday

season. I hope your business of medicine goes well for you.
    With my very best,
    William

"Medicine is a calling, not a business."

December 1, 1913   Denver, Colorado

Dear Bill,
        I write to you with Seasons Greetings, wishing
        you a Merry Christmas and a Happy New Year. It is
my hope that 1914 will bring good fortune and enjoyable
meaningfulness to your life.

Yes, the arsenic story had a happy ending for all but the
philandering husband. I might mention that I have become
greatly interested in the medicinal aspects of arsenic. It has
gained great interest as an antisyphilitic. It is known as "606"
due to it being the 606th compound tested for anti-microbial
activity by Professor Paul Ehrlich. It is now marketed under
the trade name Salvarsan and is hoped by many to be the
"magic bullet" against the Treponemal organism.

I have previously shared with you Dr. Osler's aphorism
that medicine is a calling, not a business. These words I have
lived to avoid the temptation of expanding my activities into
the greater business world. This has been particularly true
of the siren song of mining riches sung to me by the great
wealth that might wait to be taken from the nearby Colorado hills. I have seen the fortunes made by local business
barons, such as Tabor and the husband of my friend, Margaret
Brown. They have built mansions, opera houses, hotels, and
railroads. I have also witnessed the calamitous financial ruin
from circumstances they could not foresee or control. My
nearby neighbor, David Moffat, built an empire of railroads
and mines. He died three years ago in New York, trying to raise
money. While the newspapers reported the cause as pneumonia from the grip, there persists rumor that it was suicide precipitated by pending financial ruin.

Given that my sole source of income relies upon what I

may reasonable charge for my medical services, I have avoided taking on any debt. I have been judicious in lending and selective as to those to whom I have offered charity. A practice born out of necessity, but not frigidity of heart.

Unlike you, I do not have the gift of creativity. Perhaps the closest I have come was trying to solve a problem related to the treatment of female hysteria, thought to be due to congestion within the pelvic region, and relieved by massage performed by a physician or midwife. I always make referral, as there are those who garner substantial income from performance of the procedure. I have received a United States patent for an electromechanical medical vibratory device. It replaces previous devices powered by a windup mechanism, or even steam. I believe the constant, reliable provision of power in the form of electricity will reduce treatment time from one hour to no more than ten minutes. I have no experience in the necessary steps for bringing this device to commercial usefulness, and because of this, it has remained in bottom drawer of my desk. I have concluded that the wise man sticks to those things which education, training, and experience have provided success and satisfaction.

I have experienced financial reward from my assistance as a physician, but I have avoided speculative ruin. What few properties I have are paid for and require little or none of my attention. I doubt I will die with great wealth, but when at night I find it difficult to sleep, it is not about issues of my purse. I know this is easy for me to say as I serve only myself, while you have many who look to Buffalo Bill for substance, and I apologize. Far be it from me to in any way chide a man of your great accomplishment.

I close with great apology if I have in anyway caused offense.

I look forward to seeing you when you next pass through Denver.

Your friend,

Edgar

E.Y. Davidson, M.D.

1914

"I feel like a dancing bear"

March 1 1914   Cody, Wyoming

Dear Edgar,

I have agreed to Tammen's demand, and now I am preparing to travel with his circus as the star attraction. Under our agreement, I receive a salary of $100 per day. If the receipts go above $3,000, I collect 40 percent. From this I should be able to repay you the advance you so graciously offered me.

At my insistence, my travel will be via a private luxury Pullman car, with a cook, a porter, a full-length mirror into which I can look as I dress, and a driver for my carriage. Louisa will travel with me, and greatly enjoys it. I ride into the arena on horseback but must admit that getting into the saddle is often a challenge, and the process has to be hidden from the public behind a curtain. Sometimes I find it so difficult that I must enter the arena in the carriage.

I feel like a dancing bear. I work for pay, and that need is the chain around my neck.

I no longer have to put on a shooting exhibition, as the crowds just want to see Buffalo Bill in the flesh. Once I rode into the arena and thought, "People cheer me for *who I am*." Now I go in, and I think, "People cheer me for *who I was*." Well, they bought the ticket, they should enjoy the show. I just wish I'd been able to take the last bows a bit earlier while I still had hair and wampum.

I have hope for the future.

With promise,

WFC

"It saddened me during our visit to learn of your father's death."

April 15, 1914   Los Angeles, California

Dear Dr. Edgar,

I greatly appreciate your taking the time to see me last week and apologize for intruding on your

Saturday afternoon. I was only passing through Denver on the way to California. I had but little time to attend to business and my health, and also visit my dear sister May before I was off to the West Coast.

It saddened me during our visit to learn of your father's death. Having been so frequently visited by that dark angel, I share your sorrow. I knew not of his passing, and the news from you came as a true shock. I'm sure he must have found great comfort in your following him into the same profession as well as your success in Denver. The town is crowded with sawbones, and those who would rather bleed, stick on leeches, cover with camphor, and pick their patient's pocket. You, sir, use your brain as Buffalo Bill knows!

As I've often told you, your father has been a fine man and friend.

As you know, When I experienced the lingering effects of typhoid, and did not recover the fullness of health at the ranch, I telegraphed him, and he kindly, and urgently, suggested that I contact you. This is when we first met. One of my best decisions. Colonel Cody thanks you and thanks your father.

I am sure you had better things to do than listen to the complaints of a sick old scout with bad habits and swollen ankles. I feel better today, in that I no longer have to sleep with my head elevated by pillows, and my wet cough is much improved. Louisa reports that I no longer have periods when I hold my breath in sleep—an occurrence she reported as causing her much distress. One night she woke me up shouting, "WILL, BREATHE!"

I must admit that the treatment you have rendered me has caused to me to spend much of the night making more water than rest. But since certain difficulties have arisen in my financial dealings, at least it gives me something to do. It provides a distraction, when otherwise I might be walking the floor. In fact, even the momentary relief I experience is somewhat relaxing. I do believe it's helping my breathing.

That was quite the elixir you provided me for my circulation, and I pledge to remain faithful in its use. I have some curiosity as to its nature. I see so many tonics advertised, and I even agreed to a few being promoted in the Wild West program. I particularly liked the food tonic "Sanatogen" and its slogan, "Does your mirror say 'overworked'?"

I thank you for your attention and willingness to help me under the difficult circumstances. As ever, I appreciate your attention to hygiene. Since we first met, I have heeded but powerful admonition of "fingers, food, and flies." I made sure these principles were always followed in the Wild West, and we suffered no further bouts of pestilent contagion.

So simple to wash hands, and I wish I could do so of this contemptible Tammen.

Appreciatively and with condolences,
WFC
William F. Cody

"The road to be walked between treatment and toxicity is narrow,
and at some passages, treacherous."

April 25, 1914   Denver, Colorado

Dear William,
I thank you for your condolences regarding my father. He was a man of complexity, and I have come to appreciate him nonetheless for such. At his request, there were no services. I arranged for his body to be shipped to Champaign-Urbana where he was interred next to my mother. In my mind, I heard no objection from her, so I assume she was satisfied with the arrangement. I took young Mason with me so as he could see where his paternal grandparents were buried. He did ask if his parents would ever be found and buried as well. I placed my hands on his shoulders, and said, "No, but you will come to learn that is of little consequence." Whether the body is burned or buried, our remembrance is what endures. To this end, the gravesite is best considered a place for

reunion.

I smiled when I read your comments about hand washing. Over fifty years ago, the Hungarian physician Ignaz Semmelweis gave perhaps the best three words of advice to physicians: "Wash your hands." While his admonition dealt with the transmission of germs causing childbed fever, there exists no better medium for carrying contagion to patients than the unwashed hands of the doctor. I have watched this practice all too slowly be adopted by doctors. Too often, to the bedside of patients, the physician brings bacteria and bad news. It is my proposition that those who provide clean water and covered sewers do multiples more to provide for the general welfare of a community than the ministration of the Medico.

As always, it was good to once again see you. I regret that my examination disclosed the condition of which we spoke, but I trust that my assessment and recommendations were clear. I recall that Plato said, "We are imprisoned in the body, as in an oyster-shell." Therefore, we do the best we can. I hope that the medicine, such as it is, will prove of benefit. Fox leaf and calomel, when used with judiciousness, are beneficial, but must be administered with caution.

When the heart starts to fail, the body's response is to retain fluid. To a point this actually helps circulation, but over time the fluid accumulates throughout the body from legs to lungs. The digitalis has the effect of increasing the contractive force of the heart muscle.

Calomel is mercurous chloride. While a tasteless white powder, it can be quite powerful as to effect. It is used to treat various conditions because of its action as a cathartic or bowel stimulant. On their exploration of the West, Messrs. Lewis and Clark carried Dr. Benjamin Rush's Bilious Pills laced with calomel. Rush's pills therapeutic application also included treatment of various social diseases. Calomel can also be used as an antiseptic when applied to infected wounds. Women have favored calomel as a bleach against freckles on the face and hands. In conditions of failure of the heart, calomel stimulates urine flow. I have found it quite useful in treatment of dropsy conditions.

The road to be walked between treatment and toxicity is narrow, and at some passages, treacherous; therefore, please do as I say, and beware the advice of those doctors not practiced in the treatment of your condition or use of the drugs I prescribed.

Here in Colorado, tensions run high due to the coalfield strikes. Outside the Rockefeller mines near Ludlow, the Colorado National Guard and mine guards made a raid on the encampment of the striking miners and their families. The Guard soaked the tents in kerosene and set them to flame. In the cellar of one of the tents, the bodies of eleven children and two women were found. In all, twenty-five people were killed. President Wilson is sending in federal troops to restore peace. It is a dark time in Colorado.

My neighbor and friend, Margaret Brown has sent two hundred pairs of shoes and basic clothing to the miners' families. She is organizing a corp of nurses to assist in the relief, as well as organizing a committee to travel to Ludlow to review the situation. I know many—particularly men of power—see Mrs. Brown as a suffragette who does not know a woman's proper place. I find her an inspiration. She has mentioned plans to run for the United States Senate. Should she do so, my household and I shall support her.

Most sincerely,
Edgar
E.Y. Davidson, M.D.

"I am forming another company."

July 1, 1914   Sioux City, Iowa

Dear E.Y.,
 I thank you for your recent response to my telegraph asking for additional medicine you have so kindly previously provided to me. It so helps my health.

I work hard and have not yet failed to respond when I'm

called to the arena. I must admit, I do not enjoy many of the associations in this circus, and consequently keep mostly to myself. Some grumble that old Bill is a snob. Maybe a little, but I also need to save my energy. I have gone from scout, to showman, to now a curiosity. Perhaps Tammen will want me to sit in the window of his curio shop when the show season is over. Tammen has three chimpanzees in the show. I told Louisa, "This circus has three chimps and one chump."

I have to keep my eye on Tammen. His latest scheme is to have his advance men advertise one price for a ticket, and then raise it when people get to the show. I have also told him that I don't think the grandstands are all that safe. All it takes is one collapse, and people will stay away.

At our last stop I did get out to see a motion picture. I have always paid close attention to what the competition is doing. The one I saw was called "Making a Living," and featured a curious little mustachioed fellow named Chaplin. He carried a cane and wore baggy trousers. Burke tells me that it is creating quite a stir. The audience liked it, and, these picture shows work well for acting out comedy. Even though Burke suggested we add clowns to the Wild West, Nate always resisted because we were a serious show that educated people.

I am forming another company, and plan to go to Fort Robinson, Nebraska, to start making a motion picture in the Dakota Badlands. Johnny Baker will make sure we have Indians available. I'm sure people will be moved by my show, as re-enactment of battles was always the source of special enthusiasm for the Wild West.

I close with great concern about what is going on across the ocean. The assassination of the young Duke has everyone riled up, particularly Germany and Russia. I fear I shall never see England and Europe ever again.

This fall I am to meet up in Cody with the Prince Albert of Monaco and guide him on a hunt. He is the first sitting European monarch to visit the United States, and I believe one of his priorities is to pursue the game of the West with Buffalo

Bill. I shall name our hunting camp, "Camp Monaco."

With best wishes for Independence Day.

Your friend,

WFC

"I have continued on the outs with much of the Denver medical community."

July 8, 1914   Denver, Colorado

D ear William,

Thank you for your letter. Although I appreciate your dissatisfaction with your current circumstances, I read with a smile about the Cody creativity still being at work. I look forward to hearing more about your motion picture venture. On a related note, the news has been focused on a death during a movie being filmed in Colorado. In one of the scenes, the actress, Grace McHugh, was to cross the Arkansas River in a boat. In the middle of the river, the boat overturned. The man running the motion picture camera jumped in to save her. Both made it to a sandbar, but then disappeared. It appears they were sucked down by quicksand and killed.

I have continued on the outs with much of the Denver medical community. This summer Colorado has seen an outbreak of infantile paralysis both in the city and the neighboring township. Given the experiments of Abraham Flexner's brother Simon, there can be no doubt that the causative agent is infection, probably entering the body through ingestion of contaminated water and possibly food.

There remain those who maintain that the paralysis is due to toxic vapors and other environmental factors beyond the control of man. Another group is advocating treatment of children through the ingestion of radium water, even though there is not so much as a scintilla of evidence for effect.

I must tell you that I feel such frustration about the state of children's health in Colorado. The benefit of the Pasteurization process and wholesomeness of milk has been proven in eastern cities where milk banks are now common. Civic leadership continues to scoff, and on the medical side it has been proposed that formaldehyde is preferable sterilizer of milk. One local dairy even advertises that it feeds formaldehyde to its cattle!

I have also been advocating the routine use of new vaccines now available for both diphtheria and whooping cough. I have been met with condescension at best and seeming indifference to the death of children at worst. The amount of ignorance in my profession astounds me. It is all I can do get through the day, join my household for dinner, see that Mason is tucked in for the night, then to my study for relaxation and escape into additions to my library.

Forgive me for writing of my frustration, but as we both have found, there does appear to be benefit of dragging these issues into the daylight, rather allowing them to further fester and degenerate into bitterness and further poison of pessimism.

With my best hope for your future,

Your friend,

Edgar

E.Y. Davidson, M.D.

"All is not as bleak as this tired old scout would complain."
August 6, 1914   Boise, Idaho

My Dear Friend Davidson,

If I might Edgar, I must tell you that I experienced distress reading your letter. I heard a tone of darkness. Having experienced the challenges of working with other people, I can understand why it brings frustration to you. I recall with some regret when my temper has gotten the best of me. For instance, I have erupted when some acts have exited the arena of the Wild West after giving a less than convincing portrayal of historic events. I have told them with certainty that I could have done a much better job. Most have accepted this criticism as valid and well-meaning. A few have skulked away, but not daring to challenge me. Please accept some advice from an old scout, consume your own smoke, and look to the higher purpose of your professional calling. Take heart, good doctor, and remember, "It's us against the barbarians."

On to my update to you as to my situation.

As I write this, I sit at the desk in this fine office car produced by the Union Pacific Railroad. Directly behind it is pulled my parlor car with its bright coat of Pullman green, but as seems to always be the case, I must work hard to take advantage of it for sleep. Please know that I have followed your advice, and when I cannot sleep, rather than lie abed and fight with myself, I get up and read, or such as this, correspond with friends. Often after an hour or so, I find myself sleepy and able to return to bed with more successful results. I believe you called this "second sleep."

Not only do worries of finances continue to gnaw at me, but now I have the deep regret of lost friendships scratch at me as well. This damnable mess around finances caused me to lose my show, but also drink the bitter cup of obligation to continue to travel and allow my good name to be used. I once made millions, but with the ups and downs of business, the always uncertain weather, now the war in Europe, the cost of winter quarters, so regretful investments with men of no character, and my support of sisters and family, I find myself in regrettable financial circumstances.

Although I have a strong contract that should result in my receiving a considerable compensation from Tammen, the price has been heavy. I have lost my friendship with Pawnee Bill with whom I combined the Wild West and traveled for two years. I have come to recognize how things changed when old Nate left the Wild West. I am sure I told you that Nate and I started the Wild West together, and his good sense—business and common—was a good match for my many ideas. Against my wishes, he would not allow the opportunity for gambling on the grounds, and he was right. When word reached me of his death, I must tell you that I suddenly found myself feeling more alone than anytime on the vastness of our great plains. I have had partners, and he was one of the very best.

I still feel my health is not top-notch. The weather has continued damp, and I have a cough that once again rattles. You will be pleased to know that I stayed off the coffin varnish, and I mean to stick with the pledge.

All is not as bleak as this tired old scout would complain. I have come up with this excellent idea of how I can use these moving pictures to help pull me out of my hole and back onto my feet. I hope to have the opportunity to tell you more details when next I am in Denver. It is a capital idea!

Should you wish to correspond with me, you may do so c/o general delivery in Columbus, Ohio, as I plan a two-week engagement there starting in two weeks.

Every optimistically, your friend,
Bill
Wm. F. Cody

"So often it appears that the public person may be a mirror reflecting the private one."

August 20, 1914   Denver, Colorado

My Dear Buffalo Bill,
As always, I appreciated your thoughtful letter. Since our last visit, I have reflected upon your reminisces and the other issues of which you spoke as troubling you. I wish I had more to offer than a sympathetic ear. So often it appears that the public person may be a mirror reflecting the private one. I have seen this work both ways. Sometimes the apparently kind and benevolent man when on parade, behind closed doors becomes a tyrant. In my capacity of physician, I have cared for family members of otherwise well-regarded citizens of the community. Setting the bones and tending the bruises of a wife or child has made me seethe with contempt. I have made my knowledge of the cause clear to the afflicter, and this has made for some uncomfortable mo-

ments in my office or in the home to which I was summoned —not for me I assure you, but for the tormentor. I do believe I have altered some behavior to the better. Better to treat the cause of disease than the consequences.

As we also discussed, you have sincere ambition, but I must tell you that sometimes I fear you do not give credit to yourself for your obvious talents and accomplishments. While, like any human being, you have produced and encountered opportunities for regret, you have also proven generous, and as we discussed, to your own detriment.

Yes, when we last met and discussed your health, I did refer to "second sleep." I believe it is the nature of humankind to first fall asleep, then a few hours later awaken for an hour or two before once again going back to what I find to be highly refreshing deep sleep. This pattern may be in our very being, starting when we lived in caves and fell asleep when darkness set in. Perhaps we alternated taking turns during the night at the watch for danger before the sun arose again. With the coming of illumination we stayed awake into the night, but our innate sleep pattern remained. Thus, the dictum that one needs eight hours of uninterrupted sleep is against our very nature. What we need is eight hours of good sleep, with an hour or two intermission between first and second sleep. To this end we should wish one another, "Have a good night's *sleeps*."

If your cough continues, and particularly if you see the appearance of purulence—or worse yet, blood—do not hesitate to seek reputable medical attention. I implore you not to use the Powell concoction. Its dangers far exceed its very questionable benefit.

I am pleased to hear of your continued temperance. It is easy to make such a pledge, but then one must take the test. Sometime the grip will loosen, but not let go.

Sincerely,
Edgar
Edgar Davidson, M.D.

1915

"I have high hopes for their success."

March 10, 1915   Cody, Wyoming

Dear Edgar,
Greetings from the town of my name. The wind blows, and Cody is abuzz with scandal, and it has nothing to do with me! Miss Etta Feely runs a parlor house in town where cowboys, sheepherders, and workers can take their ease. Miss Etta has been brought up on charges that she sold liquor to an Indian. Her defense is she thought the man was a Mexican because—to use her words— "He spoke English better than any white man."

I have found the whole thing entertaining, and given all the business issues with which I deal, I've welcomed the distraction. There's been speculation that this will be used as an excuse to close Etta down, and chatter abides in the Irma Hotel dining room. This is a lot of harrumph. Miss Etta's customers will have nothing of it, and those charged with enforcement of a closure may well be—shall we say— "conflicted." Furthermore, Etta runs a clean and safe establishment. There is little of the issue of sanitation we discussed a few years back.

Now on to tell you of my movie. I have known the power of these moving pictures and felt that they would help tell the story of the American Indian and the misfortune of Wounded Knee. This is something that I can feel proud of as one of the accomplishments that you so often remind me that I have. I wanted as accurate a portrayal as possible and enlisted my old comrade General Miles. In order to be most authentic, we made our picture show in the Dakota Badlands. I started this project in October of '13. This allowed us to use real soldiers, arranged by General Miles, and real Indians from the near-by reservations. The General insisted that we show the actual number of troops deployed against the Indians, and because we had only 600 soldiers, we had to march them by the camera to recreate the 11,000 troops Miles had under his command. I am fairly certain that due to the cost of film, the camera, though running, had no film. Ha. Some of the Indians I used were veterans of the battle of Wounded Knee, and the army troops expressed concern that the Indians' guns might be loaded with bullets, not blanks.

You'll get a kick out of knowing that the people helping with the film were the same ones who did "The Great Train Robbery" movie. I had the very same camerist! He told me he wanted to work with the famous Buffalo Bill. That be me!

I did a splendid job of re-enacting the fight on War Bonnet Creek with Yellow Hand (some translate his Cheyenne name as "Yellow Hair"). The audiences on stage and at the Wild West demanded its recreation. It was always a winner. Over time, the scalp did become a bit rank, and I took it to my tepee at the Arizona mine.

Unfortunately, while the film was superb, I have also learned the lesson of going into business with the government. Miles disappointed me and cancelled the battle scenes, saying they were "inflammatory." Forget that the Wild West had created many battle scenes throughout the U.S. and Europe, and Miles' judgment is the only casualty we have suffered. Nevertheless, I continue to invest in my films, and I have high hopes for their success. In addition, I have a great idea. Rather than be just the silent pictures of now, with the occasional snippet of written dialogue pasted into the film, I will tour with the film and give my personal description and comments on the events portrayed on the screen. Thus, the audience will receive doubled value—the motion picture images and Buffalo Bill, himself and in person. How's that for a capital idea! This old boy still has it.

With excitement,

Will

W.F. Cody

"Buffalo Bill"

*"He was as fine a gentleman as I have had
the privilege to know."*

May 15, 1915　　　　　　McMinnville, Oregon

My Dear Dr. Davidson,
　　　I continue to travel with this damn circus. We are in a place called "The Willamette Valley." It is populated by the elders and ancestors of many who made their way west on the Oregon Trail. Promoters promised "the land of milk and honey," and "where the grass is always green, even in winter." The climate reminds me a bit of Italy, but in contrast, here there are orchards and berry farms, not vineyards.

The weather is comfortable and the crowds decent. The pioneers and their sons and daughters come to the show. A young boy asked me, "Are you the real Buffalo Bill?" I smiled, patted him on the head with my gantlet gloved hand, and I thought, *I once was, I once was...*

I have little to occupy me between shows except worry. Additionally, my brain continues to drag me back to the past. This year marks the twenty-fifth year since the death of Sitting Bull. As I believe I have told you, The Bull traveled with me, and I much admired how he conducted himself and represented his race. Although sometimes sullen and a bit peevish, he was as fine a gentleman as I have had the privilege to know.

The Bull looked right regal in a brocade waistcoat, crimson necktie, and a big old silver crucifix hanging from his neck. And, oh, how he loved his sweets, although they were no good for his teeth or girth.

I suffer from everlasting regret that I did not arrive in time to save him from murder by his own people. The Messiah craze and ghost dances among the Sioux was a very bad business in 1890. It all started with a Paiute Indian named Jack Wilson, also called Wo-vo-ka, out of Nevada who claimed to have come back to life, and those that would follow him would be immune to the bullets of soldiers if they wore a special shirt, the "Ghost Shirt." I believe he got the idea from the Mormons who wear an undergarment that's supposed to protect them from evil.

Wilson called himself the new Messiah. He even got Indians to thinking that the earth would swallow up the white man and return the red man to power and peace. The Indians started to chant a prayer they got from the Arapahoe tribe from around where you live:

> My Father, have pity on me
> I have nothing to eat.
> I am dying of thirst
> Everything is gone!

The Indian agent McLaughlin was scared to death of the Indians and The Bull in particular. The Indians called him, "Young Man Afraid of Indians." He was sure The Bull was going to lead the Sioux back on the warpath. McLaughlin sent his Indian police out to arrest him.

I'd just returned from Europe, and General Miles asked me to go out and convince The Bull to come in peacefully. I loaded up a wagon with a couple of bushels of the hard candy he liked, and some presents for his wives. I got down the road, but then got a message from President Harrison telling me to turn back.

There was a big fight, and lots of Indians killed by their own people. A few years before I had given The Bull a trick pony he particularly liked. When the shooting started, the pony took the cue from his show routine, sat down, and raised up one hoof. The Indian police thought the spirit of Sitting Bull had entered the horse, and off they went. I took back the pony, and we used it to carry the flag during the start of the Wild West in England. The Bull told me that he wished to be remembered as the last man of his race to give up his rifle. Well, he didn't make it.

I miss The Bull. I have my own set of troubles, but like the Indians, I look for hope.

Lately both my business and life in general have not been going all that well, but I know there will be a better day when some things I have put in place finally hit pay dirt. I still hold out hopes for the Arizona mines, and I hold the title to substantial land in Wyoming. My T E Ranch is proving to be popular among tourists to the area, and I have hit upon an idea to provide them with a wonderfully educational and enjoyable western experience. In contrast to when I brought the Wild West to them, now I will bring them to the Wild West. The rangers around Yellowstone Park call anyone from the East "dudes." I'll call my T E a "Dude Ranch." I'll treat them to good buckskin in their bellies and joy in their hearts. I'll slather them with love of the West. The word will spread. I'll be better off than a tick on a fat dog.

Of course, next fall season Pahaska Tepee will provide a steady income from the many hunters I will host. I also know my moving picture will prove to be a ripsnorter, people will demand to see, and the money will flow in.

My cousin has provided me with more of the remarkable powders that he obtains when he visits Canada across from his Buffalo, New York, home. They particularly help my damned rheumatism. They are also good for headache, but not the pain of dealing with disgrace and Tammen.

I am thinking of starting my own show again and have Johnny Baker and Major Burke starting to work on raising money. It will take some pluck, but at my age, my courage is the one thing that still hangs on. I have always lived by never letting courage fail, no matter how tough the trail.

I plan on being in Denver later this month to deal with some business issues, as well as visit my sister. I would regard it as a special favor if you would agree to meet with me, as I have certain additional issues of health that I would like to discuss with you in private. Of course, I will attend to the outstanding bill I believe I have for the medications you so kindly provided to me.

The weather has been constantly wet and rainy, and when clouds come in the crowds stay away.

Please give my regards to Nurse Adams.

With remembrance of The Bull,

Col. William F. Cody

"Buffalo Bill"

"There is no doubt of the injustice done to the Indian."
May 27, 1915   Denver, Colorado

Dear William,
 As always, it was a pleasure to receive your correspondence. I must admit that I was touched by your words concerning Sitting Bull, or "The Bull" as you referred to him. There is no doubt of the injustice done to the Indian. Wounded Knee was one of the vilest things perpetrated on the Indians.

We both know that the Indians were just trying to follow orders and return to the reservation. I have seen the pictures of their dead chief Spotted Elk, or "Big Foot." The poor devil was sick with pneumonia. He could not ride or walk but was wrapped up in the back of a wagon.

The Indians were on the road to return and camped. What actually perpetrated the troops opening fire on the Indians, the result was chaos. It is now known more soldiers were killed by their own guns than by the Indians. Of the 150 Indians killed, over half were women and children.

Another tragic day for Indians and the history of the West.

I find it irresponsible that the newspapers still do not mention that the army perpetrators were members of the 7th Cavalry, and there is more than a little chance they found opportunity to revenge the death of Custer and his men. What I know and don't find in the newspaper is of more interest than an article itself.

Well, Bill, there is more positive news about the American Indian. Please recall I corresponded with you a few years ago about Franz Boas, who you met at the Columbian Exposition. He has gained considerable notoriety, and now is at the American Museum of Natural History in New York City. Perhaps you could arrange to meet him sometime when you are in New York. I'm sure you would find his studies of the various races of interest and form a scientific basis for your own apparent and laudable convictions.

All the best wishes,

E

E.Y. Davidson, M.D.

P.S. As for the "little powders," you mention. I urge extreme caution. What seems best now may not serve you well in the long run. To paraphrase the Honorable Dr. Oliver Wendell Holmes, "If all the medicine in the world were thrown into the sea, it would be bad for the fish and good for humanity."

"I dream like I never have before."

August 5, 1915   Galesburg, Illinois

Dear Doctor Friend,

I trust that this letter finds you in fit fiddle.

I apologize that most of my correspondence these days deals with my continued damnable financial condition. I smoke cheap cigars and wear last year's clothes. The cigars do help me when I feel a bit on the blue side.

But I welcome the chance to send you good news about my health. I continue to take the little power pills you provided to me, and they seem to work. My dropsy is definitely better, and my ankles and feet so much less puffed up; I can now put on boots, rather than shoes. I am able to mount my horse and gallop into the arena, although sometimes I confess to still choosing to ride in my carriage. I am not huffing and wheezing when I walk up stairs or from the strain of getting astride my horse or into the carriage.

When worry escapes me for a few minutes, I can more comfortably sleep, but I have noticed that I dream like I never have before.

Oh, what dreams!

For instance, last night, I was taken back to Kansas and found myself reliving days with my father––but also the pain of his death and the days that followed. I was but a lad, but the violence of his wound and suffering till his death haunt my mind. He was a hardworking and ambitious man.

I have tried to live up to expectations and responsibility to my sisters. Father's death caused me to have to take the role of caring for my consumptive mother, as well as the younger children. Although working the wagons took me far away, and for many months, I always returned and shared my rewards with them. When my career on the stage brought success, I made sure my own children attended the finest schools and had the best in clothing. Some will say I spoilt them but knowing what it meant to have so soon lost my own childhood, I took great pleasure in providing for theirs. The home I provided for them in Rochester was most modern and particularly built to be warm in the New York winters. When death took my children away, I arranged a family plot where they rest in eternity together.

I hope I have made my father proud.

When I ascended the stage, I took great pride in my appearance. Buckskins, long boots, my signature great belt buckle, fine Stetson hat, and, of course the guns and knife I carried supported my role as one ready to protect others, even at the risk of my own life.

Protection of the innocent is so important. I recall the impact on me when, as a young man, Wild Bill Hickok came to my rescue when some teamsters started to abuse me. Bill was a bit vain about his looks, and wore his hair longish, as did I. Able to shoot equally well with both hands, he carried twin revolvers with their butts forward. He said this made it easier to sit at gaming tables. It did require that he rotate his hands inwards to draw them, cavalry-style, but Bill was a master of this. He taught me that "slow is fast." His advice was, "Cody, bring up your pistol, take careful aim, and then fire. It's not the first to jerk leather, but instead, the one who makes the first shot count." Given how Bill was murdered, he might have added, "and always remember to sit with your back to the wall!"

We enjoyed a long friendship, including when we went on to play on the stage together in New York. In my play, "May Cody, or Lost and Won," I rescued my sister from dastardly Mormon kidnappers. I am sure that the settler's cabin scene at the end of Wild West performance was so taken in by my audience because it illustrates the responsibility a man has to protect those weaker and venerable to savagery. I took care of my employees. As long as they behaved as gentlemen and ladies, I made sure they were well paid and enjoyed excellent accommodations, even when the Wild West traveled. I demanded that the Wild West be a clean show, suitable in all ways to families. I might add that this was in contrast to that Adam Forepaugh and his conspirator, my old so-called partner Doc Carver, in starting the Wild West. Their show touted games of chance and a side-show of nasty. Those two not only tolerated wicked business around their show but also demanded a cut of the action from grifters and pickpockets who traveled with the show.

I have always cared for those who worked for me. When I lost my father and had to provide my own guidance and encouragement, I learned the importance of offering direction to others. Many are those who sought out my council, and I felt duty-bound to help them, sometimes to my financial regret. In the midst of my many financial difficulties, I have always been concerned about payroll, accommodations, and the travel back to their homes of my cowboy and Indian performers.

Johnny Baker has been a life-long companion, and it has often said I have been a father to him. So too the young women of the show. I like the young women to call me "Papa." It both saddened and angered me when during the divorce trial the fact that I liked them to kiss me good night was turned so against me.

I have always protected my red brothers from white people—particularly those who called themselves Christians —who accused me of promoting "Indian-ness" and impeding their attempts at Indian assimilation. I often take out photographs of me with the fine members of the Indian race who worked for me. I particularly like the one where I am together with Sitting Bull where we are noble, well-costumed, equals.

Enough of my old scout meanderings. I assure you that dipsomaniac ways have not returned, so that is not the cause.

With appreciation and hope,

God bless you, Good Doctor,

Col. Wm F. Cody

"There is a physician in Vienna who is creating quite a stir."

August 20, 1915   Denver, Colorado

Dear William,

I am pleased to learn of your improved health, although I would caution you that your condition is not to be trifled with. Ailments of the heart can be progressive and deterioration sudden if care is not taken. I urge you to attend to your diet, particularly avoiding salt, and should you ever again consume alcohol, do so in moderation. It is best you avoid tobacco, particularly in the form of cigars, although I sympathize with your feeling that it affords you comfort when you experience melancholy, as I have experienced this benefit myself. I know we have not talked about tobacco and the gift your Indians made to the Europe discovers. As we both know, it feels good upon imbibing, whether by inhalation or pinch. In fairness to the future, other long-term effects remain to be discovered.

As regards your dreaming, this might be an effect of the pills I gave you; however, most of their effect beyond the heart usually involves slight color tinges of the vision, and, if the dosage too high, upset of the stomach and bowels.

As physicians we have only cared about two-thirds of our patients' lives. By this I mean, we have focused on events and complaints in the aware hours to the exclusion of the period of sleep. This appears to be changing.

I know you traveled extensively in Europe and thought you would find the following of interest.

There is a physician in Vienna named Sigmund Freud who is creating quite a stir with his theories about the mind and human behavior. Both Dr. Osler and a physician associate in California have alerted me to his importance. One of the key aspects of his work is interpretation of dreams. I have only started to read more widely on his theories, but it would suggest that your own experience is but a reflection of the power of our brains to hold the most wide range of information, and to present it back to us, sometimes when least expected. From what I have learned thus far, it would appear that revisiting this early period in your life is of importance to you, and thus this unconscious desire has entered the realm of the conscious. To this end, I urge you to not be distressed.

With every best wish,

E.Y.

Edgar Davidson, M.D.

"Those were the days."

September 15, 1915   Clay Center, Kansas

My Dear Edgar,

Your last letter just caught up with me here in Kansas. This country is so flat; I can see someone coming from a week away! The buffalo are gone, but now huge beasts called "tractors" are plowing up the prairie for the planting of wheat. This I will *not* re-enact in the new Wild West.

Last night I had a dream that was so real that I awoke with a sweat and a moment's question as to where I was. You asked that I should be on alert for any changes in my health, and I thought this dreaming might measure up. In the past, I've not thought much about my dreams, but now, they are so vivid, and they drag up things from my past that must have been swirling about, wanting to come out in memory. I think it might relate to when I first met you when you first visited the

Wild West.

The dream took me back to those wonderful days at the Columbian Exposition, or "The White City." The whole outfit was built on the marshy shores of Lake Michigan. It commemorated the 400-year anniversary of Columbus landing in America. When I walked the fair with Nate Salsbury, we saw many new products, including Pabst Blue Ribbon beer, Cream of Wheat cereal, Juicy Fruit gum, and a thing called a "dishwasher." Nate and I were particularly impressed with the florescent light bulbs. They make a much softer light and are said to be much more reliable than the electric ones we had hundreds of in the Wild West. What took the cake was the "Ferris Wheel." It is bigger than any waterwheel and was made out of steel that looks like a spider's work or giant bicycle wheel. People sat in seats that pivoted as they ascended and then came back down. The whole contraption was powered by a 1,000-horsepower steam engine. Salsbury and I both took a ride, and it was a fine time. In my dream, Nate was so clear. From our seat on the wheel, we could see our Wild West right next to the Exposition's main gate. Those were the days. We put 18,000 souls in our bleachers each day, and easily cleared as much as $50,000 a week. We were rich!

So that's the dream. I know not what to make of it, and perhaps I should allow it to fade away in the many draws of my remembrances.

Should you wish to reply, we will be in Des Moines for an extended period, and you can write to me c/o General Delivery. I always get my mail in Iowa.

With my best wishes,

WFC

W.F. Cody

"I find it laudable that the complexity of human behavior is being dissected and discussed outside of the usual revelations of scripture."
September 29, 1915   Denver, Colorado

My Dear Cody,
I have seen photographs of Dr. Sigmund Freud. He appears to be on a dare with the camera with furrowed brow and one lifted eyebrow. I note in one picture, like you, he enjoys a cigar.

I have increasing fascination with the study of psychology. I have dissected many a body, but the one place I have yet to plunge my scalpel and shears into is the soma of human behavior.

Did I not have the responsibilities my patients and household, and were there not the war going on, I would like to travel to Europe to study with the men bringing remarkable insight to human behavior. In reality, I must content myself to reading.

It should come of no surprise to you that Dr. Freud's theories are not without considerable controversy. I should also tell you that I have a deep-seated suspicion, bordering on resentment, of those who would speculate on meanings in the absence of disciplined examination of evidence. I have witnessed as they fall victim to the odious behavior of making up information to support their personal theories and prejudices. The effect of climate on health is one such example. Deep maps have been made of the Front Range of the Colorado foothills, claiming areas that are particularly advantageous to the treatment of consumption. The fact is, we do not know with any certainty why Colorado is good for the phthisis patient. Yet there all those who claim with surety that the mountains serve as barriers to pestilent winds blowing eastward from California.

Dr. Carl Jung has broken with Freud. I favor Jung. I cannot reduce human behavior to just being driven by perpetuation of the species. Jung, to my mind, has more depth, in that he sees a more complex subconscious at work. All though I know I simplify, he favors that much of our human behavior is passed down through the results of experience over the eons. To that degree, it is cast in, and we cannot understand how humans act without exploration of the subconscious.

I also note that Jung is a pipe smoker. It appears to me that both Freud and Jung have an appreciation of that gift of America to civilization—tobacco. There are many things we don't know about Nicotiana tabacum, but it does appear to have some favor as a medicinal for the good doctors Freud and Jung.

Both Freud and Jung quote the German philosopher, Friedrich Nietzsche. I am struggling to read Nietzsche's work. I have dredged up my university German, but Nietzsche writes in a style of German that I find dense and challenging to transition into English. In *Gotzen-Dammerug, oder, Wie man mit dem Hammer philosophiert,* which I translated as "Twilight of the idols, or How to Philosophize with a Hammer," Nietzsche wrote, "If we have our own why in life, we shall get along with almost any how." I know this is a poorly translated quote, and perhaps better said in colloquial English: "If you have your *Why?* in life, you can put up with just about any *How?*" This captured my appreciation for meaningfulness in my own life as I've dealt with my losses of loved ones.

Nietzsche was not without humor. Will, he followed his quote about "Why" and "How" with the statement, "Man does not strive for happiness; only the Englishman does that." A German swipe at priggish Britons I surmise.

I have no idea whether or not there will prove to be validity to Dr. Freud's and Dr. Jung's propositions, but I find it laudable that the complexity of human behavior is being dissected and discussed outside of the usual revelations of scripture. Although, I suspect that there is danger that if compelling explanations emerge, they may also take on the guise of a religion among the inevitable zealots.

I believe dreams are particularly important, and too long neglected as a physician's source of information about their patient. I have found that some of my patients, when asked, relate to me recurring and disturbing dreams. Freud, I believe, would say during sleep events and thoughts that trouble us emerge from the subconscious and become the subject of our dreams. Like Ovid's *Metamorphoses,* the dreams are shaped into important messages that deal with our fears and anxieties.

Thank you for your trust and confidence in me.

It is my pleasure to help you, and I look forward to our continued friendship.

With sincerity,

Edgar

E.Y. Davidson, M.D.

"I found myself dreaming of my dear, sweet mother."
October 6, 1915   Lubbock, Texas

Dear Dr. Davidson,

I must admit that having sent it, I felt a bit brainless for having written to you last month about the White City dream, but your response trimmed a bit of that edge. The day that your letter arrived, I had awakened distressed. We have had cursed rain, everyone is pestering me for money, and I had spent much of the night in my railcar with my constant curse of worry—as well as dear Lulu's snoring. She is a plain woman who favors wearing the same clothing, and no longer applies paint to her person, and she can produce a fearful racket when deep in sleep. But it is a comfort having her near and knowing I will not die alone.

I did manage to fall into a sleep about 4 a.m., but when the camp started to come awake, I found myself dreaming of my dear, sweet mother. I was but a child, but she was giving me milk, bread, and a bath. I wonder what your Viennese doctor would make of that!

My cough is better, and I now only smoke cigars in social situations. I find that I have a bit of shortness of breath, but these old lungs are also having to deal with this damn rain and damp.

Appreciatively,

Wm. F. Cody

*"I trust you will keep this in confidence, just
as I have your disclosures."*

October 15, 1915   Denver, Colorado

Dear William,

Thank you for your letter. I assure you that I found nothing "brainless" about your earlier letter. I appreciate your sharing the occurrence of the dream about your mother. Without attempting too deep a dissective psychoanalysis, and with respect to those who do, we both can conclude that mothers are a powerful force in the lives of their children, and thus your dreams quite understandable.

I write from my office in my home. I have closed the door and given the staff instructions that I am not to be disturbed. Nurse Adams is to respond to any calls I might receive.

The rest of the women appear quiet in their quarters. I may provide compensation, but truth is, they run my life. I sense they know my appreciation. My household mirrors the world in that it is men and woman together who cooperate in daily tasks; the only injustice is who is seen as receiving credit. The women of my house also reflect the strength of Denver women as a group. I have previously written to you about Margaret Brown, but she is only one of many strong women of Denver. While much is made of Wyoming giving the right of women to vote, it was not the first state, but rather the first territory to do so. In addition, its motivation was not such much egalitarian, but rather a strategy to attract more women to the territory.

Colorado was the first state to grant the vote to women, and the strategy to do so was in my mind, quite clever. When the price of silver collapsed in 1893, destitute miners streamed out of the mountains and into Denver. Denver women organized soup kitchens to feed them, and the condition was before being fed, the miners had to sign the petition for women suffrage.

As you know, an amendment to the Constitution giving

the vote to women has long resided doldrums of Congress, but not yet been submitted to the states for ratification. Given the increasing number of western states that have given women the right to vote, I do not see how Congress can continue to sit on their backsides on this important enhancement to governance and justice.

I have been giving our latest correspondence much thought.

William, you have been very forthcoming with me, and for this I have experienced both flattery and great appreciation of your trust. On this subject of dreaming, I must tell you that I personally have found the experience to be of particular benefit, although the subject matter and events portrayed, often upsetting. I often awake with my pulse racing, my bedclothes in a tangle, and with heavy perspiration. I have found it useless to try to return to sleep, so I distract my mind by reading until I feel the opportunity for sleep returning. With that, I extinguish the light and thankfully slip into a deep slumber. If I am successful in doing so, when I arise in the morning, I can reasonably expect a degree of refreshment. I believe this to be further evidence of the benefit of "second sleep."

Now on to another subject and further consideration of dreams.

I first become aware of Freud's work through conversation with Dr. Osler. Dr. Osler was particularly interested in Freud's work on the interpretation of dreams and told me that he kept a bedside journal of his dreams. As is case with many things I learned from Dr. Osler, I have adopted the habit of journaling, although I must tell you that the contents are unsettling, and the diary's existence and location is a deep secret.

As you know, I have made a yearly journey to San Francisco.

The first purpose is to visit Dr. Julius Rosenstirn—a prominent, and visionary physician. He received his medical degree from the University of Wuerzburg in Germany before immigrating to the United States. He helped found the San Francisco Opera.

I am Dr. Rosenstirn's guest at "Bohemian Club," a somewhat secret men's organization dedicated to the arts and music. After a visit to the Bohemian Club, your acquaintance, Oscar Wilde remarked, "I never saw so many well-dressed, well-fed, businessmen-looking Bohemians in my life."

Dr. Rosenstirn and I share with you a common tragedy of the loss of a child. While traveling in Germany, he received word of his daughter's illness from typhoid fever contracted from drinking contaminated water at her college, Berkeley, which is across the San Francisco Bay. She died before he could return home.

I am particularly interested in Dr. Rosenstirn's efforts to control sexual diseases in San Francisco. In this regard, he is decidedly opinionated. He believes that the "passionate call of sex" is fundamental to human life, "along with food." He also cites Sigmund—I believe I've mentioned Rosenstein's recognition of Freud before. Rosenstirn has been on the written record calling Freud "the greatest nerve specialist of the day," as showing that "many grave disorders of the nervous system are caused by suppression of the sex drive." Rosenstirn believes a particular problem exists with single working men in that they cannot not afford to marry, but still need a sexual outlet.

Dr. Rosenstirn does not condemn sexual intercourse among single persons as a crime or vice and advocates "free love" as an alternative. He is particularly progressive on the issue of prostitution. He rightly sees it as "an existing evil" providing a practical alternative to attempting to condemn or otherwise try to keep human sexual needs secret and repressed. With all this, I too agree, and believe there are important lessons for my own town of Denver.

Dr. Rosenstirn feels prostitution should be regulated and confined to particular parts of the city. He strongly believes that unregulated prostitution is the primary source of ven-

ereal disease. Only through regular examination of prostitutes, making such examinations mandatory, and confining
those found infected with VD can the spread of VD be con-
trolled.

My second reason for visiting San Francisco returns to the
topic of dreams. I believe careful exploration of the use of
medicine is the duty of the physician, but not the nickel-in-
the-slot use of unproven nostrums, but rather serious scientific inquiry. To this end, I have found the occasional smoking
of opium to both open and cleanse my mind through the resultant dreaming.

I do this with knowledge that there exists risk that the
pleasurable effects may become over-indulged and the use of
the drug habitual. I briefly fell into this trap as a consequence
of my visits to the Denver Chinese community near the Platte
River. Were it not for rescue by nurse Adams and the assistance of my household, I might have suffered sustained consequences.

Such behavior is now condemned among the Chinese
population of Denver, but in San Francisco's Chinatown, it is
easily available and tolerated. Thus, I have included a few days
of doing so during my meetings to Dr. Rosenstirn. I found it a
great comfort that abided until my next yearly visit.

I have now concluded that must no longer succumb to the
temptation. I write to you, because I must make a pledge, and
wish you to be the witness thereof.

I trust you will keep this in confidence, just as I have your
disclosures.

With every best wish,
Edgar
E.Y. Davidson, M.D.

"I have been told it is delicious."
November 6, 1915   El Paso, Texas

Dear Dr. Davidson,

    Well, what a surprise to this old scout, and trust me, your secret is safe with me—you have Buffalo Bill's word on it.

I know well the pipe.

I have been told it is delicious.

My friend Wild Bill was particularly fond of it, and given the choice, he enjoyed the hospitality of the Chinaman more than the saloon. He found great comfort.

I wish you great strength and assure you that I stand ready to help.

When I made my own pledge and gave up spirits, I did so upon advice of a doctor. You, sir, are being a good doctor to yourself.

With respect and confidentiality,

WFC

"To the road I must return."

December 23, 1915   Cody, Wyoming

Dear Edgar,

Merry Christmas and greetings from the T E Ranch. I assume that you received the official Christmas card that Louisa and I sent, but I wanted to send a personal note as well.

A fire blazes in the fireplace, and I hear the excited voices of grandchildren in the next room as they jabber to one another as to what may be in the packages under the tree. Oh, to be a child!

Best wishes for the coming New Year. It is my hope that it brings resolution of my financial challenges, satisfied creditors, and happy bankers. I so want to be able to spend more time here at the ranch and overseeing my mountain hotels.

But first, to the road I must return.

Will

"I'm not sure I believe in God, but I certainly believe in the Devil."

December 29, 1915   Denver, Colorado

Dear William,

Thank you for the card and the letter. I send back to you similar wishes.

I spent Christmas helping the Denver Elks deliver food baskets to the less fortunate in Denver. I am told that more than 1,000 such baskets were given out. At one home, I found a family of a wife and five children without any food or heat, the father in jail for drunkenness. Situations such as this will no doubt be seized upon by the prohibitionists who intend to place on next year's election ballot an amendment to the state constitution outlawing liquor in Colorado.

Colonel, there exists a dark side to those prohibitionists in that they associate alcohol with "foreigners" and "foreign ways." They appear to have adopted the horrible prejudices of the South. I fear for the future of my adopted state should these forces migrate west.

On a positive note, I suspect you saw the article about what happened on Christmas on the Western Front in the Europe war. If by chance you did not, the Germans began singing "Silent Night." The British replied with "Good King Wenceslas." With this, both sides climbed out of the trenches and began kicking a ball back and forth. It has been called "The Christmas Truce." A British officer, seeing this, ordered his men back into the trench, saying, "We're here to kill the Huns, not make friends." With this, artillery shelling started back up again. William, all too many things conspire to make me so discouraged about the current state of mankind. I'm not sure I believe in God, but I certainly believe in the Devil.

I continue at odds with my medical colleagues. Having had their former Denver medical schools shut down (as well as their access to profits and the cheap labor of students) some Denver doctors have banded together to control where medical students from the Boulder school will spend their third and fourth clinical medical student years in Denver. To accomplish this has required an amendment to the Colorado state constitution. Once it is official, it is my hope that the jealousies of the past will be set aside, and a rich course of study, focused on science and care of the patient, will emerge. As a profession, we need to rise above the tendency of some in the academy to make the false equation of intellect with and moral superiority. Should I become ill, I hope for care by a doctor who reads, learns, and is comfortable in their humility.

Enough of my negativity, but it certainly does challenge my desire for integrity of my profession, as well as finding some degree of happiness in calling myself a doctor.

I close with my sincerest wishes for your health and prosperity.

Your friend,

E.Y.

1916

"Now I have new excitement."

January 10, 1916   Cody, Wyoming

D ear Edgar,
        I know you will stand fast in doing what is right for your profession and its students. The sacrifice and hard work you put in serves as your contract with the future.

I trust that those axioms you shared in your last letter arise from your feeling a sense of meaning in your life. In my life, goals attached to meaningful motivations pull me forward, but bitterness and frustrations pull me down. For instance, creating a whole new way to tell people of the American West, its history, and its people proved so exciting. It motivated me to overcome difficulties such as those with Carver. Similarly, the promise of opening a new settlement for families in Wyoming gave me purpose, and I so enjoyed focusing on those tasks necessary to make that vision come to life. It made me spring from bed, do my Wild West duties, and then retire to my quarters to work on plans. Also, while people let me down, the energy I gained from the mines and prospecting helped me through the rough patch of my marriage and difficulties in dealing with the Bailey heirs. Now I have new excitement.

I am finally free of that beastly Tammen. He should be tied by his thumbs behind a wagon and led for two days. As you may recall, we had an arrangement whereby—in addition to my daily appearance fee—I was to receive a cut of the daily proceeds above $3,000. When I received excuses, and not money, I found that that cur had been cooking the books totally in his favor so as to cheat me out of my money. I regret it took so long for me to tumble to this fact, but I did receive relief from all my obligations to him. Tammen will always be the man who stole my show and broke my heart.

I have now agreed to join the Miller Brothers 101 Ranch Show, and things are bright. We will call it "Buffalo Bill (himself) and 101 Ranch Wild West Combined."

Like all mortals, I still have my usual fears. The last two years have greatly challenged my fear of public humiliation. I have lately started to experience a new dread, and that is the feeling of distress that time is running out.

I close with expectations of, and anticipation for, the future,

William

"I remind myself that deeds, not words, define a man."
February 1, 1916   Denver, Colorado

Dear Bill,

Thank you for your letter.

I found the counsel of your friendship helpful in reminding me that I have little inclination to sacrifice my opinions and integrity in order to avoid the criticism of the bloodless intellectuals who pontificate about their moral and intellectual superiority. I remind myself that deeds, not words, define a man.

Perhaps it is the promise of a new year, but my mood improves. I am more temperate. I have also calibrated my expectation away from the cliché of "happiness." As I have brooded upon this, I have concluded that "being happy" is a self-indulgent state of being. When Mason gives me a hug and calls me "Da" (something he has picked up from Miss Ryan, and I have not attempted to dissuade), I feel happy, but that momentary sensation quickly fades, and my mind returns to the trials and concerns that clot each day. When I sipped wine and read a good book, I felt the sensation of happiness, but that too gave way to increasing intoxication and then sleep, and I never awoke feeling happy.

This is in contrast something you touch upon in your letter—"a sense of meaning." Much more meat is found of bones of meaning. Being drawn forward—a phrase you used, and I like—and sustained each day by associated goals, is a powerful potion. I have a personal duty to use my gifts and work to improve the circumstances of other people. This may all sound a bit platitudinous, but that does not make the meaning and responsibility any less important.

I have worked out the following axioms to which I intend to adhere. They are personal daily admonitions. Over time, I may add to these four, but this is a start:

First, throttle the tendency to be judgmental of others. I need to first make sure my own life is in order before criticizing that of others.

Second, do not gossip. It appears to be a common human behavior, and I have certainly seen it in my own family. I think its roots must be in trying to exert sanctimonious superiority over others. To my thinking, it is an extension of my first admonition. I do not put sincere positive praise as in the category of gossip.

Third, don't be two-faced. I regard this type of behavior as in the toolbox of betrayal. Once someone is known to be fickle or duplicitous, not only do others not trust them, but it has the further poisoning of making them suspicious in the general motives of others.

Fourth, avoid the cult of personality. It is not because I do not trust people who have become famous—Sir William Osler a personal example of a man who has attracted well-deserved fame in medicine through intellect, integrity, and clarity of communication. Rather, I fear the mob that can grow tumor-like around the charm, promises, and superficiality of celebrities and politicians. It can certainly infect the professions.

There exist doctors in Colorado who have unquestioned obedience to certain leaders. The object of their idolatry is skilled in trading favors, advancing the favored into lucrative positions, and distracting us practitioners from those elements of our profession that need attention and reform. Nationally, the teachings of a Daniel David Palmer have attracted attention and dollars from naive students who literally "buy into" his theory of human elements being caused by the misalignment of the spine. Palmer himself relates that his "discovery" occurred when he cured the deafness of janitor by manipulating his spine. I need not name names, but I am never surprised to open a newspaper and find some fawning article about the individual, flavored with saccharine quotes from a worshiping cadre of cronies. Testimony of "cured" patients further flavors the claims of medical miracles. There is not an ounce of science behind all this, and I myself have witnessed the power of sugar pills to assuage the condition about which a patient complains.

Having written the above, I know that the final judgment of my sincerity and integrity will be whether or not the above aspirations will be meaningfully reflected in my deeds. An analysis of how I act is much more important than simple articulation of aspirations.

I also recognize that far back in my mind there exists darkness, forever wanting to move more forward. Of these, cruelty distress me the most. Whether it is by word or deed, the knowing infliction of cruelty and pain to a fellow creature is the handmaiden of betrayal. It is my hope that having tenants by which I can guide my life, I will hold such distressing thoughts at bay.

I close with my personal JOY of hearing about the improvement of your own professional circumstances. It sounds like 1916 may be a year in which good fortune returns to you. It appears your fear of public humiliation is abating, and the crowds coming to see you speak strong testimony to the legend of Buffalo Bill. As to fear of death, for the beasts, this lies with instinct of self-preservation. I believe humans—with our gift of consciousness—fear death most because of uncertainty about what lies beyond.

As to your distress about the erosion of time, I believe there is a German word for it, "torschlusspanik," which I believe translates exactly as to what you are feeling: "fear of time running out."

With appreciation,

E.Y.

> *"Spring has arrived, and with it hope for another new beginning."*

April 1, 1916   Ponca City, Oklahoma

Dear Dr. Davidson,

Spring has arrived, and with it hope for another new beginning. I am in Oklahoma at the Miller 101 Ranch where we prepare to go on national tour.

My enthusiasm is such that I greet the new troupe with the hearty to-and-fro Buffalo Bill handshake. The Miller Brothers have been long-time competitors, but a friendly bunch, putting on a top-shelf spectacle. I am to receive $100 per day plus one-third or all daily proceeds above $2,750. With war in Europe and a President Wilson who seems reluctant to accept the reality that our fine country might have to enter into the fray, we now title the show, "Buffalo Bill (himself) and 101 Ranch Wild West Combined with Military Pageant of Preparedness."

As part of this, we will have real live soldiers provided by the military. They want the public to appreciate their fine members and believe it will stir the hearts of our citizens and help gin up support for the possibility of a draft to build the army for the coming conflict. The recent Mexican raid on Columbus, New Mexico, has greatly increased interest, particularly with General Pershing and his men moving into Mexico to capture and punish Poncho Villa and his bandits. Black Jack will send those bandits packing. I hear he is chasing them with airplanes! Now wouldn't that be something to show!

I will no longer be just for show. I plan to return to putting on a demonstration of my fine shooting. It so pleases the crowd.

I hope to get to Denver in order to discuss with you a new difficulty with my bladder function I have experienced, although I'm sure it is more inconvenience than problem.

With hope and purpose, I remain,

Your friend,

William

"Buffalo Bill"

"I have continued to have problems passing my water."
September 16, 1916   Grafton, West Virginia

Dear Dr. Davidson,

Since I last visited you, I have continued to have problems passing my water, but you had warned me that such might become the case. I have spent so much time in the saddle, I suspect that it should come as no surprise that this particular region now bothers me so much. I am forced more and more to make the grand entrance in a wagon. I must say that I find this both frustrating and humiliating for one who so enjoyed the flash and thrill of riding a fine animal into the arena. I never tired of it, and bouncing behind a driver in a buggy just isn't the same. Nonetheless, I pride myself on having never missed a show.

Speaking of fine animals, yesterday I received word that my special horse Isham had to be destroyed. He developed lameness, a consequent of his age, but also the effects of his never-failing effort of speed and prance he gave me on parade and in the arena. When he heard the band begin to play, he would snort and shake, but stand as I swung into the saddle. Isham never took a bad step with me on board. As the old saying goes, "There is something about the outside of a horse that's good for the inside of a man." Unfortunately, dogs and horses die too young, and as such the good ones break a bit of your heart. Isham now lies in a grave on the T E, near where I too hope to be buried.

Isham was a favorite of mine, and when things collapsed because of that damnable Tammen, I was touched when my friends went together to save Isham from the auction. I have been fortunate to own many fine animals, and I will miss that old gentleman.

With remembrance,

Bill

Col. W.F. Cody

"I wish I could be more positive as it relates to
your condition of most discomfort."

September 22, 1916   Denver, Colorado

My Dear William,
      Thank you for your letter. I wish I could be more positive as it relates to your condition of most discomfort.

Forgive me if I give you excessive detail, but I fear that we doctors all too often error on providing to our patients too little, not too much, information.

A common short-term remedy for your bladder problem is catheterization. A tube inserted into the penis and forced past the obstruction will drain the bladder. A healthcare professional need not do this. Several years ago, I was in California Park north of Steamboat Springs. Rumors existed that wild bison still populated this rather remote area of Colorado. I found no such evidence; however, I made the acquaintance of an old sheepherder who lived with a thousand sheep, four dogs, and two horses. Around a morning campfire he told me of his bladder issues necessitating that he catheterize himself two to three times a day. I asked him how it did it. He said, "Well, since you're a doctor, I'll show you." To my amazement he took off his cowboy hat, retrieved a red rubber catheter out of the headband, moistened it with his saliva by running it through his mouth, dropped his pants, stepped to the side of the fire, grasp his member, inserted the catheter, and provided me a unique moment of medical education.

Chronic use of the catheter carries risk of infection and damage to the urinary tract. Not only can the catheter traumatize the penile urethra and the bladder, but it can also introduce bacterium into the pooled urine in the bladder. The fact that the sheepherder only left the catheter in place long enough to drain the bladder, probably accounts for why he had not developed an infection. His use of saliva to lubricate the catheter assured easy insertion and lessened the risk of trauma.

The long-term solution is surgery; however, surgery for prostate enlargement is in its infancy. Not to alarm you, but up until recently, removal of the prostate gland involved either an incision through the abdomen or in the area next to the rectum. The complication rate is high due to problems of bleeding and infection leading to sepsis and death. Although not mentioned specifically in many surgical reports, I have observed most men were left post-surgically impotent because of damage to the nerves controlling penile sexual service. Dr. Young—a native of Texas—is a pioneer who has greatly improved the surgery; thus, I am not hesitant in referring you to him. He specializes in surgery on the prostate. One of his colleagues, Doctor Edward Keyes of New York, has commented, "The prostate makes most men old, but it made Hugh Young."

Should you find yourself in Baltimore, please do not hesitate in using my name in contacting Dr. Young.

You did mention Isham to me, and I send my condolences on his passing. I have been fortunate to have a fine saddle horse that has given me much pleasure and avenue for escape from life's worries both on mountain trails and on the plains east of Denver. When the week's toil has been long, I look forward to going to his stable, looking into his kind eye, brushing his fine back, saddling him, and riding him with no particular plan in mind. His willing gait, gentle soul, and the sweet smell of his sweat put me in a place in the world that leaves me a better man.

I believe people who appreciate animals for their companionship are far richer in spirit than those who see them only as creatures for our bidding. It was your acquaintance Samuel Clemmons who said something to the effect, "If entry into Heaven was based on merit, it would be dogs, not men, that would be let in." I know I paraphrase, but the spirit is true.

William, look to life's ledger. On the left make a column of all you have accomplished. To the right write regrets. Of late,

I have found that writing down such negative thoughts serves to bleed them of their power.

At their annual gathering at the Bohemian Grove outside of San Francisco, the Bohemians do something similar. They write down their cares and concerns on pieces of paper, then they perform an additional step. They burn them in their opening bonfire.

Take satisfaction and comfort in the column of all you have accomplished, for while this world knows so much sorrow, it also knows Buffalo Bill.

With warm regards,

Edgar

Edgar. Davidson, M.D.

"I am so tired."

October 2, 1916   Fredrick, Maryland

My Dear Friend Davidson,
I write to you from Maryland where it is cold and raining. Poor Colonel Miller has left our combined show is in the hospital with a deep cold from the weather. It is a wonderment that I can come up smiling each day.

Thank you for the referral to Dr. Young. Unfortunately, he is traveling and not available for consultation.

Doctor, I must say your description of ways to care for my condition did cause this scout to squirm a bit as I read the letter.

As I have done some ciphering about what I have done in life, some accomplishments remain clear. For instance, I killed a lot of bison, and fed a lot of men. I even won a contest in which I killed sixty-nine buffalo in one day, riding my favorite buffalo horse, "Brigham," and using my fine Springfield rifle. I still have the gun, and it has always served me well, but unfortunately, on a hunt from Pahaska's lodge, the stock was damaged. It's a bit like me, broken—but unlike the gun, I still have a few parts that fire.

I loved that old gun. Inspired by my early years on the stage, I named that rifle, "Lucrezia Borgia." I took the name from a play about the bastard daughter of Pope Alexander. Born during the Italian Renaissance, Lucrezia used sex and poison to advance her family's power and wealth. I think you would agree, that's an interesting name for rifle chosen by a young scout with supposedly not much book learning!

Dear friend, my stage plays—and later, the Wild West—were a little awash in blood. Such is how I saw the frontier. Guns blazed and bodies fell, to arise again for the next act or scene. It was splendid, and the audience loved it, but not the damn critics. They had their opinions, but I had people in seats and folding money in my pocket.

Some of the events I've recreated were constructively contrived. People loved was my recreation of I the death of Custer's men at the Little Big Horn so those brave men would not be forgotten. Such was the destiny of our new nation. Yes, in the staging I arrive "too late," but it was for dramatic effect, not the claim that I could have saved Custer. (Of course, had I been there with a troop of Rough Riders, I would have turned the tide of battle.)

Some of my remembrances are a bit strange in that they seem strong, but I do wonder about particular details. I tell you in confidence that one of them is this whole battle on War Bonnet Creek. I know I was there, and I know that I procured the scalp of Yellow Hand. On stage, I held it high and exclaimed, "The first scalp for Custer!" Some continue to question why I did this, and even try to claim it did not happen. What use is there of those who disbelieve? I write this and banish it from troubling my tired, sick, mind.

What is real, and what is good showmanship? I hope to sort all this out as I work on the ledger you suggested.

Setting all the above aside, I share with you that last night I had an interesting dinner when we traveled south across the Potomac River into our great nation's capital. We dined with Stephen Mather, the first director of the new National Park

Service, and Horace Albright, co-founder with Mather of the park service.

I'm sure they enjoyed my company.

In evidence, they told me that they found me "marvelously entertaining." However, at one point in the evening, I turned to Mather and thanked him for the publicity the Park Service Director's visits had brought to not only the town of Cody, but also the Irma Hotel and the Pahaska Tepee. Mather, who had a reputation as having both a volatile mood and frankness in his speech, replied, "Mr. Cody, I did indeed visit your hostelries, but I assure you I will not again unless you take steps to rectify the sad conditions they are in."

He told me the food was bad and the service worse.

I kept a straight face as he said the Irma kitchen was "about the dirtiest, most unsanitary place I have ever seen." Mrs. Mather decided to sleep in the lobby because of "things crawling in the bed." When Mather himself went to his room, he found two men already sleeping in the bed.

He got more and more wound up, and I feared he'd pop a blood vessel right there at the table.

He told me that on their way to Yellowstone Park they stopped at the Pahaska Tepee. They found the food inedible and the waitress glitzy and loud. He asked me if I was operating a combination eating place and brothel.

Well, my years on the stage gave me a pretty thick hide when it came to suffering critics.

They can judge, but they don't create.

I smiled, did not fire back, but rather roared with laughter and asked that the Director send me a list of the sad conditions, and promised that they would be corrected.

As we concluded dinner, we enjoyed cigars imported from liberated Cuba.

I instructed the maître d'hôtel to forward the bill to my attention at the Hoffman House hotel in New York City, but not before adding a generous tip for his conscientious supervision of staff.

Following dinner, I rounded up the party and swept us all back off north across the river to enjoy the dazzling 101 Ranch Show. Doctor, what they did not see was me being carried from my dressing tent to a curtain shielding me from the audience. Once on my horse, I held my hat high and sat ramrod in the saddle. The curtain parted, and I rode out once again to the cheers of the audience. At the end, the crowd gave me a standing ovation. My heart sang.

I am so tired. Major Burke thinks that come November, that will be my final appearances until I can return to rejuvenate in Wyoming.

With my very best wishes,
Bill
William F. Cody
"Buffalo Bill"

"Violence is everywhere; I hate it but I am so drawn to it."
October 16, 1916   Lumberton, North Carolina

Dear Dr. Davidson,
I trust that this letter finds you doing well and tolerant of the complaints of a rusty old scout. I say rusty, because my skin is dry and itches, sometimes so much that those around me must think I have fleas.

I have also noticed that my shortness of breath at night is such that it not only wakes me up at night, but I find myself lying in my berth conscious of each breath and the fact that my breaths come and go. One moment I am fine, breathing regular, and then I am short of breath and breathing fast and deep.

A few years ago, while hunting big horns in the mountains not far from the Pahaska Tepee, I lay in my bedroll and had a similar thing happen. Then I thought little of it, other than the effect of a strenuous day on horseback and trail, as well as perhaps a little too much good chow. When I have these spells, I can feel that gallop rhythm of my heart that you said you heard on my last visit and my legs cramp as if I have had a long day in the saddle.

I must also tell you that headache in the front of my head is becoming more of a problem. I swear that I have been temperate. In the past when my head hurt, Dr. Powell told me that I need to be bled, but I kept him and his lance at bay.

On a positive note, I have recently had the pleasure of enjoying a refreshing drink, now available in a very distinctive bottle. In the past, I savored it at soda fountains, which I found to be a suitable alternative to going to a saloon. It is called "Coca Cola," and it was concocted by an Atlanta pharmacist. I think the beverage's name may betray one of the ingredients he chose to include. It's caramel color and fizzy taste slakes both thirst and the constant terrible taste in my mouth. My favored drink has been lemonade, but this new concoction may elbow forward on my palatal desires.

I have to say that I am troubled as I continue taking inventory of my life and put it in the ledger.

Particularly, I cogitate about all the ways I have seen that men practice violence on one another. Not to say that I haven't done my part. I think about that poor Indian, Tall Bull. At Summit Springs battle, as you have noted, he put the knife to his horse and fought to the death while his family escaped up a gully. Then there was that nasty business I've shared often with you about Yellow Hand, and the first scalp for Custer. I also know that the things that most brought people into the stands involved guns, robberies, hunting buffalo, attacks on settlers, the Custer Fight, and even the Boxers. Violence is everywhere; I hate it but I am so drawn to it. When I get into these thoughts, my mood becomes as foul as my breath.

Well, enough of my tired old ramblings.

Your friend,

W.F. Cody

"Your 'taking inventory' and conflicted feelings place you within those members of our race who have conscience."
October 21, 1916   Denver, Colorado

Dear Buffalo Bill,

Thank you for your recent correspondence.

My friend, your "taking inventory" and conflicted feelings place you within those members of our race who have conscience. I recall assisting a surgeon during my years as a student at Johns Hopkins. He took pride in both his surgery and instruction. While demonstrating a particularly interesting piece of anatomy laid open by the incision, he nicked himself with the scalpel. The wound suppurated, and a few days later he lay dead. To this day, I feel he gave his life while trying to give me an education. To serve, practice self-sacrifice, is to take risk—sometimes fatal of reputation, but then again, even worse.

It appears to be within our nature to be drawn to violence. My work in charitable casualty wards, as well as the words of our daily Denver papers, reaffirm the inescapable conclusion that a beast beats within the breasts of very many and it wages war with our aspirations to be civilized. I hope you give yourself some comfort in your efforts to try to bring together a brotherhood of man and give no ground to the devil in the fight for the souls of our species.

On the medical side, I note that you did not mention bladder function. Am I to take from this that it remains unchanged or better?

As for the itching you describe, of course, this is a common problem with those of us who choose to live in the otherwise healthy high, dry altitude of the Rocky Mountains; however, since I know you to be traveling, it may be due to something other than locale. It is also possible that the breathing problem and headache are also related as well. We have spoken of concern about the function of your kidneys, and what you are experiencing relates to alterations thereto.

Sometimes a tepid bath will help with the itching, although I have also found that others respond well to bathing in hot water. Addition of light oils and perhaps a bit of salt to the bath may also prove salutary.

As you are aware, many travel to the mineral springs of Colorado and other states of the West to both enjoy the waters through immersion, as well as ingestion. I fear many of the claims are far overstated; however, I see little harm, as long as one avoids some of the associated treatments often foisted upon those in whom hope exceeds good sense. In particular, I would take caution in suggestions that purging and so-called bowel cleansing treatments would be restorative.

I believe it wise that you limit your intake of meat to no more than once a day as both the salt nature of flesh and the amounts of disagreeable chloride may have an adverse effect on your health, and strain upon your heart and blood vessels in particular.

I advise you in the strongest of terms to not allow any blood-letting. While this form of treatment may be useful in far-advanced disease where tension of the blood vessels and congestion of the heart severe, it has no place in the treatment of this condition. In fact, taking some iron in the form of a half to full drachm of perchloride of iron may be helpful, since anemia is often an attendant condition.

As regards to your breathing, I suspect it is of a type called "Cheyne-Stokes," originally recognized and described by physicians, one Irish and the other a Scot, early last century, John Cheyne and William Stokes. I must say that I am not surprised by this occurrence. If it becomes particularly troublesome, we can try judicious amounts of morphia, as this has proven to be highly beneficial when used with caution and prudence.

With every best wish for your happiness,

Edgar

E.Y. Davidson, M.D.

"I can say that the expectancies of the world about the life of Buffalo Bill were only exceeded by my own."
November 11, 1916   Norfolk, Virginia

Dear Dr. Davidson,
        I thank you for your many kindnesses to this worn-out old scout. I am coming to peace with the folding of the tents and packing up for the final time. Today the tour ends here in Virginia.

I have enjoyed success with the Wild West. It gave me great wealth as well as notoriety. I only now wish I'd known when to quit. Oh, how I hate that loathsome word "quit." Perhaps I need to think differently.

I have written my attorney, Henry Horsey, to move forward to the sell the Irma Hotel, the Pahaska Tepee, and the Irma Farm that provides produce for the hotel.

So many people have betrayed and abandoned me. I appreciate your friendship more than you shall ever know. Wild Bill Hickok, Texas Jack Omohundro, and my long-time business partner, Nate Salsbury were good pards, but we did not always part on the best of terms. In these cases, the feelings of betrayal flowed in both directions. The true snakes in my garden came in the form of Tammen and his partner, Bonfils. I so hold them in contempt, but given circumstances, I felt the bitter taste of pride as I swallowed and did business with them.

The glanders disaster in Europe really got the ball rolling down the hill. I had to mortgage everything just to keep the Wild West going. Even when I started making money, I had to keep feeding my debtors. I wish I'd filled in the hole, and kept doing what I was good at. Now in the blinding light that shines on the past, I should have stopped trying to be a business tycoon. I no longer get my neck hairs up when called a "showman." Do what you're good at, and be satisfied. No one ever went broke putting a nickel away from every dime he earned, providing you put them in the right place. Good advice from a snake-bit old scout.

I have had many good fortunes, and perhaps some of the things that now weigh so heavily upon me will prove successful—if not for me, perhaps for my loved ones. I still have the mining claims in Arizona, and maybe the land I still have in

Wyoming will someday be worth more than just a hat full of promises.

I still have obligations to meet and money to make. As Pawnee Bill once put it to me, "dog's gotta eat."

I had hopes when I learned that winners of the Congressional Medal of Honor were receiving a small pension. I wrote to the Department of the Army and told them of my medal that I'd won in the Indian wars and how I needed the money because of business reversals and because it rains all the time. The bastards turned me down. Damn the government I once so loyally and nobly served. They even took back my medal, saying it was only meant to go to soldiers, and not civilians.

My dreams again come back to me of my life on the prairies, and the many experiences I have related to audiences throughout the world, as well as the books that tell the tales. I have enjoyed my life, but I feel I have constantly been on the stage. I can say in all truth that the expectancies of the world about the life of Buffalo Bill were only exceeded by my own.

When the Wild West was performing outside the Columbian Exposition, a man named Frederick Jackson Turner gave a talk to a pow wow of historians that created quite the stir. He used lots of figures and numbers to support an argument that the American frontier was no more. Well, one thing I have always believed is that facts get forgotten, but stories remembered. People welcomed my stories of the wonderful American West, and I am certain that they will recollect them long into the future.

I am preparing a series of articles for *Hearst's International Magazine* entitled, "The Great West That Was." It goes with my dude ranch idea where T E should best become a ranch where people from throughout the world can come and experience the American West. As my guests, they will learn from Buffalo Bill. It should provide funds that I need, and I will make a fortune again.

As I write this, I am preparing to travel to my sister's home in Denver. I have a bad cold. My sister May has recommended that I attend the healing waters of Glenwood Springs. It is only a day's rail journey away. I am told the mineral springs and vapor caves have been known for healing powers, going back to their use by the Ute Indians. Evidently Doc Holiday sought their benefit for his consumption. He is buried in the cemetery that overlooks the town; although, I've heard that a flash flood might have moved his burial site. Where a man's bones land is much less important than the deeds they done. You can take that to the bank, Pard.

No need to reply as I hope to contact you upon my arrival in Denver.

I also plan to bring you a special parcel.

Faithfully your friend,

Wm. Cody BB

"Pain comes in many forms."

November 27, 1916   Denver, Colorado

Dear "Bison William,"

I start with this greeting because I have both read of you referring to yourself in such a way, and also because it gives a bit of breadth to the wide affection so many feel for you. Although you said not to write, I couldn't leave your last letter unanswered, even if I should see you when you get to Denver.

Pain comes in many forms, and for you, I feel the pain of betrayal flow through the words you have written. Each betrayal begins when we commit to trust. But recall that this is theme of the human circumstance. Shakespeare in *Julius Caesar* so well taught us that ambition supersedes loyalty. You attracted and supported many talented people, and I have found that those with talent also have ambition. Rather than bitterness, pray you should find satisfaction in having provided opportunity to set loose their ambitions.

Let the guilty burden fall on them, for they are the ones who brayed your loyalty.

I do have a bit of news to share with you. Please recall

my sharing with you how I deduced the death by arsenic of a husband was accidental. I have found that I derive interest and excitement examining the circumstances of a death when the possibility exists of an associated element of novelty or even crime. I have recently consulted in the case of a woman with severe episodes of vomiting and diarrhea that eventually resulted in her death. A brother suffered from a similar condition, and concern existed that there was a familial association. Upon postmortem examination of the woman, she was found to have ulceration of her stomach, but not characteristic of those of peptic cause. I was also struck that her body, although several days dead, showed little evidence of the expected onset of decay.

I took a sample from the contents of her stomach, sublimed it with copper, and saw under the microscope the characteristic crystals of oxide of antimony. Antimony is known to have a particular quality of preserving the body after death, and there have been cases reported in the literature where victims of poisoning have been exhumed and appear as natural as in life.

Suspecting foul play, I instructed the constable to search the home. Under the bed of her husband was secreted a large porcelain jar of silvery white antimony salts. When confronted, he confessed. He had been slow poisoning his wife and brother-in-law in hopes of capturing control of her family's business interest.

Colorado, as well as some other western states, has a system whereby the coroner of each county is elected. Furthermore, it is not required that the corner actually have any medical expertise whatsoever. If autopsy is necessary, a qualified medical examiner must be brought in. Starting next year, I will make myself available, of course for an appropriate fee, to provide such services. There is a win for all, in that the coroner will get the recognition craved by those who seek election, and I will get the satisfaction of putting my brain and experience to work.

I look forward to a visit with you in Denver. I should be available, but I do plan to journey to San Francisco shortly after Thanksgiving for meetings and the holidays. Should you need to contact me, please feel free to send correspondence to Dr. Julius Rosenstirn in San Francisco. As you know from my previous correspondence, he is a prominent physician, and I'm sure it will get to him. I anticipate that I will return to Denver no later than the third week in January.

Please be advised that Sister Adams will also be absent from Denver as she plans on visiting her family in Philadelphia during the Christmas season, as well as welcoming in the New Year with them.

With my sincere best wishes for comfort,
E.Y. Davidson

1917

"I might honor us both by allowing the future to experience our past."

September 30, 1917   Denver, Colorado

Dear William,

It has been almost nine months since your death. I have held off writing to you as I knew not what to say. In addition, it might seem foolish to correspond with the dead, but do we not do so when we look to history for understanding and advice? If nothing else, writing this letter provides a form of therapy. We both agreed that writing down feelings robs them of some of their negative effect on us. This is important because in the lives of humans, the memories of bad times have much more power than those of the good.

For seventeen years we corresponded. While I initially provided medical service to you, and continued to do so, our relationship evolved into a special friendship, though our ages, experiences, and circumstances greatly differed.

Unfortunately, in the end, I was unable to care for you. I did not return from San Francisco until after your death. A further misfortune is that we two alone knew of our relationship. At the end, as your conscious state slipped, there was no way to communicate with me so as to speed my journey back to Denver. I do feel a tinge of guilt that I abandoned you.

You should know that the life of Cody continues of general interest, transcending races, classes, and continents. Even in war, the Western World still mourns your death. I hope you smile when you learn that the Boy Scouts are collecting pennies to assure that a proper monument stands at your gravesite.

What do I now think of our letter exchanges?

Well, at first, we focused on issues with your health. Patients often come to me with complex problems. Early in my career I recognized need to have patience with this and listen. I have found if I listen long enough to patients, they would eventually tell me what is wrong. I also believe it is important to remember a good physician identifies with the patient, not the disease.

In our case, the tables became a bit turned. As time went on, you provided me a way to share my thoughts and issues without concern about professional consequences, personal embarrassment, or regret. When my wife—and then my son— died, I slipped toward self-pity. I also developed some behaviors that I recognized as self-abusive. Writing to you proved to be a powerful restorative that set me back on the proper path. From your days as a scout, you know it's one thing to look at a map, it's quite another to set foot on, and then down, the trail.

All this has put me in a better place.

Now I wish to tell you a story.

As a result of the Flexner report, the medical schools in Colorado have consolidated into a single entity under the University of Colorado. I have been asked to participate in the committee overseeing the curriculum and its implementation. I immediately warmed to the invitation as I knew exactly what should be done.

Then I discovered two important things.

First, by exercising patience in the meetings, I let everyone else have their say, knowing full well they will eventually be compelled to accept my recommendations. For instance, I knew what courses should be part of the early student curriculum. By allowing others to participate, they were satisfied that at least they have had an opportunity to be heard, and therefore accept my proposals for a rigorous scientific curriculum. The committee wholeheartedly agreed.

But then, I found a second curious thing. Sometimes someone had a better idea! For instance, it was proposed we have a weekly conference for discussion of interesting cases, particularly if learning existed from pathological examination. It would be termed, "Clinical Pathological Conference," shortened to "CPC." This would serve to help tie in the science with the actual care of patients. In my mind I agreed, and thought they'd be a good way to start the week by having them on Monday, when minds would be newly fresh from the salubriousness of the sabbath.

Before I could present my proposal as to when, an unexpected alternative emerged. And it came from Dr. Ian McGregor, a tough old bird I thought didn't have much interest in students. I'd wondered why he was on the committee.

"Let's do them on Saturday morning—we've wrapped up the week, the pressure is off, and it would be great to involve the students," said Dr. McGregor. Sometimes people pleasantly surprise me, though not near often enough.

It was agreed to have the conference on Saturday mornings. I made a mental note to ask Mrs. Kelly to cook up a batch of her donuts for me to bring to the first conference. I brought them to the first CPC meeting, and they were a great hit. I wished I'd brought more.

My practice of medicine goes well. Humans are united in the commonality of suffering. Those who seek my care have many forms of suffering. This week I have seen the turned-out miner with "miner's consumption" from the dust he must inhale at work, the barkeep captive of the product he sells, and the businessman whose bills exceed his income and in despair tries to take his own life. I have discovered that helping those who suffer, even if it is just giving them of my time and ear, adds meaning to my own life. I have also found it is easier to bind a broken bone than heal a fractured spirit.

I now turn from school and clinic to the larger world.

The World War continues to chew through Europe. In April, the United States declared war on Germany. The country is mobilizing. A draft has started, but as many as a third of young men called up are found to have tuberculosis and sent home.

Hospital units are being formed for service in Europe. I pondered joining, but when I considered my obligation to my patients, Mason, and household, I concluded it was impractical, as well as irresponsible. I do plan to volunteer my services to a large army hospital that is planned just east of Denver. It will be dedicated to soldiers who return to the United

States with tuberculosis. It will also treat those whose lungs damaged from the gas attacks—a new horror of this war.

It is my hope that the war will quickly be over and this century, which has started with the butchery of the battle-field, will ultimately prove to be one whereby mankind corrals its base instincts and peace will prevail. President Woodrow Wilson, who counts himself a pacifist, justifies his action in entering the war because it will be "the war to end all wars." Forgive me if I remain skeptical. I have concluded, "A cynic is an idealist who has had their heart broken one too many times."

In one of your letters to me you wrote of violence and how you hated it, but were so attracted to it. We humans may have to accept that violence is ingrained in human nature. As you know, I am greatly interested in human behavior. Freud writes that when humans' aggressive instincts turn outward, they appear in the form of violence toward others. Jung argues for "the shadow" as the dark side of the human psyche. Perhaps Dr. Freud and he would agree that war is a collective societal manifestation of these parts of human nature. I see the violent homicidal behavior of men daily in the streets of lower Denver, but also in the homes of the prosperous and the well-to-do. I would also submit that the increasing popularity of American football is just another, ritualized, manifestation of human attraction to violence. That good-natured Wild West sport in which your cowboys and Indians competed on horse has now become a sport of flying wedges and tackles that leaves shattered bones and fractured skulls. Last year, several deaths occurred on the gridiron of college football.

Bill, you will recall my writing to you about Sir William Osler. This month I received a distressing letter from Sir William. Although an American by birth, his son Edward Revere Osler volunteered for service in the British Royal Army and was sent to France. In the process of moving artillery during the Battle of Ypres, a German shell struck near Revere. He received wounds to abdomen, thigh, and upper chest. Ironically,

Dr. Harvey Cushing, who I also mentioned to you in previous letters, headed a nearby hospital unit of Harvard volunteers. The aid station in which Revere lay summoned Cushing. In spite of blood transfusion and surgical treatment, Revere's wounds proved fatal. The great, great grandson of Paul Revere was buried in a muddy grave bedded with juniper boughs and wrapped in a British Union Jack flag.

Lady Grace Osler and Sir William had a first son, Paul Revere Osler, who died within a week of being born. Dr. Osler shared with me in his letter that he composed a letter supposedly written from Heaven by their baby son. It assured the grieving parents that he was in a good place with other children. It was an attempt by Osler to deal with his own pain and console the grieving mother. Again, evidence that somehow the process of putting words down seems to have a salutary effect on the human mind and heart.

Osler wrote to me, "A sweeter lad never lived." Lady Grace and he take a small bit of comfort in knowing their friend Cushing sat at Revere's side as he died. Sir William closed our last correspondence with, "Call no man happy until he dies."

Osler joins the two of us in having lost a son.

Returning to the positive, I continue to enjoy my medical examiner work. I'm currently working to understand why a young man struck by a train outside of Colorado Springs had mustard colored teeth but no evidence of decay. When his family arrived to identify his body, I noted that they too had such dental discoloration. When I examined them, all had remarkably strong teeth with no caries—an oddly curious finding. I feel there is an important clue and a mystery to be solved.

I have recently been in consultation about axe murders in Colorado Springs that share some eerie similarities to murders reported in Iowa, as well as along the Southern Pacific Railroad. In the Springs case, the killer or killers went to the trouble of covering up all the mirrors in the house, as well as covering the home's windows with bed sheets. I wish to find why people do to one another such morbid malice and the associated aberrant behavior. There is still so much to be explored and explained.

My staff continues in their support of Mason and me. Meals are hardy and punctual, the home is spotless, and all else is in order. The governess, Miss Ryan, does express sadness that she will never again see her native Ireland for she is understandably terrified of ocean travel, and no alternatives exist. It troubles her sleep, and sometimes in the night I hear her door open downstairs and then footsteps as she retreats to read in my library. She apparently has no interest in marriage. She confides in Mrs. Clarke and Nurse Adams, but never me.

I miss you Bill. From my front window I can see Lookout Mountain where you now lie. To the west you have a great view of the Rocky Mountains. The mountains sparkle with early snow. To the east you overlook Denver. On a clear day, I think you might be able to see all the way to Nebraska.

I have a new automobile, a blue Overland Roadster. It sports yellow spoke wheels and can fit additional people in the back with what is called a "rumble seat." Last week I drove it up the road to where you lie, and I swear I heard you say, "Doctor, it's a dandy!" And it is.

That's about it, Buffalo Bill.

You should know I believe history will treat you kindly. I hope this gives you comfort.

I am in receipt of the collection of letters you sent to me, and I have placed them in a secure spot, along with the letters I wrote to you. I assure you that our letters will remain our secret. At some point, when both of us have moved on to a different dimension, I might honor us both by allowing the future to experience our past.

To those that might read our letters, I would ask that they particularly look past the popular image of Buffalo Bill. I read one of your early letters to me. In it you wrote that you wanted to be remembered as someone other than a "just a showman." I have recently read of a French economist, Jean-

Baptiste Say. He wrote of "entrepreneurs," which translates from French as "adventurers."

Adventurers have imagination, and they have the courage to take risk. Whether on stage, in the arena, or in business, William F. "Buffalo Bill" Cody was an adventurer. You took many risks, and unlike pallid bankers and bureaucrats, you had skin in the game. As you would say, Hah!

Buffalo Bill created the American Wild West so others could write about it.

Finally, and simply, you touched something in people's souls that made them have a few moments of happiness, even if that joy faded as they left the Wild West or finished a story about your life. As a doctor I submit, "You were good medicine."

"Your pard,"
Edgar
E.Y. Davidson

Epilogue

I n early January 1917, Cody journeyed by train to Glenwood Springs as suggested by his sister May Decker. He drank and bathed in the warm mineral waters. He also consulted the spa doctor. The news was bad. After examining Cody, the doctor told Cody he had less than two weeks to live.

Cody returned to his sister's Denver home, feeling too sick to travel back to Cody, Wyoming. His condition worsened. In Davidson's absence, the physician caring for Cody was John H. East. East was quoted in *The Denver Post* as attributing Cody's rapid decline to a recent eclipse of the moon.

After "a bad night," Cody lost consciousness at 10 a.m. and died at 12:05 p.m. on January 10, 1917, in the Denver home of his sister. At his bedside were his wife, Lulu Cody, and sister May Decker, as well as May's family. Prior to passing on, Cody converted to the Catholic church and received last rites. The administering priest had immigrated from Ireland, drawn to the American West he said by the tales of Buffalo Bill.

Cody died the good death. Dying not in the sterile and often chaotic environment of the hospital. He didn't suffer in a battlefield, or other site of trauma. No, Cody died in bed, in the home of his sister, surrounded by family.

Nationwide, Western Union flashed the message to "Hold all lines open," and then dot-dashed throughout the world the news of Cody's death.

The undertaker was called. He embalmed Cody in the home. Cody's body lay in the front room of May's home until January 14 when it was taken by horse-drawn caisson to the Colorado State Capitol. Colorado and America took time out from World War I to recognize the death of Cody. Cody lay in state in the rotunda under the gold dome of the capitol. Thousands of people filed by. Late in the afternoon, he was taken to the Elks Hall where the Elks conducted his funeral. Following this, the Knights of Columbus transferred him to the Olinger Mortuary.

Behind the scenes, controversy raged. Cody had expressed

his desire to be buried on Cedar Mountain overlooking Cody, Wyoming, and Cody, Wyoming, wanted him back. North Platte, Nebraska, home of the Cody ranch, "Scouts Rest," thought it too had a claim. But Denver had Cody's body, and it wasn't giving it up. Even in death, Cody was going to promote *The Denver Post.* Lulu reportedly accepted $10,000 from Tammen and Bonfils in exchange for consenting to have Cody buried in Colorado.

Over the next six months, Cody's gravesite was blasted out of solid granite on top of Lookout Mountain, just west of Denver. During this time, the Olinger Mortuary re-embalmed Cody six times.

On June 3, 1917, Cody's body was taken to the grave. It remains the largest state funeral in the history of Colorado. Denver police and Boy Scouts guarded Cody's coffin. Masons conducted the funeral. Lulu asked that the casket be opened for one last view of Buffalo Bill. One improbable, yet entertaining, report stated that when an old girlfriend of Cody's passed by the casket, she kissed the glass covering Cody's body, and the inside of the glass steamed up.

As Cody's body was lowered in the steel vault of his twelve-foot deep tomb, a bugler sobbed out taps, and artillery from the Colorado National Guard boomed a twelve-gun salute—usually reserved for a brigadier general.

Rumors circulated that Cody, Wyoming, was coming for Cody's body. The grave was reopened and concrete poured on top of the old scout's casket.

Fifty-one years earlier, a young Cody had ridden past this mountain on his way to the Black Hawk and Central City Russell's Gulch gold fields. Looking up at the mountain, Cody would not have imagined that his body would rest on its top and visited throughout each year by thousands of people. They drive the winding Lariat Trail road to his grave, on which some toss coins for good luck. In a nearby museum sit Cody artifacts. A gift store sells souvenirs. Toy guns are a particularly popular sale item. Television and radio transmission towers sit next to Cody's grave. Even in death, Cody can't get away from show business.

Death continued winning.

Three months after Cody's death, Major John Burke, Cody's longtime press agent, checked himself into Providence Hospital in Washington, D.C., and the next day died of pneumonia.

William F. "Buffalo Bill" Cody named his hotel in Cody, Wyoming, "The Irma" after his daughter Irma Cody Garlow. Irma and her husband Fred Garlow died in the 1918 influenza epidemic. In that same year, Dr. Davidson's Hopkins mentor, Sir William Osler, also succumbed to influenza. Close to death, he expressed regret that his was one autopsy he would not be able to witness. Those that knew Osler felt he never recovered from Revere's death, and he died of a broken heart. Dr. Harvey Cushing returned from World War I to innovate new techniques for surgery on the human brain and became the father of modern neurosurgery. In addition, in 1929, Dr. Cushing received the Pulitzer Prize for his two-volume biography of Osler. It is still considered one of the premier works of American literature. Dr. Davidson received a personally inscribed first addition from Cushing.

Louisa "Lulu" Cody died in Cody, Wyoming, in 1921. She is also buried on Lookout Mountain. Her coffin is said by some to have been placed on top of William Cody's. If someone wanted Cody's body, they'd have to go through Louisa.

Mary Hannah Cody Decker ("May") died in California in 1926. Her home in Denver where William Cody died still stands.

Julia Melvina Cody Goodman died October 26, 1928 in Honolulu, Hawaii. She is buried in North Platte, Nebraska, not far from Scout's Rest Ranch.

Johnny Baker, Cody's "adopted son," opened the museum and gift shop that is next to William Cody's grave on Lookout Mountain. He died in 1931.

Harry H. Tammen died in 1923, leaving half of a multimillion-dollar estate to children's healthcare in Denver.

Phoebe Ann Mosey, "Annie Oakley," continued to set shooting records. At age 62, she hit 100 targets in a row in a contest. She died of pernicious anemia in 1925, aged 66 years. After her death, her husband of fifty years, Frank Butler, stopped eating and died eighteen days later. Oakley is enshrined in many halls of fame, including the National Women's and the Cowgirl halls of fame. Annie inspired the hit musical, "Annie Get Your Gun."

Margaret Tobin Brown, "The Unsinkable Mrs. Brown"— Titanic survivor, socialite, and tireless worker for miner and children rights—died in 1932. Her autopsy disclosed a brain tumor. In life, she was only known as "Maggie" as a child and "Margaret" as an adult. In 1960, Richard Morris and Meredith Wilson wrote the book and stage play, *The Unsinkable Molly Brown.* They chose the name "Molly" because it was easier to sing. Even though estranged in life, she is buried next to her husband J.J. Brown in the Cemetery of the Holy Rood in Westbury, N.Y.

Harry Tammen's *Denver Post* partner, Fredrick Bonfils, died at home of encephalitis in 1933, still fighting a newspaper war with the *Rocky Mountain News*. The Denver blood bank bears his name.

Gordon William Lillie "Pawnee Bill" successfully invested his show earnings in land, cattle, banking, movie production, and an Oklahoma oil refinery. He died in his sleep on February 3, 1942 at age 81 in Pawnee, Oklahoma.

In a letter dated April 23, 1944 to Thomas Hornsby Ferril, columnist for the *Rocky Mountain Herald*, Mari Sandoz noted western author and director of research for the Nebraska State Historical Society, characterized the Cody claim of killing Yellow Hand as "a lie." Sandoz wrote that Cody may have paid a soldier five dollars for the Yellow Hand scalp.

Dr. John H. East, who attended Cody at his death, died June 24, 1944. As he died, he was asked if he wanted a minister. He declined and replied, "I am willing to die as I have lived—on the square."

In 1947, a contest was held to name the Buffalo, New York, All-American League football team. In homage to Cody the frontiersman, the name "Bills" was chosen over "Bullets," "Blue Devils," and "Nickels." Though the league folded, when Buffalo was later awarded a franchise in the new American Football League, the name was resurrected.

After going through multiple owners following Cody's death, the T E Ranch, southwest of Cody, Wyoming, was sold in 1972—the year of Dr. Davidson's death—to Charles Duncan, the president of the Coca-Cola Company. Cody might have raised a Coke to the transaction. Today the ranch headquarters Cody loved so much is on the National Register of Historic Places.

In 1989, under pressure from the Wyoming congressional delegation, Cody's Congressional Medal of Honor was restored by the Army Board for the Correction of Military Records; however, none of the associated back pay was awarded to the Cody estate.

David Eagleman, an American writer and neuroscientist wrote: "There are three deaths. The first is when the body ceases to function. The second is when the body is consigned to the grave. The third is that moment, sometime in the future, when your name is spoken for the last time."

Cody, the rascal, definitely cheated third death. He lives on in stories, myths, museums, and even a professional football team.

Cody would like the name "Eagleman."

Dr. Edgar Yorick Davidson died at age 99 years in 1972. An article in *The Denver Post* remarked that an attractive young woman attending to him in his last days reported that he was frustrated over not making it to 100. At his request, Dr. Davidson was cremated. Some of his ashes were interred in the graves of his wife and son, the remainder spread over an undisclosed location.

Acknowledgements

Though this is a work of fiction, and resemblance of characters, living or dead, is purely coincidental, there are some real people who need recognition.

First, I'd like to thank the staff at the McCracken Research Library in the Buffalo Bill Center of the West in Cody, Wyoming. They gave me access to the many letters in the collection. The same is true for the Western History collection of the Denver Public Library. Steve Freisen, then director of the Buffalo Bill Museum on Lookout Mountain, was particularly generous with his time and access to the museum's collection of letters. "Did Buffalo Bill Visit Your Town?" compiled by the Buffalo Bill Museum and Grave under Freisen's leadership proved a valuable resource in producing cities and dates for the Cody correspondence. All and all, being able to read all these letters gave me a feel for Cody's issues, writing style, and hints as to the health challenges he faced. I still owe the world my take on Cody's cause of death.

Good people read the many drafts of this novel and offered criticism and encouragement. Among them were Dr. Patty Limerick, Dr. Steven Shoemaker, Dr. Tamar McKee, General Andy Love, Wren Schauer, and Patrick Wolf. Early on, Michael Keenan made the suggestion of focusing the epistolary style on just the letters between Cody and Davidson. He sat my modern-day narrator and commentator down and told him to shut up.

Patrick Wolf continues to be a critical source of technical expertise, particularly on those days I questions why I am allowed access to electricity.

Anne Wright provided close editing. Her "book doctoring" was good medicine for Dr. Davidson in that she argued for giving him liveliness and complexity that made this something more than another "Buffalo Bill book." Thank you, Anne.

And also my appreciation for the proofreading and fact-checking of Katie Dvorak. In an era when apps abound for spelling and grammar, still the best work, and fewest mistakes, resides with the wetware of the human brain.

Clyde Mason produced the cover art, but also gave me the pleasure of lively interchange and the opportunity to watch creativity at work.

Finally, there's Karen Scoggin. Her support and patience holds my life together. She is my "Good Medicine."

About the Author

Chil Scoggin lives beside a creek outside of Boulder, Colorado. He cohabitates with his wife, horses, various other creatures, and he suspects, a few ghosts. His professional career has included a tenured medical professorship and bio-technology startups. He has particular interests in Medicine and the American West. He falls off of or under a horse every two years. In addition to medical and scientific publications, he has authored op-ed articles and essays for The New York Times, Chicago Tribune, Denver Post, Boulder Daily Camera, and Scripps Howard newspapers. Good Medicine is his first work of fiction.

Made in the USA
Monee, IL
18 April 2020